T0128208

The Tempest:

La Tempete:

The Diary of Simeon Gereau

A Novel

By

Lee A. Kolesnikoff

Order this book online at www.trafford.com
or email orders@trafford.com

Most Trafford titles are also available at major online book retailers.

Print information available on the last page.

ISBN: 978-1-6987-0156-1 (sc)
ISBN: 978-1-6987-0158-5 (hc)
ISBN: 978-1-6987-0157-8 (e)

Library of Congress Control Number: 2020909606

Trafford rev. 06/18/2020

 www.trafford.com

North America & international
toll-free: 1 888 232 4444 (USA & Canada)
fax: 812 355 4082

To Eugenia, beloved wife and companion;
Thank you for your patience and support.

To Nick Kling;
Thank you for your encouragement and understanding

Contents

Surprise

From his perch on the second floor terrace of *Plus Amour,* his café, Jacques Tremaine believed nothing could compare with early morning in Saint Raphael; feeling the refreshing Mediterranean breeze pass across his face, inhaling the familiar odors flowing from it, hearing the shrill screams of birds first searching out and then diving into the sea for their breakfast. Savoring this kaleidoscope of the senses was his way of indulging himself as he began the day. His café was the fulfillment of the dream he and his wife had when they honeymooned here over a decade ago, before the Great War. They fell in love with everything about the town and its inhabitants. From that time forward, they reminisced with fondness about their too-short stay there. It made a much deeper impression on them than they realized. While her husband was engaged in training in the military, Marie often mentioned and later wrote to him about their favorite little hideaway, and how they might settle there after he came home. It was her way of sealing the certainty of his return from the service. Many believe strong thoughts such as these provide the impetus many soldiers need to survive the misfortunes of war. Her scheme worked. Jacques returned almost unscathed, a German sniper's bullet passing through his lower arm but leaving him otherwise intact.

The couple migrated to Saint Raphael shortly after his completion of service in the French Army. Spontaneously, but not really, Jacques concluded that owning a business would be just the thing for them. He purchased an abandoned storefront called Jean-Pierre's Patisserie. Working hard and cleverly, he renovated the dull establishment into an avant-garde bistro that provided an exciting venue for those who just had to submerge themselves in conversation and libation while being surrounded by a provocative splash of ambiance.

The *Plus* owner's daily ritual also mandated that his second order of business was to sort the mail. The first stack contained requests for payment; the second, two letters. The first was from his sister Janette who wrote that all was well, but unbearably hot in Paris. She invited herself and husband Henri for a visit, sometime soon, most likely in August. Jacques smiled. Saint Raphael's appeal extended far beyond its borders. Other families and acquaintances also offered to visit during August.

The other was from a student requesting an interview for a summer job. His excellent character far exceeded the quality of his penmanship. The owner knew the youth and was well disposed toward him. The boy would have his wish. Jacques made a mental note to contact him.

Suddenly, a visibly excited Marie appeared at the top of the stairway.

"What?" her husband asked, "What is it?" Unfolding the newspaper in her hand, she placed it on the table. All she could say was "Jules, Jules Ronda; and Charles, Charles Brousseau, they are alive. Jacques - they are alive!"

TWO OFFICERS FOUND!

Designated as 'Missing in Action' and likely dead after the Aprile 1917 battle in Soissons, two officers recovered from their amnesia and were discovered last week. . .

The headlines and the story that followed explained everything. The pair had experienced amnesia during the period they were missing from the battlefield and had after all this time, over ten years, without reason or warning, once again become aware of their identity. Both were discovered in separate places, Brousseau in Soissons, and Ronda in Saint Germaine en Laye. The paper called them heroes. The remainder of the article explained how the military would be managing their sudden appearance, military discharge, and other matters. Relatives would be able to take them home as soon as they were processed.

Jacques put down the newspaper. Not especially religious, he nevertheless uttered a 'thank you, God.' He had served as an officer in the French cavalry with Lieutenants Ronda and Brousseau in

Captain Simeon Gereau's unit. They had all experienced the bloody April 1917 carnage that was Soissons, a wasteful squandering of good French soldiers slaughtered by the withering fire of German automatic weapons and artillery. He empathized with the growing reticence of French troops as they awakened day after day to prosecute an ever-weakening assault. And, he understood why, after almost a week of unsuccessfully gaining any ground, they refused to form up and continue to press on. It was pointless. But their decision called forth consequences; horrendous consequences.

The cafe proprietor was not an ambitious man. It was not a crime. He simply wanted to live his life as fate allowed, and live it as fully as possible. His father had been a sweeper in a foundry where moulds were constructed and hot metal poured into them. It was his job to keep the floor clean by sweeping away the bits of slag so that they would not contaminate the castings. Working alongside the men who poured the molten metal was devilish work. Pierre Tremaine swore he would do everything in his power to prevent his son from following in his footsteps. The paths that led away from poverty were but three: the taking of the cloth, serving in the military, or being educated. The last was not possible for it required a great deal of money. Neither was the first, for son Jacques was plainly unspiritual. He wouldn't last a week at seminary. The second, however, showed promise. Pierre had a second cousin who was in the military, and an officer.

Papa Tremaine contacted him and explained the dilemma. Before long, an 'arrangement' was fashioned. The post carried two hundred francs to the cousin who responded by return mail, with a glowing recommendation lauding the fine character, high intelligence and suitability of Jacques Tremaine for the military officer's academy, a person he had never met. Mama Tremaine was thrilled, Papa felt victorious. The son dismissed the scheme as folly.

All that changed. Officers' Academy seemed to be just the shock treatment Jacques needed. Serving La Belle France, duty, honor, integrity and the thought of being special invigorated the young candidate; it became his chrysalis. He befriended fellow officer Jules Ronda and their association added to his self-esteem and desire to excel. Carrying the relationship even further, both wives were brought into the circle of comradery. The connection between the men and now their wives deepened. The couples became inseparable; dining, picnicking, and stealing as much time as possible. Following suit, the wives stayed in touch while both men were soldiering. The trip to the training school was not convenient, but Marie and Annette endured it without complaint. It helped that each felt it their duty to encourage the other when that occasional 'dark day' of depression made its appearance. Marie was as happy as Jacques at the wonderful association. She and Jules' wife had formed a bond that time could not erase. They too, were comrades in arms. Still, it was eminently clear that when it came to friendship man-to-man, Jules Ronda's best friend was his superior, Simeon Gereau.

Charles Brousseau was another matter. Of noble descent, arrogant, lover of self and distant, he refused to lower himself and associate with his comrades, even though Ronda was of his kind, born of aristocratic lineage. There were many tales of his incompetence as an officer. Rumors persisted about his bungling of an assignment to protect a foreign dignitary, and how he mistakenly shot the dignitary, believing he was an intruder. More tales followed, but some were so preposterous that one might conclude, and correctly, that they were fictitious, simply icing on the cake. Ronda and Tremaine did not like him. So it was no surprise that Jacques and Marie viewed Brousseau's recent resurrection with less enthusiasm.

The good news about Jules elevated the spirits of owner and wife. Their customers could not help but take note of the added brightness and kindness of spirit they had suddenly attained. It seemed *Plus Amour* had acquired new owners, and a much happier pair at that. As the months trickled by, husband and wife developed a growing desire to see friend Jules and his wife Annette. Enjoying a late supper one night, both were uncharacteristically silent. Then without warning, they simultaneously expressed their need and agreed that next month, August, they would close *Plus,* contact the ministry, find out where he was, and go there. Preparations began.

As the day of departure neared, time seemed to pass more slowly. The week prior to the closing felt two months long. With the weekend nearing and the end in sight, the owners began reducing their stores, passing on perishables to customers and friends. At eighteen on Friday the cafe was closed. The weekend was set aside for packing and correcting those innumerable omissions one encounters when preparing for a trip of elastic duration.

Then, as if some divine plan had been put in motion, Jacques received a letter in Saturday's post.

Dear Jacques

I can imagine your surprise hearing from me like this, convinced that I died on that bloody field in Soissons in 1917 where so many of our comrades needlessly gave their lives. I have much to tell you about what has happened since then, things you will find hard to believe. After I clear up some personal matters I hope to visit you soon and explain everything more fully.

Our dear friend Simeon Gereau is dead. Charles Brousseau, his warden, buried him in an unmarked grave, wrapped in cloth so rotted anyone else would have discarded it. But that is Charles, corrupt even when it comes to burying the remains of one of his comrades. Simeon died the victim of a treachery so great that I feel compelled to explain its circumstances. I found Simeon in his cell; still sleeping, I thought. I was his jailor. When I went to wake him, he was cold to the touch. Strange as it may sound, I was happy for him because he had finally escaped the terrible existence he was forced to endure since Soissons, trying to survive in a stinking three by four meter masonry room with a tiny window so high he could not even reach it to look outside. That window and its location symbolized what his life had become; so close to the world he loved, yet unable to take part in it. Simeon, Charles, and I were forced to endure this existence, incommunicado, since Soissons. It was so bizarre it defies reality.

All that last month Simeon had been saying he wanted Father Danilou to have his diary when he passed. Father had been visiting him for over four years. He found out about the three of us after I let it slip to Marcel DeParque the head deacon of Father's church. One night I got drunk at the café and he, God bless him, helped me back to the chateau. After that, Father saw to it that Warden Brousseau stopped taking the food money for his own use and started giving Simeon better rations.

One night, Simeon told me he was going to die. I made light of it and said that most likely he would survive me. He smiled and then coughed that terrible cough which for years had been robbing him of his strength. He reminded me that Father Danilou should be getting the diary. During the night Calista Planiere came for him and took him to heaven; I'm sure of it. I found the diary lying on his bed. He never could rid himself of the guilt he felt about how she died. Night after night her apparition would come to him in his dreams, trying to console him. But she could not. He had tried, convicted, and sentenced himself. He felt responsible for her death. That was all there was to it.

My dear friend was a good man, more honorable than any I have ever known. His imprisonment resulted from the madness that pollutes everyone during war. He committed no crime; he didn't murder anyone, and he didn't steal from anyone. It was Captain Simeon Gereau's love for his men, and his desire to save them from being slaughtered in that fruitless Soissons assault. That was why he ordered his men not to engage the enemy. It caused his superiors to scapegoat him in order to save face. The General in Charge had promised at the beginning of the operation that he would call off the assault if it got too difficult. He did not.

I will be sending you Simeon's diary. Since I was his friend, Father Danilou gave it to me. It should arrive in a few days. Read it, and, when at last I meet with you, we will discuss the terrible injustice it chronicles.

It will be good to see your face again. It is a gift I never expected.

Jules

The letter changed everything. The closing was rescinded. How could he meet with his comrade without first having read the diary? Jacques became sullen. When his wife questioned whether anything was wrong, he mentioned receiving the letter and revealed its contents. It had the same effect on her. Now there were more questions than answers. There was no other choice but to wait for the post to deliver the diary.

One, two, then three days passed. On the fourth, the package arrived. Jacques and Marie could hardly wait for the café's closing time to start reading. They didn't. They closed at twenty four, four hours early. Opening it, they found Simeon's diary to be terribly worn, and filthy. It was obvious that rodents had been chewing on its covers and that it had been wetted and dried many times. The odor of mold was very powerful. Marie retired to the boudoir, retrieved a vial of bath fragrance and doused the covers and all of the pages. The *eau de Marie* achieved the desired effect. Jacques and his wife began reading.

29 Aprile, 1902

My name is Simeon Gereau and this is my twelfth birthday, Tuesday, the 29th day of Aprile of the year of our Lord, 1902. I am starting this diary because I am sure I will become famous, perhaps a pilot, fireman, or village postmaster; even a president of some great company. I might find I am brilliant and become a doctor, teacher, scientist; even a religious person like Jesus our Saviour, but that is not likely. The stiff white collar priests wear is not for me. I will never become a politician because Papa says they are dreadful people, dishonest and not to be trusted. It is nighttime now and I am in bed and supposed to be sleeping, but I have lit a candle and am writing down my thoughts and events of the day, as all famous people have done.

Today school was boring. Monsieur Pruveur our teacher told us about the battle of 1870 and how the Germans beat us because they cheated and surprised us before we were ready. Everyone else may have believed that, but I think one of our generals must have been on their side. Everyone knows no one can beat a French soldier in combat. Spies must have tampered with the weapons or ammunition. Our soldiers should watch their equipment more closely. The Germans don't like us very much. We don't like them either. While teacher was talking about the war I saw Claire looking at me. She let out a little smile so I smiled back. My face felt hot when I did, so I stopped. Emil saw me. After class he started to make fun of me so I pushed him. I told him I would push harder if he did not stop. He did.

Now that I am strong, Papa wants me to spend more time helping him with the farm. I don't mind because I have gotten really big for my age. Everyone says that about me. I'm stronger than I look but I keep it hidden. I'm not a braggart like that Emil Juste; he shows off his strength to all the girls and tells the boys they'd better listen to him or he'll make them pay. I could take him in a minute, but I don't want to get into a fight. One of us could get thrown out of school. I don't want that. I want to have a good record. If I'm going to be famous, I don't want people saying 'look at that Simeon, he beats up anyone he doesn't like.' Is that any way for a famous man to act? I'll help Papa as much as I can. He breathes heavily when he lifts the hay into the barn, so I hurry and lift more than my share so he can rest.

This is the second time we have owned the farm. Papa sold it to a man who didn't take care of the land so we bought it back. But we didn't know had badly the man had treated the fields. He didn't put one pound of fertilizer or manure on them. The first year the crop was so bad we almost lost the farm. We had the worst harvest of all the farms in Saint Germaine. Papa had to take a night job and Mama went to work in the post office. But we survived that first winter. I helped all I could because I knew Papa would be tired after coming home from his night job.

He is getting old. He stays at the house longer than usual. He doesn't want to go out to the barn because 'it's too cold.' The first time this happened was right after Christmas. But Mama didn't say anything. She didn't nag him to go out and do chores. She knew what was happening; Papa was losing his strength.

I think Claire Perot likes me, but she tries not to show it. I like her, too, but she's so quiet. She never laughs or gossips with the other girls. I know they tell secrets about the boys, but when they do, she is always somewhere else. I wonder why?

That's enough writing for today. I'm getting tired so I'll stop. I know famous men write a lot, but I'm new at this. Next time I'll start writing earlier so that I don't get sleepy so soon. For my birthday Papa gave me a very fine pocket knife, one that folds. He said it I should use it when I have to cut the strings to open the sheaves of straw or hay.

Simeon Gereau

9 Jun, 1902

    It's June already. I haven't been keeping up on my diary. It's so easy to set it aside when there is so much to do. After school I always help Papa in the barn; I clean the stalls and sweep up the grain that has fallen to the floor. He always leaves the cleaning of the milk pails for me. I don't complain because I know that he might be getting tired by the time evening comes. He works all day. I'm glad it's not that hot yet. It's a long day when you're the only one doing the work. He hires a man now and then, Alfonse, especially when the hay or grain needs to be brought in. The three of us do it all. There is so much work even I get tired, and I am the youngest. I don't see as much of Claire during the summer because I have to work. I don't like that but what can I do? I must help Papa. It is my duty as his son, and if I am to be a famous man, how can I be one if I shirk my duty to my family? Giselle likes me. She's all right, but I like Claire better. When there is not that much to do on the farm, I play football with Emil and some other boys. Giselle is always there watching. Claire has to help her aunt so she doesn't come often. When she does, I sneak glances at her while I play. When Emil sees that, he screams 'the ball, the ball,' because it rolls past me and gets closer to the goal. I don't care about the ball. I want to watch Claire.

    I am promising myself to write every night. Someone who does as much work as I do still must find time to record everything no matter what.

                         Simeon Gereau

The couple continued reading; it was the diary of a youth, full of hope and excitement about his future, the vast possibilities it held, and where it might lead. It was a love story about a life in its early stages of blossoming, and the desire to reach out to another.

But end of day has its own demands. First, the anticipation, and then the excitement of receiving the diary, takes its toll. Add to that the energy required in running a bistro. Thus, it is not surprising that Morpheus eventually overpowers husband and wife.

"Soon it will be three; that's enough for tonight," a tired Marie exclaims. "We'll read more tomorrow."

And they did. Night after night the couple could not wait to close their establishment and resume their reading. Though the regimen was demanding, they found the strength to persevere. One morning, Marie came to breakfast and observed her husband chortling.

"Something humorous?" she asked.

"I was recalling how Simeon met Jules. On the first day of cavalry school, the cadre commanded every new cadet to participate in a horse race. I think they wanted to see how well everyone rode. Whether or not that was their goal, it was still a good idea. Most of the riders sped off at top speed, unaware of how difficult the course might be, and not fully in tune with their mount. Most fell to the ground in short order. Many never advanced to the second obstacle. Simeon, unlike the others, took time and familiarized himself with his mount, a beautiful graphite black stallion. In the last group to enter the race, he and his steed flew over each obstacle effortlessly. It looked as if he was easily going to win the prize, a bottle of very good wine. The one additional condition besides completing the course was that the rider remained mounted during the entire race. As he approached the most difficult obstacle, a brash young fellow raced past him at full gallop. Heading for the next jump, the young rider did not plan well for the leap and his horse tripped on the highest part and smashed to the turf. Easily clearing the same obstacle, Simeon dismounted and rushed to aid the fallen rider. Oh, what a mess he was. The turf was wet. Grass stained the entire front of his jacket. After Simeon helped him up, both spent a few moments picking some out of the fallen rider's moustache." Jacques laughed.

"It was a sight to see, I tell you. What made it worse was that afterward, Simeon mounted his horse and negotiated the final obstacle flawlessly. Watching from the sidelines, Jules, who prided himself on his horsemanship, could only watch and no doubt wish it was he who had won the bottle of wine. That was the beginning of their friendship."

By now Jacques was grinning and so was Marie. While the diary was acquainting them with the youthful Simeon, it was also serving to resurrect memories long forgotten.

"It is a fact of life that we rush to recall pleasant experiences - not the others. Still, it is not always the case that we can choose to recall only the beautiful without also calling forth some of the experiences we wish to forget."

This was becoming Tremaine's dilemma. Reveling in the diary of a young man about to take his place in the world, he also had been present at the annihilation of all his friend's aspirations. He assumed his friend had been killed. As the truth was beginning to unfold, he feared the alternative might have been worse.

After several weeks the couple had progressed from the observations of a twelve-year-old youth to the more mature lamentations of a nineteen-year-old. It seemed Simeon had much to complain about. What caused such a reversal of sentiment remained a mystery. Although they did not know it, tonight's reading would provide the answer.

10 March, 1909

> *I'm not waiting any longer, I'll ask her today. I have promised myself so many times to speak to her about how I feel, but I always make excuses for not doing it. Almost everyone we know has paired off: Charles and Elise, Alfonse and Sigrid, Paul and Marie. All that's left are Claire, Marianne, and Camille. And there are only two boys, me and Emil, and I know he has eyes for Camille. Could there be someone else? She's always talking to that young new teacher Robert what's-his-name. Oh, no, it can't be him; he's too fat for her. What would she want with a stuffed sausage like that? I bet he's a smooth talker. He probably gets a lot of young girls like that. She doesn't seem to pay any attention to me. Still, she smiles a lot. What am I to take from that? Is it an invitation? She's so quiet, not loud and laughing and giddy like the others. Is that because she thinks too much of herself? Maybe she doesn't think that much of me. I've made up my mind - this afternoon I'm going to ask her. I'll find her; I'll tell her I have feelings for her. What should I say? I love you? That's silly. She must already know that I like her, I'm always where she is and as near as I can be to her. Why doesn't she say something? 'I like you' would be enough. Claire, please say something, that's what I'll say.*

This afternoon at fourteen, right after history class, I'll speak to her. I'll know whether Claire Perot likes me or not.

I did it. I spoke to her. I said 'Claire I care for you but I don't know how to show it. Please help me.' She answered 'I will.' I took her hand. I was in heaven. We walked and talked. She told me that she always liked me, but since I was so shy, she, too, didn't know what to do. What a cabbage I have been. All that time she was waiting for me to do something while I was waiting for her. Well, it's over, I mean the waiting. Now we can see each other all the time. Thank you God, thank you. Her eyes are sometimes green and then other times brown. Isn't that mysterious? Her hair shines in the sunlight. I'm going to see her in school tomorrow and then afterward we're going for walk in the meadow.

What am I going to talk about? I don't want to be boring. I can tell her about Papa's farm, how he sold it and then bought it back and about how he sold it again. I'll leave out the part about how hard it was after he bought it back. I'll mention that later. I don't want her to think badly of my family. I asked her if she had a photo I could have. She said she would look and see if she had any. She asked if I had one. I said I didn't, but would see if I could get one. I lied. I had a lot of photos but they all seemed too childish to give to her. I wanted a good one to give to her. That's enough for now. I'm going to go to bed. I hope I can sleep; I'm so excited. I think if I die tonight I'll go straight to heaven. I love God so. He has given me Claire.

S. G.

Marie closed the diary. She looked at Jacques. Much was conveyed in that glance. Given the privilege of peering into the soul and emotions of a youth falling in love for the first time, they had been given insight into that innocent overwhelming rush one feels when uniting with another; the exhilaration, the joy, the wondrous anticipation of the future. Marie grasped her husband's hand.

Morning brought with it an unexpected serenity. One might have considered that strange; after all, comrade Simeon Gereau had passed. Further, Jules Ronda had suggested that the circumstances surrounding his death were heinous. But Jacques and Marie had not arrived at that point in the diary. At the moment they were reveling in the budding love of a youth for his maiden. It was touching; it also brought to mind the time when Jacques and Marie were just getting acquainted; they recalled those silly meaningless things each performed to inform the other they cared. Their love-dance was serious, and none of their offerings, from the inconsequential to the most profound, was ever taken lightly.

The unfolding story of Simeon's early life posed no surprise. It brought to mind the old adage 'the man is the shadow of the boy.' Even at an early age, Simeon's excellence of character was already making itself apparent. Jacques' reaction was fatalistic, for he dreaded to what end that nobility would ultimately lead.

A second letter from Jules Ronda came in the mail. It seemed he was satisfied with his progress in becoming 'civilianized.' Fortunately his wife had never remarried, so what remained to be accomplished was the difficult task of reuniting after a ten-year hiatus. Ronda seemed confident it could be accomplished, mentioning that the necessary adjustment was well under way. He inquired about the diary; how far had they progressed in reading it, how did they find it, and when might they expect to have finished it so that all might meet and discuss its contents and what actually transpired after the Soissons assault.

Jacques penned a reply stating that he and Marie were just beginning to read it and were enjoying Simeon's reflections about his early life and all its episodes. They regretted their slow pace, explaining that they had a business to run and that at day's end they were spending as much time as they could, at least two hours a night, reading the intriguing document. Skimming over pages would be an injustice they claimed, both to the author and to Jules, who had indicated that he considered the diary important. They promised they would give it the attention it deserved and would he please be patient and give them more time.

But the sense of urgency Jules' conveyed convinced Jacques and Marie that they had better not take too much time reading the diary. So they decided that *Plus* would close regularly at twenty-four instead of four. The owners explained to their customers the change would only be temporary, and that, no, they were not selling, and, yes, both owners still were in good health.

12 July 1909

> *Today Claire and I went to a vineyard. It was owned by the father of one of the students in school. We spent the entire day there. Monsieur Blamat gave us a tour of the farm; the pressing vats, the store room, the grape-fields and the workers' living quarters. After, we were allowed to roam through the meadows by ourselves. Claire spied a large oak tree atop a hill in the distance and we made for it. Sheltered by its shade we viewed the entire valley below. I kissed Claire on the cheek and told her that I loved her. She whispered "Always, always." I took her in my arms and kissed her. Suddenly someone shouted*
>
> *"Hello, hello, where are you? Are you coming to lunch; hello, hello."*
>
> *It was the owner, God bless him, and at just the wrong time. Food was the last need we were thinking of. I responded and we went to lunch. Papa wants me to attend military academy. He says my future lies with serving France and making it my career. On the way home I spoke with Claire about it and she encouraged me. She thought it was a good idea. I didn't tell her but the Germans have always been at odds with France and the relationship has always been fragile. I don't want to have to go to war and leave Claire a widow. That doesn't seem very likely right now; things are peaceful, though strained. Why is the government seeking candidates for the military? Do they know something they are not telling us? I worry too much. I spoke to Papa and he says our nations have been bickering since Charlemagne divided his kingdom and gave pieces of it to his sons. He doesn't seem worried, so why should I?*

S.G.

The Tremaines read on, closely following the blossoming relationship between Simeon and Claire. By this time, the prevalent impression shared the readers was that they would eventually wed.

25 December 1911

I gave Claire a beautiful shawl for the holiday. Mama had one of her friends make it. She loves Claire so. They are like two sisters; they cook together, they shop together and they spend time conversing with each other. They talk so often I wonder what they can be saying. Men don't do that – unless they are talking about girls. Then the conversation can last for hours. We men are just like them; when the subject is of interest time doesn't matter. Mama and Claire made a wonderful dinner for the family. The gander was tender and delicious. Papa raised the bird and named him Gerard. I escorted Claire to her home and then returned to chatter with Papa and Uncle Alfonse while Aunt Juliette and Mama cleared the table and tidied up. I wasn't careful; I drank too much and had to excuse myself. I am getting dizzy so this is all I am going to write tonight.

S.G.

2 February, 1914

I have been called to service and will be attending the academy for officers. I leave on Monday. Times have changed. It seems there is a lot of talk about the Germans increasing the manpower in their army. Many say that doesn't bode well for France. Claire is concerned. I can see her point of view. Still, she has no reason to be upset, at least for now. I promised her that upon my graduation we would be married there, under a phalanx of crossed sabers. She was pleased. She's already making plans to visit me regularly. I told her to wait until I found out what my schedule was. I didn't mention what my mother heard at the post office. The mayor told her that France was expecting war, and soon. It seems the Germans are getting ready to invade; they're just waiting for an excuse. I'll tell Claire about it later. Right now, it's just talk. I don't want her to worry.

God, I love her so. Thank you, God, for giving me Claire.

S.G.

"That's about the time I had to report," Jacques told Marie, "they were calling many men to serve. They must have taken the threat seriously."

She smiled. "You mean when Papa sent the two hundred francs to your cousin?"

Jacques scowled. "I was a good officer."

Marie grasped his hand, "You were."

6 May, 1914

Today they had all the new candidates engage in a horse race. The race course had a number of jumps and water obstacles. The prize for winning was a good bottle of wine. Everyone raced over to the horse stalls, chose a horse and raced off. I was the last one there. It seems they all overlooked the best horse of all. Can you imagine that? By the time I rode out on to the course, there were cadets lying on the ground all over the place. They had missed the jumps or had been unhorsed while attempting them. My stallion made all the jumps easily. Approaching the second-to-last one, one cadet sped by and made the last one before me, but he misjudged it. The horse stumbled and he crashed to the ground. I made the jump and then stopped to help him up. He seemed unhurt so I remounted and finished the course. Even though I was the only who finished, I knew I wouldn't get the wine. The one condition was that the winning horseman had to stay horsed during the entire run. When a Captain LaBarge approached and offered me the wine. I told him I was not eligible for the prize. He seemed annoyed and told me to take it because 'that was an order.' I took it.

I believe I found a comrade. An officer cadet named Jules Ronda complimented me on my ride. Before long we were at the barracks sampling the contents of my prize. He seems like a good fellow. I like him. I think it will be good to have him for a friend.

S.G.

7 May, 1914

Winning that horse race has done some good. Not only did I win the bottle of wine but Captain LaBarge has taken an interest in me. I wonder if anything will come of it. He was impressed by my horsemanship. From the little I saw of his riding, there's no need for him to take riding lessons; he's a master horseman. Maybe I make too much of it. Perhaps he was just being courteous. I'll turn in now; I feel tired. The first day has been exciting: meeting new comrades, *racing, the new surroundings, it has drained my strength. Good night Claire, I love you.*

S.G.

8 May, 1914

The orderly awakened me at four. He told me my horse was already saddled and a Captain LaBarge was waiting outside. I dressed and went out. He took me riding. I think he has a burden to teach me about the strategies a good cavalryman should possess. The lesson lasted almost three hours. I returned just in time to report for regular training. He told me I should expect to ride with him each morning from now on. God, that man rides hard. I can hardly stay up with him. All this, mind you, in the pre-dawn light. Either he's mad or the best horseman I've ever seen. I'm going to ask around and see what I can find out about him. My first impression is that he's an extraordinary soldier. The man is intense. By the way he behaves I'm sure there must be a lot of stories about him. I can't wait to hear them. It's been an eighteen hour day and I'm tired. It's as if he is teaching me because time is short and he has to prepare me as best he can. I can't dismiss the feeling that it has to do with the Germans. Does he know something I don't? In a few days I'll choose the right moment and ask him.

Sweet dreams Claire, I miss you so. I wish all of this were over, the school, the service, and the black cloud of the German invasion hanging over us. Then I would be with

*you and we could get on with our lives. No one should have
to live with this uncertainty.*

S.G.

In bed, Marie rolled over and reached out to touch her husband. He wasn't there. That was not a surprise. Everyone experiences the urge, even during sleep time. She waited for him to return. After a time she wondered why he hadn't. She decided to get up and find him. Jacques was on the veranda.

"Is everything alright?"

He nodded. "Reading Simeon's diary is resurrecting the past, those terrible times I worked so hard to drive out of my mind. Now they are back and I am dealing with them once again. This time, I can't seem to get rid of them. I'm afraid, Marie. They tore me apart once, but I managed to fight back and overcome them. I don't know whether I can do that again."

"I'll help you," Marie responded, "We'll fight them together. Now come to bed. I want to nibble on your ear." Jacques smiled and took her hand.

"This is the true price of war, the one few pay attention to, the destruction of a person's peace of mind. Soldiers try to bury those terrible things they have seen, but they keep returning. Some cannot manage coping with them and they turn to drink or take their own lives. Others become silent – forever - they cannot bear living in this world anymore, but their body lives on while their spirit has expired. I have seen a few of them and looked into their eyes. They are lifeless. They seem alive but the enemy, the war and its brutality has beaten them. They are dead men – living."

"You are not one of those, my Jacques, you are a good man, and I will not let the war, no matter how ghastly, take you away from me. Now come to bed, before I go out into the street and find someone else."

This time the pair had won the skirmish; with Marie's help Jacques had restored himself and driven away the images that plagued him. Whether they were gone forever one could only guess, but he was indeed correct, the smiling youth that waved goodbye upon leaving for the war was not the same person who returned. The burdens placed on his soul should never have been carried by anyone. But such is the nature of war; all the implied glory, the flag waving, the patriotic songs, the blessings by the clergy fall to naught when the first soldier sheds his blood and it is seen by his comrade. Absent all the former, it is the latter that sears itself into the memory; that look, that last unknowing glance of a mortally wounded comrade before he expires, the 'why' that lingers during that last instant before the eyes glaze over, vacant forever.

Reading Simeon Gereau's diary shocked the Tremaines; Marie realized this more than her husband. To counteract its effect Marie decided to schedule a trip to Metz. A fact not well known by their friends and confidantes, Jacques had one addiction; he loved Spaghetti ala Bolognese, and the restaurant he frequently mentioned as having the best ever was in Metz, a small establishment he and Marie had visited some years ago. He was so impressed by the chef's preparation that he tried to finagle the recipe for the sauce from the proprietor. He adamantly refused. Of course the next best thing would be to pay a visit to said establishment and try again. But running *Plus* and the other cares of life caused husband and wife to repeatedly postpone the trip. But now necessity dictated that everything else be set aside. For all its revelations, Simeon Gereau's scribblings would be relegated to a minor role as the couple journeyed to Metz. Marie hoped it would dissipate the moroseness that was overtaking her husband. To lighten the mood Marie even purchased a bottle of good cognac for the trip. Women have been known to do that.

So, one morning Marie said, "I'm hungry for some spaghetti - let's go to Metz." It was as if she poked Jacques with a hot iron.

"Good idea," he responded, "And this time, we'll get the recipe for the sauce. The owner is older now; perhaps he's thinking of meeting his Maker. How could he justify not being kind and giving a fellow merchant his recipe? I recall he had a slight limp. I'm sure it's worse by now. I could sympathize and reflect 'Oh, I'm so sorry for your trouble. Is there anything that I can do to help?'"

"When do you want to go? Is next Monday too soon?" Marie tempted.

"I'll make the arrangements," her husband answered. Metz was at least two days distant if one wished to spend each day driving at least seven hours. Allocating three days for the trip would be less demanding. Jacques was already experiencing enough stress reading the diary.

〜

When the German and French military and government officials from both nations entered the railroad car where they would be signing the armistice, many must have breathed a sigh of relief that the war was at an end. For others, the event was moot, for they had already resolved what the war meant to them; they rested beneath green sod in some distant field. As in all wars there are times when honor and morality are set aside by some need to behave otherwise. Lieutenant Jules Ronda experienced this. While he did not have the convenience of being as morally bankrupt as Charles Brousseau or as unfeeling as the military tribunal who mandated their incarceration, he well understood the injustice that had been perpetrated.

For over a decade he and his comrade Simeon had been negotiating the valley of the shadow of death. Ronda even fed him part of his own rations as that swine Brousseau pocketed the food money by cutting back on quantity. As Ronda watched his friend's health deteriorate, he cursed his superior for his greed, and his insensitivity to his former commander's plight. He hoped relief might be at hand when he told the priest of his burden – his friend was dying, not only because of the dank and dark environment but also from near starvation, because the warden was misappropriating the funds targeted for rations. The priest managed to correct the nourishment problem by hurling veiled threats at the perpetrator, but could not set aside the punishment the tribunal had determined for his friend.

Faithful Ronda experienced deep anguish when one day he witnessed his friend start refuse food. All through the years of his incarceration Simeon had been tormented by visitations from his little deceased friend Calista Planiere. He felt responsible for her death when she was fatally wounded by German artillery shrapnel on that fateful Sunday afternoon. April, 1917 was the time when all those bad things happened, events that altered the course of Calista Planiere, several other young communicants, and a number of army officers who were involved in the Soissons stand-down.

The lieutenant had used all of the resources available to him to keep his friend alive and well. It was a pyrrhic victory, because he was simply keeping him alive to spend more time in his cell. The countercurrents that were in play frustrated and deepened his sorrow. Still, he did not back away from his obligation. He kept Captain Simeon Gereau as comfortable and in as good a humor as possible. Many days he would leave the cell holding back tears. When beyond earshot he wept.

Ronda had returned from the valley of the shadow. His friend did not. In his heart of hearts where logic and reason have little sway, he sincerely believed that Calista had returned in a dream one last time to take him to heaven. On many occasions she had pleaded with Simeon, telling him that neither she, nor God held him accountable for her death. The agony he underwent was not caused by the imprisonment mandated by the tribunal, but his belief that he was responsible for his little friend's death.

Now the caveat set by the tribunal began to take effect. With Gereau's passing, Ronda and Brousseau were free to take up the lives they had left upon entering the service. All that remained was the concocting of a plausible explanation for the pair's sudden reappearance.

Amnesia was the ploy of choice. The two 'were discovered' after they approached authorities and stated that they 'could remember again.' France was overjoyed at their resurrection as were their families.

But the unjust deliberations of the tribunal demanded a response.

After returning home and beginning the daunting task of reestablishing his relationship with his wife and children, he returned to evaluating the circumstances of the last decade: his incarceration, the actions of the officers empowered to judge what had happened, the commands the troops were expected to follow in the face of withering German fire, their eventual refusal to engage the enemy in the light of the glaring preponderance of fire power against them, and the lack of cover between the assaulting force and well-fortified German automatic weapons.

The injustice of the entire affair gripped him as if he were in the jaws of some great beast that was unwilling to let him go. The breach of civility, of military strategy, of decorum, of a fair trial where the accused was represented by council and the presumption of innocence prevailed – these issues haunted Jules Ronda as much as Calista Planiere had Simeon Gereau. Of everything that he experienced in his new-found existence, the behavior of his children upset him the most. They were free to do as they wished, think as they wished, come and go as they desired, be late for supper, or not attend at all. They could meet with their friends, or not; go to the cinema, dance, swim, or stroll along the banks of the Seine. But their father, of noble blood and a military officer of some stature, could not. A military tribunal had sat in judgement of him and several comrades and determined that they were no longer fit to remain free or see the light of day; one of them to never see it again.

Who would dare to issue a *Carte Blanche*, that innocuous instrument of targeted derision used in olden times, where a soul disappeared from sight secretly whisked away by those of unknown and dark intent? Why was there not a public trial? Why weren't relatives informed of the accused whereabouts? The vilest criminal enjoys these fundamental rights. Why were soldiers, officers, who had served with distinction, denied these?

Unchained now by the unjust treatment, the formerly proud and noble Jules Ronda was experiencing a resurrection. No longer responsible for his friend's well-being, no longer subject to the whims of that corrupt and miserable warden Charles Brousseau, he was seeing the event set against the broader horizon of his beloved France and the qualities it proudly cherished and protected.

He determined he would set a course aimed directly at those who were still in power and who had orchestrated the terrible injustice that followed the April 1917 'mutiny.' The primary need for secrecy was to protect those in command and to dampen any reports that contradicted the official version of what had happened on the battlefront. The French High command had erred first, by miscalculating the strength of the opposing forces on the hillside and second, by pursuing a strategy based on what they *thought* was the situation. When the troops refused to engage, their decision was considered mutinous.

Just recalling the entire affair enraged Ronda. That was why he sent the diary to the Tremaines. After they finished reading it, he would be sending it to others, perhaps at some point to legislators. His intent was to shed light on the whole disgusting miscarriage of justice, to make those who initiated and signed the modern day *Carte Blanches* to answer for their actions.

Jules Ronda loved *La Belle France* too much to let the travesty pass unanswered.

⁓

Driving west along the Mediterranean, the sunny day, its warmth and mild breeze were exhilarating. Soon husband and wife headed west-northwest, bound for Avignon. The long-awaited respite made the couple feel brighter, younger. Marie must have nuzzled Jacques ten times while he was driving. He could not return her affection because he had to concentrate on negotiating the unfamiliar road; but at the first opportunity he stopped the car and responded.

As they approached the city, an out-of-place seagull flew across their path. Its speed suggested another was chasing it, but when Jacques scanned the sky, none was seen. Then he saw it; a reminder of what had transpired not soon to be forgotten. One of the houses still showed the pockmarks that dotted French real estate; the unmistakable signature of bullets. The owner had patched most of them, but their outlines were still discernable. Someone used a plaster of different hue. Whoever it was, they must have tired or run out of material, because two lines remained unrepaired. The sight affected Jacques deeply but he exhibited no visible signs of his discomfort. Besides, Marie was otherwise engaged, taking in the splendid scenery as they sped through the countryside.

The unexpected reminder also brought to mind what had occurred at Soissons during the rebellion and the events that followed. Whatever he did – it was for the good of the company, the corps, and France – he had done the right thing – the only course of action available to a man of honor.

His train of thought was interrupted when Marie tugged at his sleeve; she wanted him to stop. There was a roadside vendor selling items she thought she might fancy. Over the course of the day they had repeatedly done the same, pulling over to peruse the wares of vendors; items of dubious value. But that was the crux of Marie's plan; to divert her husband's attention from thinking about the diary, to cleverly seduce him into pondering why Marie had an interest in this or that totally worthless trinket or scrap of cloth.

As the day wore on, Jacques was becoming visibly perturbed by his wife's unexpected behavior. An ever-watchful Marie finally decided that enough was enough, and suddenly reverted to her previous practice of enjoying the ride and lauding the beauty of the day, the countryside, the summer breeze, and whatever else came into her mind. Jacques was elated; now he could relax and just drive. Having passed through Avignon, now they turned north. The road they were taking paralleled the Rhone River. In a few hours the Rhone would turn away and the Saon River would take its place paralleling the roadway.

Marie's unexpected penchant for shopping had prolonged their journey to such an extent that they would not be reaching Lyon, their first overnight, before dark. Unfamiliar with the road, they decided to seek lodging. The sun was setting and still they had not come upon a place that met their needs. In the distance they spied a lovely cottage. They slowed, hoping the owners offered rooms for the night. Regardless, they still considered stopping if only to visit the quaint and beautiful home. Nearing, they saw a woman planting flowers along the entryway. Plump and red-faced, she seemed absorbed in what she was doing. Upon hearing their approaching vehicle she stood upright, smiled, and waved. Marie glanced at her husband. Their roadside sign offered a bed and breakfast. Nothing could have prevented them from stopping. This was the place for them. It was fate. Thinking back on the events of the day, Jacques was happy that Marie had squandered the day shopping; how else would they have come upon this lovely home?

Madame Mercedes Bouchard and her husband Andrei had built the cottage many decades ago. He, a carpenter of repute, and she a seamstress of good skill had frugally saved their money, bought the land and erected their dream home over several seasons. The building schedule depended on revenue, so construction progressed unevenly. Still, they persevered and their home was completed. Madame birthed two children. The first, Vanessa, died during a difficult childbirth but their second, Alfonse, survived, only to be killed during the war. Now, approaching the twilight years of their lives, their thoughts often turned to their children, fate, and what might have been, had tragedy not befallen them. The one redeeming activity they enjoyed was having the occasional guest or two spending the night with them. Their *pension* gave them purpose – and company.

"I am Jacques Tremaine and this is my wife, Marie," the husband began, "we would be delighted to spend the evening in this beautiful home. How did you come by it?"

"We built it, all by ourselves. Andrei is a remarkably skilled carpenter, you know. He can do everything," Madame Bouchard proudly stated. "Isn't that so, my love?"

A visibly embarrassed Andrei answered "I suppose so. I put my heart and soul into this place. I am very proud of the results."

"And well you should," Jacques responded.

"You must be tired," the hostess observed, "I will show you your room. Supper is at twenty. The bath is at the end of the hall. Please see to your own things. We are not that young anymore." As she led the way the Tremaines followed, excited to be staying in such a wonderful edifice and with, already evident, a remarkable and lovely couple.

In bed and weary from the numerous stops Marie required, Jacques turned to her and whispered,

"You know, I was very disappointed today. You had me make so many stops it prevented us from reaching Metz." Marie turned and looked into her husband's eyes. "But, I'm glad you did. Otherwise, we wouldn't be spending the night here. I feel there is a reason for all of this. I can't tell you what it is, but I expect we will find out." Marie gasped. She took hold of her husband's arm.

"I feel that way, too," she answered.

Tinkle, tinkle went the bell that signaled supper was ready to be served. Husband and wife were already dressed, washed and ready to eat. Their short nap had the proper effect; no longer were they tired; they were ready to meet their hosts.

The table was covered with a beautiful tapestry, too elegant to be used as a tablecloth, while the variety of prepared food resting on it exceeded any expectation the Tremaines might have had for meals at a *pension*. Before too much time had passed it came to be known that Madame had made the tablecloth and prepared the meal while Andrei had fashioned the beautiful table and chairs "in his spare time." The conversation fell to the Bouchard children.

"We lost our first child during her birth at the hospital. We were never able to bring her home. She was beautiful," Madame Bouchard related. Tears were forming in her eyes.

"No matter, we loved her from the start," her husband added, "and we miss her even now."

"God is seeing to her needs," Marie comforted, "She is not alone."

"There are events in life that seem to have no answer," Jacques opined, "But someday, God may give us the wisdom to understand them."

The meal continued as the Tremaines explained that they were on their way to Metz, an old haunt they were eager to revisit. The reason they had stopped at the Bouchards was that Marie, bless her, had frequented too many vendors, thus delaying them just enough to have to seek lodging for the night.

"You look like a military man," Bouchard noted, "did you fight in the war?"

"Yes," Jacques replied, "I was in the cavalry. The last place I fought was at Soissons in April, 1917. I was wounded and had to be sent home." Bouchard glanced at Madame.

"That was the place our son was wounded. They kept him at the field hospital for a time, but then they sent him to Paris. They couldn't help him there, so they sent him home. Three months later he died. There was nothing we could do to save him. His body was torn to shreds by the shrapnel. It was terrible. He told us how the general kept sending them out every morning to be killed. Then one day, they refused to go. There was no point to it."

"Yes, I know. I was there." Jacques replied.

Marie reached over and gently stroked his neck. "He tries not to bring it to mind. It upsets him."

Madame Bouchard collected the dinner and salad plates and returned with dessert, a delicacy she dubbed 'Bouchard Surprise.' The treat served to turn the topic of conversation to why Jacques loved Spaghetti Bolognese so and just what made the Metz version so special. As the hosts sought an answer, the addict provided none.

All was resolved when he finally admitted "I can't give you a specific reason, I just like it, that's all."

As Madame cleared the table, her husband escorted his guests to the parlor.

"Let's not mention the war," Marie whispered into her husband's ear, "It just brings back painful memories." Jacques nodded. Andrei sought a well-worn chair facing the fireplace. It was apparent he must have spent many winter nights there enjoying the roaring fire and the warmth it offered. He struck a match and lit his pipe. His guests took their seats on a divan that faced their host.

"I used to sit here with my boy on my knee. Sometimes he complained the fire was too hot. I had to move the chair. See here," he pointed, "those are the marks. Every time I sit here, especially during the winter, I think of that. It's all I have left of him; memories." Jacques and Marie did not respond; there was nothing to add.

Madame Bouchard entered the room, went over to her husband and gently kissed him on the forehead. "It's all right, dear, it's all right. Our boy has done his part. Now we must be brave and endure the rest." Andrei took his wife's hand and placed a kiss upon it. He smiled.

"It is as you have said many times before; it's hard being brave, it's hard." Tears formed. "Excuse me, I didn't mean to. . ."

"It's all right Monsieur Bouchard, we understand," Marie consoled, "we are experiencing the same as you."

"You have lost someone?" He asked.

"Not exactly, well yes, we have. We just found out one of comrades has passed away; someone who was at Soissons. We are reading his diary."

"What is his name?" the host asked.

"Simeon Gereau," Jacques replied, "He was my commanding officer."

"Mon Dieu, I know that name! Alfonse my son spoke of him. He was the one they spirited away, along with two others. No one ever heard of them again. He assumed they were taken somewhere, court martialed, and executed before a firing squad. When the officials came from Paris to investigate, the first thing they did was to remove the general in command. Then they started looking for the soldiers and officers who incited the mutiny. Many replied that either they did not know their identities or they would not give them up. As a last resort the investigators decided to interview the wounded. There, they found success. One officer, slightly wounded, gave them six names, saying they were the ones who told the troops not to fight any more. They arrested twelve, executed three, exonerated three, and imprisoned three. The others were taken away. As I mentioned, Alfonse assumed they were tried and shot."

"Who was the officer? What was his name?" Marie asked. "He was never told, but it was from someone who served with the accused," the father replied.

Jacques placed his hand over his mouth and yawned. "Please excuse us. We have been travelling all day and the excitement, the fresh air and the wonderful meal Madame has prepared have all taken their toll," he said, "A hot bath and a warm bed seems in order."

"Of course," Madame Bouchard replied, "Breakfast is at seven, later if you wish. Do you have a preference?"

"Seven is fine," Marie answered. Madame nodded her reply.

"What kind of person would do that?" Marie said as she continued disrobing, "Give up one of their own when they were just trying to prevent more senseless killing? I don't understand why someone would do that."

"Perhaps there was a reason," her husband replied, "We don't know all the facts – let's go to bed – I am tired. All those stops. . ."

"All right," Marie responded. Without any more being said, Jacques climbed into bed, pulled the covers up to his chin and, in what seemed an instant, fell asleep. But his wife was uneasy. *That's strange,* she thought, *why is he tired? The trip wasn't that strenuous – and we had already napped.* Marie noticed something else. Jacques became tense when she inquired about the officer's identity. *Could he have been somehow involved? Could it have been him? No of course not. He would never do that – never! Still, what was the reason for his reaction?* She did not sleep well.

The next morning the couple bid the Bouchards farewell and resumed their journey. They approached Lyon. The Saon meandered away. Dijon was not far ahead, then Nancy. They saw the Meuse River nearing. It, too, shared the valley with the road. Marie could not forget what she had heard last night at the Bouchards. She was still thinking about it when a road sign stated 'Metz 5 KM.'

"We're here at last," she observed, finally breaking her silence. Suddenly she became aware that her husband had also remained silent for the duration of the trip. "Is everything all right?" She asked. She received a nod and a murmured response she could not understand. Jacques had answered in this way before, when he was frustrated or did not wish to discuss a topic that irritated him. Perhaps he expected Marie to resurrect elements of the conversation of last night. "I can't wait to get there, I'm getting hungry," Marie offered. Her husband, obviously relieved at the change of topic, answered

"So am I. I'm looking forward to getting a good meal and acquiring that recipe. It's been on my mind since we left." Metz came into view.

A Voice in The Wilderness

He clapped his hands together softly, so his client would not hear. He paced back and forth. The portrait of Napoleon hung on the wall above the mantle. He glanced at it and thought to himself: *what would you have had to say about this? What would have been your response?* The image remained silent as Advocate Henri Graton expected it would, but his queries did not bring him any closer to a solution. He continued pacing while his client, seated, became more and more impatient. Graton was reluctant to look his way, afraid he might detect the discomfort the advocate was experiencing. Every counselor lives in fear of having to defend that one situation which offers no respite, no safe harbor – 'damned if you do and damned if you don't – a defense *sans* reprieve. Jules Ronda was the client and the matter at hand was his insistence that the French Army, the General Command, and by implication the nation, answer for the secret and unlawful incarceration of Lieutenant Charles Brousseau, Lieutenant Jules Ronda, and Captain Simeon Gereau.

Graton removed his handkerchief from his pocket, wiped the sweat from his brow, and then, just above his collar. He had never recalled how hot it had become this time of day. The words *Liberte, Fratenite, Egalite* were coursing through his thoughts. The possibility of challenging the entire legal apparatus of the French Government was unnerving him. He was a good advocate; in fact, an excellent one. He was well known and admired by many of his colleagues. Those who didn't, were either jealous or had been beaten and professionally humiliated by his strong courtroom defenses. But to present in open court the allegations of this one man, accusing the Army and the Government of such treachery was suicidal, not for Ronda, but for him. How many more referrals from government offices could he expect after representing the plaintiff in a case which would certainly gain national if not international attention? How many judges would look unfavorably upon him after he represented Monsieur Jules Ronda? True, his client had some standing because of his noble birth. His allegations would certainly carry more weight than the ranting of some commoner. Still, both the client and his advocate would be challenging the French government and the French Army. They would be accusing them of engaging in criminal acts. For the second time Graton wiped the sweat from his forehead.

Noting the erratic behavior of his lawyer, Jules Ronda correctly concluded that he was afraid – no – panic-stricken – by the thought of alleging that French authorities had engaged in criminal and perhaps treasonous activities. There was also the possibility that a crime against humanity had been perpetrated. The lieutenant had seen such behavior before, soldiers who turned pale and froze at the thought that they might be killed. The nervous twitching, the sweating, the placing of the hand over the mouth – as if to stifle an oncoming scream; all these manifestations were apparent in Advocate Graton. Ronda wondered how he would have fared as a soldier at Soissons; seeing scores of his comrades dying day after day, the green meadow turning redder and redder with their blood. And what would he have said in that room when the tribunal; deliberating in secret, sentenced three men to prison while informing their families they were 'missing in action.' Even before the answer came, Ronda already knew what it would be. Couched in high-sounding and legalistic terms, the short answer would be no, he would not agree to advocate for the lieutenant.

"After considering the elements of your complaint, I feel there is not enough evidence to bring this before a court for a hearing. Of course I believe every word of your story, but proving it in a court of law, with no documents verifying the tribunal's decision, no record of pay stubs or purchases of food recorded anywhere, I would be like Don Quixote, engaged in a fool's errand."

"But he was a man of honor, he believed in his cause, impossible as it was. The difference here is that an injustice has occurred, a grievous one. How may any soldier feel safe if he knows that one day under the right circumstances, he may be spirited away never to return to his family without even being allowed to defend himself openly in a court of law. The most horrendous criminal has that right. Why shouldn't those who have chosen to defend their country? Where, Advocate

Graton, is the *Fraternite,* the *Liberte?* Are we living in *La Belle France* or elsewhere? Besides, I have his diary."

"You don't understand. . ."

"Oh but I do," replied Ronda, "A case like this could put you on the bad side of those who have power over you – they won't mention your name, they won't send you clients, they won't speak favorably of you anymore – you will be an outcast. I do understand." He rose and started for the door. "Thank you for your time."

"I'm sorry. . ."

"You're not sorry, you're frightened. Be careful or you'll piss your pants."

Graton was the fourth advocate who would not take Ronda's grievance before the courts. He was not surprised. The legal community is tightly knit and no one who is a member would dare to question the integrity of the government or any of its institutions without seriously weighing the consequences. It would be professional suicide. In those rare instances when such quixotic attempts were made, the advocates were older and of significant repute – able to retire when the inevitable tide would have turned against them. It was their last hurrah – to be able to allege something purely for its merit, not whether the case was an affront to the establishment.

It was fifteen; Ronda was hungry. Turning the corner, he noticed a blue red and white awning advertising in bright red letters the name of the café, *'Montemarte.'* He took the table closest to the corner; the breeze was the strongest there. *Who will take my case?* He pondered, *where can I find someone with that kind of courage?* At the next table two men were engaged in a heated discussion.

"I won, can you believe it? I won! Of course I knew the judge and I have had some words in other cases, but this time he took my side. He is a real Frenchman – he understood what had happened to my client – and that I was right."

"But won't that put you in trouble with the legal community? They don't like having their decisions questioned," his companion replied.

"To hell with them, it's the justice of it that counts. After they get done cursing me they'll go home and say to themselves 'I wish I had the balls to do that.'" The advocate noticed that Ronda was eavesdropping. "Excuse me," he said to his friend, "I must see someone."

"You seem interested in our conversation, Monsieur, is there any reason for that?" Advocate Mercal's manner was not friendly.

"I have been seeking an advocate to represent me. Four have refused to take my case – no balls. I have just heard you state that you have them. Are you my man?"

The advocate sat down. "I'll see you later, Pierre," he called out over his shoulder, "Have you ordered yet?"

"No, I haven't." The advocate reached into his jacket and produced a business card. "Finish your lunch. I'll be waiting for you at my office."

Walking briskly, Ronda arrived at the advocate's doorstep in less than half-an-hour. Step by step he climbed to the second floor. The elaborate script on the door announced 'Bernard M. Mercal, Advocate.' He turned the door knob and entered. A strikingly pretty young lady seated behind the desk greeted him. She had been prepared for his arrival. "Monsieur Ronda? Go right in," she said, "He is expecting you."

The new client entered. With a sweep of his arm the advocate motioned that he sit. "How may I be of help?" he asked. The client began. "Stop, stop, I have heard this story – more times than I would like. Everyone advocate, judge, and courtroom employee knows of the injustice you and your friend have suffered. No one wants you to even visit his office. If any client has leprosy – legal leprosy – it is you."

"Finally; I have found someone who will speak to the real issue of why no one will hear my plea. What is it? Why are you all so afraid? A terrible injustice has been committed. Are you blind to what has happened? You say you know the story – why then are you not enraged? Where is your humanity?"

The advocate sighed. "You expect me to go after the army and the government; why? War produces many indiscretions, injustices, even criminal acts – they're all a part of the insanity we call war. Why is this instance unique?"

"If I am to be shot or hung for treason or cowardice, my family *will* be notified; my name *will* be read aloud, my rank, and my crime. That is the law; its strength lies in its justice – the treatment of all equally – and openly. My family surmised I was dead, so did Simeon's and Charles.' Which perpetrator is incarcerated *secretly* without being allowed to have their family visit or know where they are? Is there one?"

"I cannot help you. I have fought against overwhelming forces and won - but this, this climb is too steep; it is the most daunting Everest of them all. Every newspaper will carry the story – day after day they will catalogue the victories or defeats made by the plaintiff's or the defendant's advocate. I will be maligned as being unpatriotic, trying to bring the government down and who knows what else? My career as an advocate will end – I will have to wash dishes or become a farm hand or truck driver. I will never be able to enter a courtroom again as an advocate. I will be finished, finished, with no chance of restoring myself – the government will see to that, you can be sure."

"My friend lies buried in rags. He was an honorable man. I shall not rest until the truth about his death is made public. Somewhere in France there is an advocate who will take my case. I shall find him. I understand your fear. But all the time I was in Chateau Germain I experienced no such fear. I was too busy trying to keep him alive. It's simply a matter of values, sir; which is the greater; career, or restoring honor to a man's name?" Ronda took his leave.

There were other advocates in Paris, many – but not enough. As Gereau's friend and protector visited one after the other, the news of his plight preceded him. Forewarned of his impending visit, some refused to see him while others gave him his due and listened. It was a tired and angry Jules Ronda that opened the door of his home, only to trudge up the stairs, undress and fall into bed. The physical demands of his quest had overwhelmed him; he was not discouraged – he was disappointed. The thought that kept surfacing again and again was *Are these the people we fought for?* He understood that justice and fairness did not reside everywhere; that the world had more than its share of scoundrels and ne'er-do-wells, but if there was a place where the former flourished, he saw that it was in the court system of his beloved France. In the past several weeks his idealism slammed headlong into reality; justice was being dispensed by those who accepted its limitations. The principle was being gamed, and by those who most vociferously exclaimed that they were its defenders.

Several more weeks passed with the same results; no one would take his case. Some agreed with its merits while others exhibited a discernable reticence while feigning interest in his complaint. It became more and more apparent that he, Ronda, was a marked man. The last half dozen advocates seemed to know about his needs even before he could fully present them. Checkmate, was the only impression he could envision. *They will not listen,* he mused, *they have made up their minds or someone has made it up for them. Which way now? To whom can*

I turn? For the present he decided to turn away from his pilgrimage and spend time with his family, mount his favorite steed and gallop along the trails of his estate, the ones he knew so well, and to spend evenings reading or sitting in front of the fire with his wife. It was time for restoration. After a short respite he would try again.

He received a letter.

27 May1929
Monsieur Lieutenant Jules Ronda

> *I have decided to represent you. If you have not retained someone else, please make an appointment to see me when it is convenient.*

> *Bernard Mercal, Advocate*

———

The sojourn she had so cleverly planned had not achieved its objective. Her husband, though appearing happy from time to time, once more was sliding into a state of gloom. Three days of strolling and driving around the city, visiting historic monuments and eating at the same restaurant every night had the effect she had hoped for, but, left idle for an hour or two, Jacques' countenance changed, and for the worse. Marie knew it was the diary. Jacques decision to leave it at Saint Raphael did not diminish its effect.

They prepared to leave the city. The plan was to pack after they frequented their favorite eating place, get a good night's sleep and leave early the next morning. Already on very good terms with the owner, the son of the man who had owned the place previously, the couple enjoyed their last meal dining and conversing with him.

"Will you be going home now?" He asked.

"Yes," Marie replied, "We also have a café. It is called the *Plus*. We love it."

"We may take a slight detour," Jacques added, "We haven't decided." Marie glanced at her husband. His stone-like expression gave her no indication what he was thinking.

"Where are you thinking of going?" The proprietor asked.

"Soissons," Jacques replied as he stared at Marie, "We have important business there. His wife turned away.

"Pardon me. I see some friends coming in the door. If I don't see you again, have a wonderful trip. It has been a pleasure meeting you – and the history – the story about my father and you meeting him – it has been precious. I wish he were alive to greet you as he did when you last came. But you have succeeded; now you have the recipe. I'm sure that would have made him happy."

"I thought we were going home?" Marie questioned.

"When we get back to our room I have something to show you," Jacques whispered. The rest of the meal was eaten in silence.

In their room once again, Jacques reached into his travel bag, retrieved the diary and showed it to her.

"So that's why you are still sad. You've been reading it – I thought you were going to leave it at home?" His wife said.

"I couldn't. I read it while you slept," he replied.

"Soissons, is that where we are going?"

"Yes; it's about something I left there."

"What?"

"The person I was before I entered the war, the one you loved, the one who felt things like love, warmth, tenderness, hope. I left him back there on that field of battle where Calista Planiere died. I must find him. You can't help. I alone must find him."

"And if you don't?"

"Then I will be the one you know now, somewhat good, somewhat happy, somewhat loving – but with my spirit chained to the past. I am going to Soissons to reclaim the me you once knew – if I can."

"Then let us start," Marie replied, "We will try."

Husband and wife felt a new and urgent need to continue reading Simeon Gereau's diary - as if Jacques' comrade had left him a message from the hereafter and that his resurrection was bound up somewhere in those rotting and barely legible pages. It was the only artifact they possessed that connected them with the past. Searching, weighing every word, they read far into the night. One entry in particular touched them deeply.

21 May 1914

> *I have not written in my diary for some time now. This is because every morning I ride with Captain LaBarge for at least two hours. Then I report for regular*

duty with the rest of the cadets. We drill, ride, practice cavalry maneuvers, and study tactics until eighteen. We have supper at twenty. By that time I almost fall asleep at the table. I do not complain because every day we get reports about the Germans massing their troops at the border. More and more it seems that there will be war. LaBarge feels they are just waiting for an excuse, some sort of political event that will justify their invading France. I don't want to worry Claire, but that is the situation and it would be wrong for me to withhold it from her. Today we received word that the government has called for full mobilization of all armed forces. We will be getting two weeks leave. After that, who knows how long it will be until the next one. We discussed running off to Paris for a few days. I'll write her and tell her this would be the right time. I expect to be home by the end of the week. If she gets packed in time we can go. I will make the arrangements from here. At last we can be together, even for a short while. I'll tell her I don't think we should marry right now because I wouldn't want to die and leave her a widow – I won't tell her that. Oh God, no, I wouldn't want that.

Good night, my love, I shall see you soon.

S.G.

"Soissons has the answer," Marie exclaimed, "I pray to God we can find it." Jacques slowly nodded.

—

The office of Advocate Bernard Mercal seemed cheerier; the receptionist more amicable. The sunlight streaming through the window brighter, the oak chair Jules Ronda was seated in more comfortable. It was his strong feeling that this was going to be a good day. It would be the first step on the road to righting the wrong done to his comrade. His thoughts were interrupted by a squeak from a door knob being turned. The advocate opened the door, smiled, and beckoned to his client.

As he sat down Ronda noticed the portrait on the wall behind the advocate's desk.

"Graton has Napoleon over his desk. Who is this person?"

"That, my friend, is Baron de La Brede and de Montesquieu. Charles – Louis de Secondat was his given name. He was a famous French lawyer and jurist. His Spirit of Laws published in 1748 is still admired for its legal theory and philosophy. He is no Napoleon. I keep him there to remind me of what the law should mean – so I don't forget."

"What changed your mind?"

Mercal glanced at his client. It was the glance a youth might have had when he admitted he had broken the family heirloom or soiled his Sunday suit. It depicted shame and inescapable guilt. It also pleaded that judgement be set aside because a redemptive act had been planned and was in progress.

"Recently one of my clients was sentenced to hang. He deserved to be punished for the heinous acts he perpetrated. The court allowed his family to visit him before sentence was passed. I could not help but think of your friend. He was an honorable man, an officer in the French Army. You are correct. France needs to hear of his travail – and yours."

"I also have given the matter more thought. You realize that taking this case could ruin you – your practice – your reputation. I struggle with that thought; do I have the right to ask you to do this? I know the details of all the events. I know where the just and unjust acts are. I have made my judgements and I have decided to carry my fight forward – win or lose. I do not need a jury to tell me a terrible thing has occurred. My reasons are clear; this must never happen again – to anyone – the world must realize that Simeon Gereau was an honorable man – and a faithful French officer."

"My career has been founded on defending those who have a just cause but have been rejected by others for a variety of reasons, mainly self-serving. Many in our profession feel it is not productive to defend those who have no means or are unpopular for social or political reasons. I, however, have found that many complaints have merit. In a way I am the Don Quixote of the legal profession – but I defeat many of the windmills I attack. I have thought a great deal about your case and have found its realities unsettling: how can anyone be tried secretly – without a jury – and have sentence passed without the opportunity for appeal – why has the family not been notified – and if the person has passed, why has the family not been able to attend the funeral? The more I think of it the more I become unsettled. Then, I see a monster, my former client, sentenced to death; his family is allowed to visit him on the day of his death. I think; where is the justice? One, an honorable soldier, is treated inhumanely, while the other, a perpetrator of heinous crimes, is afforded humane treatment at the sunset of his life."

Mercal stared at Ronda. Something about it was primal. "I must take this case; otherwise I will have abrogated my pledge to uphold the law. Is there any evidence to support your complaint?"

"I have his diary. He has written in it since he was the age of twelve. During his younger years there are times when he did not write faithfully, every day, but when incarcerated he wrote daily, sometimes prodigiously. It gives an accurate account of his stay at Saint Germain."

"Did you bring it with you?"

"I sent it to a comrade."

"You must retrieve it immediately. Such a powerful article of evidence must be guarded and guarded well. The validity of the entire complaint and its credence rests on the existence of that document. Leave – leave now – and don't come back until you return with it in your hand."

—

The aide rapped twice on the door and entered. He stood at attention while the adjutant continued to speak on the telephone. Placing his hand over it, he mouthed the order 'at ease.' "What?" he whispered.

The aide snapped to attention, extended his hand and placed a communique on the desk. The adjutant nodded. Turning his attention back to the conversation he was having before being interrupted, he replied

". . . and who do you say is going to submit this complaint; one of those who were there? You say he is of noble blood? He is going from office to office seeking an advocate? Well, he won't find one, I'll see to that. No one would dare to allege that we committed a war crime or even a malfeasance – it would mean the end of their career. No one would be that stupid."

Adjutant De Voux returned the phone to its receiver. *This is France,* he thought; *yes, there might just be someone who would take this case – but who?* He had all but forgotten the incident, that day when the officers from Paris headquarters travelled to Soissons to 'clean up the mess.' They sentenced several soldiers to be executed and forgave most of the others – except the three who were to be incarcerated in Chateau Saint Germain. It was intolerable; he regretted having been one of those tasked to do it. Now, unexpectedly, one of the survivors was attempting to resurrect the whole affair. To what end? It had to be squelched.

The adjutant's interest was personal. At the time of the Soissons incident, his rank was captain. He assisted those who made decisions regarding the identification, charging, and sentencing. He played a significant role during this period because he believed his enthusiastic support of command would be noticed and become beneficial to his career. He was correct. On returning to Paris, he was reassigned to a more important unit, the one that dealt with negotiations and matters of a delicate and covert nature. Once again those in charge were impressed by the quality of his work. His rise to the present position of adjutant was driven from the impetus that began with his behavior at Soissons. The approaching inquiry to be brought by Jules Ronda demanded a response. He sought to expunge any reference for his part in the decision-making process at Soissons. Skilled in the covert arts, he intended to initiate surveillance of his adversary and the advocate who would represent him should he have the good fortune to find one.

———

The trip from Metz to Soissons was relatively short. After an early lunch, the Tremaines arrived at the bridge that spanned the Aisne and led to Saint Waast Church. It was bright and warm, the birds were singing and everyone in sight was taking full advantage of the glorious day. As they came closer Marie noticed a change in her husband. He seemed unaware of her presence; he observed every house, the bridge, the terrain surrounding the area, and especially the green field that lay on the other side of the bridge. He swerved to the side of the road and stopped. As if he was aged and carrying a heavy burden he started toward the bridge. Each step seemed to require a great deal of effort. Now his gaze was fixed on one area in particular. Marie, following a few steps behind, could not see any object that justified his attention. Jacques crossed the bridge, stopped, and burst into tears. His wife approached.

"Here is where Calista died." Someone had scratched a small cross in the pavement – it was barely visible, but it did not escape his scrutiny. "This has to stop, I can't bear it anymore. Marie, help me."

Now his wife began to realize what war meant – its true cost – not only in lives lost, but in lives ruined – families having to bear for decades, perhaps a lifetime, the memory of the horror its citizen soldiers experienced. She began to doubt whether or not she could help her husband free himself from the feelings and the utter remorse that was draining him. What tools did she have to fight with? Was her love enough? Could it overwhelm and put to sleep what her husband was feeling? Did logic have a place in this confrontation with past episodes, memories, and emotional eruptions to horrific memories? All she could do was to approach, kneel, and embrace him as ferociously as she could. Its violence toppled Jacques and they both fell, rolling down the grassy slope and finally coming to a stop at the edge of the water. Both were grinning. The impromptu faux pas had released them both from their travail. Laughing, he helped his wife to her feet. They embraced again, this time using appropriate caution. Moving any farther would have landed them in the river. For the present the cloud that hung over her husband had lifted. Neither could explain why it had, nor which event had initiated its clearing. But they didn't care; it was gone and that was enough for them. Touring the immediate area on foot, Jacques pointed out various points where certain events took place. While some were heinous, he was able to maintain his composure. The guilt he felt had vanished.

They found a room in a nearby hotel. They went to supper. How soon would they be leaving Soissons and what routes might they be taking were the topics they discussed. There was no question they would continue reading the diary every evening because now they could do it without being burdened with the ghosts of the past.

6 June 1914

Dearest Claire,

> *I want to marry you – as soon as possible. Who knows what the future will bring? There is talk of war everywhere. I don't want to wait; I don't think it would be wise. We must use the time and opportunity allotted to us.*
> *Please say yes. I love you. NO – NO – NO!!!!!!*

6 June
1914

> *Dearest, I miss you so. I've been thinking. Perhaps we*
> *should marry – immediately. Why wait until my service*
> *ends, it seems so stupid to wait. You feel the same way*
> *about me as I do you. I can ask the commander for a*
> *week off – we can be married in Paris. We can tell our*
> *parents later, when things settle down. I know this is*
> *sudden but I also know that you've been thinking about*
> *it, too. Remember how we talked about it the last time we*
> *were together? We could have been married then, but we*
> *hesitated. Why? I want to spend the rest of my life with*
> *you – have babies and grow old and fat together – what's*
> *wrong with that? I won't say anything about it to the*
> *company commander until I hear from you. I hope you're*
> *excited about my proposal. It's all I've been thinking about*
> *since our last trip.*
> *Please say yes. I love you. That's better!!!!!!!!!*

S.G.

Marie was touched. Simeon was experimenting by first penning
the letter into his diary. How many times he had he written and
rewritten those words, hoping to insert the properly crafted invitation
to his proposal? She reflected on her own experience with her husband.
Almost all the soldiers and officers in the service at that time had
never seen war. They had been called to serve in anticipation of what
seemed more and more to be the probability of an invasion. They had
no sense of how it might disrupt, or even end, their lives. Despite it
all, here was a couple desiring to marry and to hell with whatever
was to follow. How many others felt the same way, gazing into war's
maw, defying it by daring to carry on with their lives? Marie could
not in any way envision what her husband, Simeon, Jules, and Charles
had experienced; but she did, just for an instant, perceive the heroic
aspect of insisting to carry on with one's life in the face of adversity.
How young we all were, she thought, *what did we know about war,*
or politics, or revenge, or of long-standing adversarial relationships?
Nothing; we were naïve – both as a nation and as individuals - and
how heavy a price we paid for it. Other thoughts were resurrected:

how one family, all feeling safe after the French had driven their foes back, were annihilated by an unexploded artillery shell buried nearby. Everyone: father, mother, grandmother, children; the entire lineage was obliterated. Moving forward, history would no longer include their ilk.

How is it that one not appreciate life, its beauty, its fragile nature, Marie thought. *Is it not enough to feel the morning sun's warmth on one's cheek, to inhale the odor of the early summer lilacs, to feel the momentary stillness as the sun descends below the horizon and evening approaches, to caress another human being in an act of love? What is it that drives men to make horrible war machines; each refinement being more terrible than the last?*

Aware of what had happened on June 28, 1914, the assassination, Marie and Jacques read on.

16 *June 1914*

I convinced the commandant to grant me ten days off. I will leave here on the nineteenth. If traffic is light, I should arrive there no later than fourteen. Be packed so we can make for Paris right away. I have already made arrangements with a priest who will perform the ceremony. One of the fellows suggested we stay at this particular pension which he highly recommends. I made arrangements. We have a room there. Claire, I love you. It will be so wonderful to be man and wife. I love you dearly, dearly, my precious one. I know God will greatly bless our union. I am so happy. What more can I say? I shall see you soon, dearest. Yes, this will do!!!!

S.G.

Jacques shook his head; Marie knew why. "I wonder when he will find out," he said, "it will ruin everything for them." "Let's read on," Marie suggested, "we'll see what happens."

22 *June 1914*

Today Claire and I were married by Father Ferdinand. She looked beautiful with her wreath of white flowers, and her beige dress. If anyone could have married an angel, it was me. I was so happy I could hardly answer the questions the priest asked me. When no words came out, he smiled and patted my hand. "It's all right," he whispered, "now take a deep breath and answer slowly." I succeeded. He must have seen such things many times before – he knew just what to do." We had supper with Father and the two witnesses; that was our wedding repast. There was a surprise. Even though I insisted, Father Ferdinand and the witnesses paid for the meal, stating that I was a soldier and it would be an honor to do this for Claire and me. We thanked them.

It was still not too late so we strolled through the streets hand-in-hand - not speaking - just happy to be man and wife. Claire wanted to see the Louvre so we decided to go there perhaps tomorrow or the next day. But tonight would be ours.

Time stood still. Each moment was one of forever, entwined in each breath, each kiss, and each caress. I could feel her breathing, close, passionate, yet loving and tender. As the moon shone upon her face I knew in my heart her silver smile would remain in my memory until I passed from this place; a moment like this could come only once, and I was thankful that it was I to whom it came. I loved Claire, I was making love to her, but these moments were not only that. Was it God's way of blessing our marriage; was this night one of eternity? I felt it was. We were not in bed, we were not in Paris – we were in paradise.

I love you, Madame Claire Gereau.

Monsieur (your husband) Simeon Gereau

30 June 1914

Terrible news today – the academy was in chaos - I must write Claire. Archduke Franz Ferdinand of Austria and his wife Sophie were assassinated in Sarajevo the day before yesterday – and on the Feast of Saint Verus, mind you. Some are saying it's just the excuse the Germans need to start a war. The commandant is leaving for Paris tomorrow to attend a meeting. Everyone is worried - this might be the event that thrusts us into conflict. I hope not.

I won't tell Claire about all of this, just the news about the assassination. Besides, the rest is pure speculation. Captain LaBarge was at my doorstep this morning – four. He seemed more intense than usual, though that is hard to imagine. He was uncommonly silent today – he just kept watching me. He always critiques my riding or my choice of trails or some little thing he noticed, but not today. Why?

Madame Claire, I love you

S.G.

"He found out; it's a terrible after-wedding surprise. I feel sad for him," Marie said.

"It was bad news for everyone, those at the academy and all of France. At that time we were only speculating, but when they invaded Belgium we knew there was no turning back; it was war," Jacques responded, "Simeon was distraught – he worried about how Claire would react – more concerning was that he might leave her a widow. They were expecting."

"Are you all right?" She asked, "I know reliving this must be difficult for you. We can stop reading if you wish."

"At first I experienced some dark moments, but they have dispersed. Now I am anxious to see how Simeon reacted to all of this. I am living his life through this diary and I can only admire the courage of the man that I knew. Now I can have an insight into what made him so remarkable. Turn the page."

3 August 1914

The commandant tells us he has received reports of German troops moving toward the Belgian border. He speculates they will invade as soon as all their troops are in place. He believes they have been preparing for this for some time. Years ago the press, quite by accident, learned of the Schlieffen Plan. It was a strategy, first, to invade France, and second, encircle and take the French capital, all within five days. Surely they will not stop at Belgium but continue onto French soil. It seems their plan will soon be placed in motion. I can't avoid it – I will have to write Claire tonight and tell her the truth. It will be better if she hears it from me than from some story made even more sensational by the press. I won't mention the invading of France – it hasn't happened yet, so why worry her needlessly. Perhaps it can be avoided through negotiation.

Sleep well, Claire –Madame Gereau – I love you.

S.G.

7 August 1914

Yesterday Belgium was invaded – they are resisting - I bet that surprised the Germans. I'm sure Claire has heard of it by now. But that's the least of my troubles; LaBarge has been driving me harder and harder. It may have something to do with the invasion. I'm going to wait before I say anything – he can't keep driving me this way without telling me why. There's a rumor he may be promoted. God only knows he deserves it. He's a magnificent soldier – everyone admires him, though they shake in their boots when he calls them out for some shortcoming. I've been with him long enough to sense that he has something up his sleeve. Perhaps it's the maneuvering for the promotion. I can't wait to see what it is. Tired – must rest – the orderly will be knocking on my door at daybreak – I have another date with the old lion. Everyone calls him by that name – not to his face!

I love you, Claire. Sleep well, I wish I were with you.

S.G.

Marie put the diary down.

"We were all taken by surprise. I don't think many of the men thought there would be war. The assassination changed everything," Jacques opined.

"If not the assassination, then it would have been some other excuse," Marie replied, "They wanted war and whatever reason they could manufacture, that one would be their excuse. It was inevitable."

"I can't imagine what their objective was," Jacques answered, "they defeated France in 1870; they proved their battle-worthiness then, why did it need to be reaffirmed?"

"There are some things we will never know and I feel this may be one of them," Marie lamented. Her husband nodded in agreement.

———

Night was fading fast. In a few hours dawn would be breaking. It was one of those times during the month when the moon seemed to be elsewhere. The sky's unforgiving darkness made the stars appear more luminous. But it all went unnoticed. Charles Brousseau stared out of the window and perceived none of this. His thoughts were elsewhere.

"What is wrong? Tell me – for heaven's sake, tell me. What is it – what's wrong with you? Tell me, please." It was the cry of his despondent mate, confused, concerned and unable to respond to the needs of her companion. Her steps, soft and cautious, had patted down the stairs and into the kitchen. There, in the half-light shed by a small candle, Jasmine Broussaeu came upon her husband. He was sitting in a chair and staring in the direction of the window, observing that which one could only imagine. This had been his habit for some time now, ever since he had regained his memory, come home and married Jasmine. The kitchen and the particular seat he chose had become his nocturnal refuge. Whether the night sky was moon-lit or otherwise, her husband sat stone-still, finding some undefined tranquility in its infinite expanse. She had borne his behavior without comment, expecting that one day Charles would cease his somnambular excursions and return to her bed, where she would greet him affectionately – very affectionately.

The reverse however, was occurring – he seemed to be sinking further and further into a state of catatonia; he spent many of his daylight hours sitting in his favorite parlor chair. He seldom smiled; he showed no recognition of his wife's presence, and he did not respond to any of her comments. When summoned for meals, he arose, dusted off his lap and meandered into the dining room. While there, he answered questions grudgingly. His answers were curt and, when asked further about a topic, he avoided clarifying his initial response. His wife was concerned, but she was unable to see any way to improve the situation. If there was a malfeasance on her part it was not to seek professional help from a medical or psychiatric specialist. In the aftermath of the Great War his condition was far too common among those who had survived.

Jasmine was unaware of Charles' real burden; she thought it was the result of the war. She was incorrect. There was more to her husband's malaise than she could ever have imagined.

He had been married before, although he never told her. For a short period in his life he experienced an epiphany, when he returned to life after having served as 'warden' to Captain Simeon Gereau in Chateau Germain. He married his lover Lily and became a respected person. But when the influenza robbed them of their first child, his dark side reappeared. Resuming his previous ways, he abandoned Lilly and sought out another, any other. It was Jasmine's misfortune to be the chosen one. The plain truth was that he was a bigamist. And now, his plan for the future was to abandon Jasmine as well and take up with that woman in the brothel he had come to know so well, Clarisse.

Charles was never a man of principle. From the time he was able to take charge of his life he yielded to the urges driven by his desires. The needle of his moral compass was broken; there was no high calling, compassion, empathy, regret, or self-recrimination – he was Charles Brousseau, of noble blood, and that fact gave license for all of his calamitous behavior. Jasmine ignored his boorishness, strategizing that it was more important to be wed to an imperfect man of nobility and means than to a principled and admirable one of lesser stature. It was a decision that cost her dearly every day of her married life. The same week after they had returned from their wedding holiday, one of her friends mentioned that Charles had spent an afternoon with an old flame currently in the employ of the most famous procurer in Paris. She did not respond. She remained silent on the issue to this day. Evening soirees proved to be Charles' Achilles Heel. Having imbibed aplenty, he stumbled from Madame to Mademoiselle, groping, touching, kissing and caressing anyone who happened to fall within his grasp. Embarrassed, his wife smiled, ignored her husband's philandering and maintained a proper and brave countenance through it all.

And then, it stopped. He descended to his present state. It was as if he had been mortally wounded.

Men of wealth remain so because they ration their pleasures and are brutally miserly with their expenditures. Those who do not, soon fall into that painful pit referred to by many as 'formerly wealthy, but currently in serious debt.' Charles Brousseau was approaching that pit with remarkable speed.

The following episode fully describes their state of affairs.

Jasmine was having her hair done at the usual place. She had been a client for as long as anyone could remember – at least five years. She received the best service and, until recently, had paid on demand and tipped generously. As her hairdresser was adding the final touches, she noticed the proprietor approaching. She rose quickly, asked to be forgiven for not paying because she left her purse at home - for the fifth time. She made for the door, but this time the proprietor moved more quickly than previously and blocked it. She stared at her, saying nothing. Still, her gaze clearly conveyed the message. "I'll have something for you next time," she whispered to the owner. "Madame might consider paying in full," was the reply. She moved forward as the proprietor stepped aside and let her customer leave. Neither woman smiled. The same tense relationship existed between the Brousseaus and artisans, butchers, grocers, and clothiers. Using their services was accomplished with ease – paying for them was another matter.

As bleak as their circumstances were, her greater concern was her husband's recent behavior. If someone were to ask what she thought the problem was, she would reply that he was possessed. The profound change in Charles' behavior left her no other choice. He had become celibate. He refused to attend any affair on their social calendar, even those that had been structured as a tribute to his return. He had survived the war, he had survived a ten-years-long bout with amnesia, but he had not managed to exorcise the demon plaguing him.

What could it be? She thought; *if I knew what it was, we could fight it together.* Her last resort was prayer.

"Where are you going?" Madame Ronda asked.

"I must go to San Raphael – the Tremaines have Simeon's diary – Mercal needs it as evidence to support my allegations. It's crucial to the case – it's the only evidence we have other than my account. Of course there is Charles, but what kind of testimony would he be willing to give? I don't trust him – I never trusted him – neither did anyone else."

"Once it becomes known that you are going after them they will stop at nothing – I am afraid – you are challenging the establishment. Be careful."

"I will," he consoled.

Leaving Paris and heading south to San Raphael, Ronda was actually closer to the Tremaines than he would be when he reached his destination, for they were heading to Soissons not nearly as far from Paris as the town where they lived. Unknowing, he sped south, while they, north.

Finally arriving at the café, he tapped then pounded on the door. No one answered. A person passing by paused, surveyed the stranger who was trying to knock down the door of *Plus Amour*, and inquired,

"Are you looking for the Tremaines? They are on holiday. I believe they went to Metz."

"When are they expected to return?" Ronda asked, "I need to speak with them – it's very important."

"If you want to wait for them, you can stay at the hotel. It's on the next street – that way."

There was no other alternative – he had to take lodging and wait for them if he wanted to get the diary. He could afford to wait, having done so for so long in the bowels of Chateau Germain; what did it matter if a few more days were spent achieving his goal. Time was on his side; he had the evidence and he had the stature to bring his complaint forward – no one would dare deny that.

The young desk clerk greeted him with a smile. "May I help you sir? She asked in impeccable Italian.

Ronda responded, "I am French, I would like a room."

"Will you be staying long?" She answered, now in as impeccable French.

"I cannot say. I am waiting for someone. I don't know when he will be returning to San Raphael. I hope it will be soon."

"Then I will give you the room on the second floor that faces our main street. That way you will be able to observe who comes and goes. Is that satisfactory?"

"Thank you." Arriving at his room, he entered, opened the shuttered window and stepped out onto the small balcony. He could see the *Plus* and a good portion of the road coming from the west, the one the Tremaines would be using. *What a strange odyssey this has become,* he thought, *when I entered the military, my only thought was to fight for France, to protect my family and to repel the invaders. Now I have been shown that it is not only the invaders that I must defend against, but others of my own kind. All those times I thought I would go mad as I observed my dear friend waste away in that cell. How I beat my fists against that cell door until they bled. I could have helped him escape, but that was not the honorable thing to do. Why did I think it so? What honor was there in hiding a man from his family, from his right to an open and fair trial? That was why I beat my hands against the door – I could not decide – which was more honorable, to save the soul of an innocent man or to follow the sentence imposed upon him by the tribunal?* Tears came, then sobbing. It blurred the images of the road and. It approximated the justice administered to Simeon; blurred.

There was a soft rapping on the door. "Is everything all right, Monsieur?" He wiped away the tears. It was the desk clerk. Ronda wondered what she wanted. Opening the door, he found the smiling young woman carrying a tray containing a bottle of wine and a goblet.

"I was told you were looking for the Tremaines. I could never face them if I did not do everything I could to make you comfortable. This is for you – compliments of the house – and me. We are good friends." In a moment she was gone. *Army intelligence could learn a thing or two from the residents of San Raphael,* Ronda mused; *news certainly travels fast in these parts.*

———

Sitting in his chair with his fingers locked together and forming an inverted V over his nose, he was deep in thought. Could this one decision be the start of his plummet downward from the acclaim and respect he had worked so hard to achieve? The question was beginning to dampen the outrage he felt after hearing about Captain Simeon Gereau. It was not fear that he was confronting but the cold logic that characterizes the legal mind. His deliberation was an exercise, weighing the good and bad aspects of his decision. There had been situations in the past when his ardor had caused him to make irrational and frankly stupid decisions. Being new to the profession at that time, the more experienced colleagues in the profession forgave him his unbalanced impertinence. But he had to work hard to restore his stature. Fortunately several god-sent opportunities allowed him to demonstrate his credibility as well as his reasoned clarity in the defense of his clients. It took seven years, but Advocate Mercal finally reached the upper echelon; highly regarded by all but a few envious detractors.

His experience and understanding of the law and its unassailable essence had convinced him that the scenario that Jules Ronda had described should never have occurred, certainly not in any nation that called itself civilized. But he also understood that at times circumstances and political pressures produced heinous results. And the most bizarre of these was the tragedy of events called war. This was not the first time Mercal had heard of military 'indiscretions,' – but they were acts of momentary insanity, outrage, the desire for revenge; 'to make things right,' – an honorable man's response to something he considered barbaric. Simeon Gereau's travail far exceeded those parameters. He was cold-bloodedly, and with malice targeted and sentenced on the unsubstantiated word of someone who identified him as one of the major conspirators. Mercal imagined how he would cross-examine him. It would be a terrible and embarrassing spectacle. By the time he was finished, everyone would know not only who this man was but how low he had fallen by accusing the captain without proof.

To hell with it, he thought, *I have to do this or I'll never be able to look in the mirror again. I have always respected what I have seen there and I'm not going to change that now.*

His secretary opened the door a crack. "Do you want to be alone? I won't disturb you if you do – it's just that there is a message for you. I wouldn't have interrupted except that it's from. . ." The secretary hesitated.

"Who is it from?"

"It's from an adjutant – he would like you to come to his office."

"When would he like that?"

"Immediately – he hoped he could see you today, but I told him that was not possible. Should I contact him and suggest tomorrow?"

"Yes; tomorrow, but after lunch. I don't want him to ruin my appetite – you won't tell him that, will you?"

"No, I won't," she answered coyly.

———

"He will see you now," the aide said as he ushered Mercal into the adjutant's office.

"Please," he said as he motioned the advocate to sit. Once he saw his guest was seated, he wasted no time in indicating his intentions. "You have a good reputation; that is why you are here. There may be something coming up, serious allegations concerning the French Army - me – can you imagine it? It's about something that happened years ago – I'm sure you've heard about it. Some lunatic is going from advocate to advocate claiming we jailed some soldiers without a trial, adequate counsel, and all of that kind of rubbish. I want it stopped and I think you're just the man to do that. "What do you say?"

Mercal could see that the adjutant was perturbed. "Can you give me more information about what happened?"

"I could, but I'm sure you've heard about it already."

"I do know something about the allegations, yes. But now I need to hear your version of what occurred."

"I don't want to discuss it if you don't mind."

"Then I can't take the case. I have gone to trial unprepared twice and it cost me dearly. I won't do that again. If you want me to consider taking your case, you will have to be honest with me – tell me everything."

The adjutant wagged his head from side to side. One might have thought he had a toothache, but it was far worse. "All right," he said, "You want to hear all about it, then I'll tell you."

The adjutant began - it was as if a floodgate had finally opened and everything behind it cascaded forth. He had been bearing the guilt for a long time. He well understood that what he and others had done was wrong, morally and perhaps criminally – even rising to the level of a war crime. Mercal listened intently. While the story corroborated Ronda's, certain aspects were omitted, either on purpose or because they had been forgotten.

"That's all of it," the adjutant explained as he wiped the sweat from his brow. He seemed more at ease now. "Will you defend me and the French Army? We, France, need you. Everyone speaks well of you. Will you be our advocate?"

"I can't"

"Why not; it will give you exposure. And after it's over, every governmental entity will seek you out first if they need an advocate. You will have become their favorite."

"I already have a client – Lieutenant Jules Ronda. I'm sure you know him. You sentenced him, Charles Brousseau and Simeon Gereau to Chateau Germain to 'clean up the mess.' And, to your credit you did it very skillfully – there was no trial, no defense and no court martial or public sentencing. In the old days, I suppose someone would have said that you were simply carrying out a *Carte Blanche* – but Bastille

Day put a stop to that. Rest assured, Monsieur Adjutant De Voux, all of this will become known to the public. I shall see you in court."

"I should have expected you would be the one to take his case. They said you were good but they also said 'be careful' because you were a rogue. I see that now. Well, Monsieur Advocate this is one windmill that will beat you – take this to court and you're finished. After this, you'll be picking grapes for a living.

"Having my hands colored red from grapes is nothing. Having them reddened by someone's blood is another matter – the way yours are."

"Leave."

"Marie, I'm waiting. The car is at the front door. Are you coming?" Jacques' impatience was understandable. The diary had captured his wife. Though at times uncomfortable to read, she still could not stop absorbing the musings of the author. Her zeal might have been attributed to curiosity, or interest in her husband's comrade, or hoping, perhaps, to unearth some hidden activity of her spouse.

Regardless, her husband had spent the last twenty minutes trying to get her into the car. "Please, Marie," he entreated, "Let's go." Hastily descending, she raced out and got into the car. Once seated, she opened the diary again and read on.

12 August 1914

> *Great news; I have been promoted to captain. The colonel ordered me go to a dinner for officers whose grade was captain and higher. I was the only lieutenant there. Most snubbed me, as if they were thinking 'what is he doing here?' LaBarge came over and introduced me to a General – Field Marshall Berget – he approved of me. I took the colonel aside and asked "What am I doing here? Only captains and above are supposed to be at this dinner." He called me a cabbage. Did I think the General approved of me because he liked the color of my eyes or the way I carried myself? He was approving the next officer, a captain, to take his place. Then he called me a cabbage again. Tomorrow I will*

*be Captain Gereau. I will write Claire and tell her. I'm so
excited I can't sleep even though I'm very tired.*
    I love you Claire. Sleep well.

S.G.

14 August 1914

    *Colonel LaBarge wants me to take over his
assignment. I will be in charge of training the cavalry
cadets starting the day after tomorrow. He said he would
help me get started. There is talk of accelerating the
program because the Germans have now invaded France.
We will need as many cavalrymen as soon as possible.
That will be very difficult. Most cadets are not experienced
horsemen. Those that are, are from aristocratic families.
The most ferocious fight they ever had was fighting over
dessert at supper. But I will train them as best I can in
the time allotted. They say he going to the front. LaBarge
has asked to form a quick response cavalry battalion to
be held in reserve and respond to breaches in the line. On
horseback, his men could move quickly to fortify the sector.
I think it's a good idea but I suspect he just wants to get
into the fight. He loves soldiering.*
    Tired – must sleep.

S.G.

It was late afternoon when the Tremaines stopped in front of
Plus Amour. They had made good time. Traffic was light and they ate
while in transit. It was vastly different from the way they left; Marie
didn't ask to stop at one vendor. After all, why should she? The trip to
Soissons had solved the problem. They proceeded with unloading the
baggage. Finally home, the couple retired to the veranda above, opened
a bottle of cognac and intended to loaf away the rest of the long, hot
afternoon.

Someone was knocking on the door. Jacques went down to see who
it was. Jules Ronda was standing in the doorway. In a few moments he
was at the place where Marie was just having her third sip of wine.

"Jules!" She exclaimed as she rose to embrace him, "Oh, it's so good to see you. Why didn't you tell us you were coming? You're very lucky, you know. We have just returned from a trip. Had you come any sooner, you would have missed us."

"I did – I've been waiting three days for you to return."

"I'm so sorry," Marie answered, "If we only had known. . ."

"I came because I must have the diary. My advocate says we need it to prosecute our case."

"Your case?" Jacques asked, "What case?"

"We are going after those who incarcerated Charles, Simeon, and me – the High Command and the French government."

"But you had amnesia, isn't that so?" Marie interjected, "That's what they said."

"Come to the hotel and dine with me. I'll explain everything. I see you haven't gotten to the important part of Simeon's diary."

Dinner lasted three hours. Jules' friends could hardly believe what they were hearing, tales of intrigue, secrecy, utter disregard for the law – and somehow all justified when performed for the greater good.

"When I tell someone about this, at first they don't believe it. When I tell them of the diary, they are willing to believe, providing I show them the diary. When I refuse, they return to their disbelief. I don't care. I have the proof and the only ones that need to see it are the judges, the advocates, and perhaps some high-ranking government officials. I have an advocate. We are going to court. The entire nation will hear of this treachery."

"Won't that be dangerous? People do very bad things in order to protect their station in life. They might come after you." Marie voiced her concerns and Jacques nodded in agreement.

"What good will all this do? It's over with – you are home, safe; you can enjoy your family. Haven't you had enough?" Jacques implored, "War is insane enough – it has stopped. Why risk becoming another casualty?"

"You didn't see Simeon at his last. He was lying there, clothed in rags, filthy and stinking. He was smiling; waiting for Calista to come and take him to heaven so that they could be together. She had forgiven him – she said it wasn't his fault that she was killed. She came every night in his dreams and kept telling him that. At the night of his death he accepted what she had told him." Ronda burst into tears. "I cannot be silent about this. The world must know – whatever the cost."

"How can we help?" Marie asked softly, "Is there anything we can do to assist you?"

"Give me the diary. As this moves ahead, I may require more of you, but, for now, this will serve. Thank you."

"When will you be departing?" Jacques asked.

"I thought I might leave tonight, but that might be foolhardy. I can't afford to compromise this valuable evidence I have in my possession. Before I could be cavalier; now I have to be careful. Oh, and please give my regards to that lovely hotel clerk. She treated me well when she found out we were friends."

Ronda returned to his room and the Tremaines to *Plus*. Having experienced success in his quest, he slept well; the couple, fitfully.

While the events they had heard about seemed inconceivable, they were valid. Jules Ronda would be confronting the establishment, a conglomerate of some principled and many unprincipled officials. To some, their oath of allegiance to France was the code they lived by. To others, it was the path to the first rung of the ladder of opportunity; they cared little about their nation.

Morning arrived. Ronda thanked the desk clerk for her hospitality and bid her adieu. He met the Tremaines at the hotel restaurant and had breakfast with them. The couple would have liked to retain the diary, but they understood its importance and why their friend needed to take it to the advocate.

As he prepared to leave, Marie embraced him and whispered "Safe voyage, and God be with you."

"We are here if you need us," Jacques said. The couple watched as he drove off, but at a reasonable speed.

He retraced the route that his friends had used in coming home; first to Avignon, and then turning north. Suddenly, and without warning the impulse to visit Saint Germain and the chateau became very strong. During the year that followed his release, if someone were to ask him would he like to visit Chateau Germain, he would have emphatically said "No!" But now the visit seemed imperative, as if he had to go there to settle some unresolved question. What it was, he could not say – but the need existed and it cried out for an answer. Who could say what thoughts cascaded through his mind as he approached?

It was an issue, a confrontation, which had to be answered only by him. The closer he came, the more apprehensive; past memories were overshadowing the present. He did not notice the rushing rivers, the overwhelming beauty of the forests, the vast green meadows, the singing birds, the coolness of the early morning, the sweltering heat the mid-afternoon sun imposed; these were all relegated to non-entities. Ronda was on the way to confront his demons.

It was evening, nineteen, of the third day when he parked his car at the curb at Saint Germain en Laye and approached the chateau. Not having seen it for some time, the edifice appeared strangely unfamiliar. It was difficult for him to concede that he had lived in it for over a decade. He walked along the path that led to the overlook. He had not previously taken the time to go here. *Imagine,* he said to himself, *I was here for such a long time and did not take the opportunity to see this beautiful view; I know, it was me – there was no place in my heart to savor it. I was full of frustration and hate – I was dead to beauty.* He turned and surveyed the chateau.

Suddenly, it was as if a strong wind rushed into his heart - he could feel his chest tightening, as if a huge hand was squeezing the life out of him. He gasped. The pain in his chest was intense and getting worse. He grasped the parapet and held it tightly – it prevented him from falling. A young child came into view. She was kicking a large ball across the lawn. It reminded him of his own children – and why he should try to conquer the pain that was draining him. *Calm down,* he thought, *calm down. That child is the same age as your Helene - calm down. You want to see her again, don't you? You won't - not if you don't calm down.* The sweating stopped, the invisible hand released him.

He had to get away from the chateau – now. Crossing the street, he made his way toward the Rue de Republique; he passed the church located a short distance from the chateau. Why did I never go in? He thought. Then he remembered; he was angry with God, angry for his friend Simeon, angry at Charles, angry for those living and dead who were sacrificed – yes, sacrificed, during those days at Soissons. Imprisoned here, there was no place for God in his heart. He sought out the place where evenings he occasionally spent an hour or two having a glass of wine. It was an unreasonable expectation, but he wondered whether he would come upon the man who helped him that night, the one where he drank too much and could not negotiate his way back to the chateau. A Ronda in despair told him about Simeon, his imprisonment, about Charles and his pilfering the food money. It would be an impossible coincidence, but Ronda expected to find him there. Entering, he scanned the tables and bar, hoping he might recognize the person he sought. He saw no one he knew. Moving to the dining room, he sat at the table that gave him the broadest view of the tables and those at the bar. He failed to notice one person sitting alongside him at the adjoining table. Ronda ordered wine. The waiter then stopped at the next table. Ronda thought he recognized the timbre. *Could that be him,* he thought? He felt a rush, a cascading of emotion. He turned and looked at the man. Each surveyed the other.

"I know you," the man said, "but I can't remember your name. Weren't you that soldier at the chateau?" In a moment they were both seated at the same table and shaking hands. They were comrades, two people sharing the same memory.

"You were the one who told the priest about us, weren't you? What is your name?"

"I am Marcel DeParque, I was Father Danilou's chief man at the church. He saved me, too, you know."

"How is Father?" Ronda asked, "I must thank him for what he did to make Simeon's circumstances better."

"You will have to get to heaven. Father is with God and his angels. His work must have been done here, because God called him home. I will never forget him." Marcel gazed into his glass of wine as if it was a crystal ball, as if he was searching for something inside. His gaze still fixed, he opined "Life moves on. Even those who are dear to us do not live forever. Still we keep them alive in here, loving them with our thoughts."

"I see that you, too, have been carrying a heavy load," Marcel noted, "I suppose everyone in this room is the same as we are; they have their own cross to carry."

He leaned forward and said on a low voice "You know we were in prison in the chateau."

"How so, I saw you here a few times a month – you weren't in prison."

"I was the guard – I kept watch over the prisoner."

"What kind of madness is this? I've never heard of anything so crazy. When you told me about it, I thought you were drunk. Drunks say anything."

Ronda told DeParque the entire story – everything.

"So the Army sentenced you; did you deserve it?"

"We did," Ronda answered, "but it was done in secret, that's what was wrong about it. Even our families didn't know we were alive. They thought we were missing in action. We were just whisked away to some unspecified place."

"If you deserved it I can understand that. But the rest – I don't know about that. Two of our boys from here were in that battle. They were killed. The mothers cried for a week. One grandmother got so upset – she wouldn't stop crying – the death of her grandson killed her. They buried her a month after everyone found out about the boys. And you say they died for nothing? How terrible. How do you know that? You say you were there; in which capacity? Were you an officer?" Ronda's answer was silence; then, a labored nod. "You were an officer? If everything was so impossible, why didn't you stop it? Oh, I see. You saw the situation but those above you did not. Hmm, that's sad, very sad."

The conversation continued far into the night. This time, Ronda did not leave drunk. On the contrary, the chance meeting proved beneficial – how much so he would only learn much later.

—

"My club membership is in jeopardy; how can that be? I am one of your most distinguished members. How is it in jeopardy? You can't say? Why not? I'll drop by this afternoon and we will get this 'jeopardy' situation solved. When? I'll be there by fourteen at the latest. Thank you." *It's De Voux*, Mercal thought to himself, *he's applying pressure.*

His secretary interrupted. "Monsieur Ronda is here."

"Send him in."

"Here it is," he said as he handed the diary to the advocate, "Everything you need is in there; the entire story – all ten years - and more. I'm sure reading it will make many uncomfortable. I hope the public gets to hear all that went on. Perhaps it might do some good."

"Now, we stop."

"Why? You have the document."

"I must read it. Since it is our only tangible evidence other than your testimony, I have to be able to defend what it says, the conclusions it draws, and the sanity of the man who wrote it. Was your friend sane or was he delusional when he wrote in it?"

"He was as sane as you or I."

"Sane? Talking to a dead child every night? How can that be? And you expect me to believe he was of sound mind? How could I?"

"You insult me, sir. I knew my friend – well! He was a good man and of sound mind. It was his guilt that burdened him, nothing else. I'll find another advocate!"

"SIT DOWN. Now you see why I must read this diary. Those will be the questions – the attacks - they will raise questions about the validity of this document. I must be more prepared than they to defend the writings of your friend. As far as is possible I must know him intimately; what he thinks and feels. I need time to do that."

"I'm sorry. I thought you were becoming concerned about proceeding – your future, and all that."

"I'll begin reading this evening. Don't worry, it won't take long."

The arguments Mercal had presented to his client were formidable. What was the mental state of someone who had been living in solitary confinement for a decade? Who could vouch for it? Perhaps the words written in the diary could, and, perhaps, his friend, who of course would be biased. The advocate had already discounted the possibility of any help from Charles Brousseau. His assistant had investigated him and found that he was a dilatant, a rogue, and well on his way to bankruptcy. In other words, his testimony would be for sale. The advocate felt the central argument he could present lay in the contents of the diary; he had to get to know its writer, his depression stemming from the death of his friend Calista, his only hope of salvation through the mercy of a loving God. These would be the pillars of his defense.

The illegality of what the government and army perpetrated was a substantive issue, but secondary. The main question weighed by any jury would be the mental state of Captain Simeon Gereau – everything stemmed from that. If they came to the conclusion he was acting to save his men from further bloodshed, then the rest would flow logically. How could any man of such high ideals be judged insane? Seeing what had occurred to his men on the battlefield and the death of the young girl who was his friend flung him into a state of depression. Under the conditions that existed at the time, who wouldn't have experienced the same? Worse, his sense of duty forced him to take on these great burdens all by himself.

Ronda burst into Mercal's office. "Marcel DeParque; have your investigator talk with him."

"Who is he?"

"He is the head layman of the local church. I stopped at Saint Germain-en-Laye on my way back from San Raphael. I wondered if I might find him again. I did. He's the one who convinced Father Danilou to force that pig Brousseau to stop absconding with the food money set aside for Simeon."

"What food money?"

"I'll tell you about that later."

"And where can I find this priest? He would be a valuable witness."

"He passed away."

"Where can I find this man?"

"He's in Saint Germain–en-Laye, I can help your investigator find him."

"Good; that might make our case stronger – every bit helps. Give everything some more thought. Perhaps there are others we can use to help our case."

Ronda left again. Mercal felt better.

—

13 September 1914

> LaBarge is leaving for the front. He has chosen those riders he desires for his cavalry strike team. He has instructed several other officers to form up their own units and rendezvous with him when they are ready. He is choosing only the most experienced soldiers and horsemen. There will be no time for training. Everyone in these units must be ready to ride and fight. Before he left we met and had a few moments together. He is an old veteran – I hope nothing happens to him – France would lose a great soldier. He will return if he has anything to say about it. He wished me well and I wished him the same. I don't want him to leave – he is such an inspiration.
>
> War – what madness – souls thrust into battle at peril to their lives, and why? Because someone somewhere has decided it must be so. I'm sure they won't be standing in front leading the attackers. They will be far from the din of battle while young men who have hardly tasted life will be maimed or dying for some high – sounding rhetoric, and not an encyclical by the Pope. I will continue to train

the cadets as quickly and skillfully as I can. If they have to see war, I want them to be as well prepared as I can make them. God help me that I can. I have decided that we must spend more time than previously scheduled. I know it will be hard on both instructor and cadet, but I feel I have no choice. Mother of God, help me. Give me strength and wisdom to accomplish what I must.

I love you Claire. Stay well. Perhaps someday this insanity will come to an end. Holy Mother, protect my love while I am away.

S.G.

Mercal paused in his reading. *Is this the man I am to defend,* he mused; *who would dare question the motives of so noble a soul? Still, I am certain some will try, if only to save their own necks.*

It was at this moment the advocate recalled his days as a student; how proud he was to be pursuing an education to become an advocate. He would be a defender of the innocent, those wrongly accused, and those who could not afford counsel. Only now did he realize how far he had drifted from those pristine objectives. He ate in the finest places. His home was magnificent and expensive, and situated in a section of Paris where those of lesser circumstance would never dream of visiting. He associated with educated men and women, people who reflected and spoke with authority.

When have I had one of those people in my office, he mused, *the innocent, the wrongly accused, those who could not afford me? Not for some time.* The advocate had pronounced judgement upon his own behavior. Now it would be different; he was in the process of correcting his own malfeasance. He *had* to defend Captain Simeon Gereau.

He found the place where he stopped. He resumed reading.

4 October 1914

I am letting too many days go by. I should be writing in my diary more often but I am so tired from the long hours training the men and meeting with instructors afterward. This pace is inhuman but I have no other choice. The Germans are advancing and our troops are waiting for them in the trenches but they don't come right away. First they bombard the sector with artillery – day and night. Our men hear the shells exploding all around them. Many are killed. By the time the Germans do attack, those who remain are weary from the noise and explosions – trying to stay alive. They fight bravely but they are easily overwhelmed. It has been reported that we have lost many, not from the fighting, but the barrages. French soldiers' body parts are strewn all over the field. It must be a terrible sight. I hope I never have to see such things. We are fortunate. The academy is not in the direct line of the German advance. For the time being I can still train cadets here. It seems the enemy's goal is to take Paris. If our resistance does not stiffen, the invaders may be spending Christmas atop the Eiffel Tower.

No word yet about LaBarge. I'm sure he's in the thickest part of the fighting. I can just imagine the old tiger – up to his hips in Germans, slashing them with his sword and screaming obscenities. I hope he survives all of this. He doesn't deserve to die this way though I think he would rather go down fighting than in some obscure place with nurses running around his bed tending to his needs.

Goodnight my love. I wish I was by your side tonight. Your kisses would make me feel whole again.

S.G.

12 November 1914

The word from the front is that the old tiger has been wounded. The story they tell seems to be fantasy. He turned a rout into a counter attack by standing his ground and fighting off three of the enemy after being unhorsed. When the retreating soldiers saw that, they turned around and rushed into the advancing hordes. They fought like wild men and turned the enemy to rout. LaBarge was sent to a field hospital. When it was decided that he needed more care, he screamed obscenities at the doctors and tried to leave, but his wounds prevented it. Still screaming his disapproval, they loaded him into an ambulance and carted him off to a proper hospital. He threatened to

> *court-martial anyone who would not permit him to return*
> *to battle. Who would have expected anything else?*
> *Good night, my love. Sleep well.*

S.G.

Providence seems to have interceded. As the advocate continued his reading of the diary, his case load diminished. His required appearance before a magistrate was infrequent. Research and investigation for other pending cases he delegated to subordinates. Thus, he could devote much of his day to reading and making notes pertaining to the mental status and high moral character of its author. Simeon, through his writing, was exposing himself and his innermost feelings to his advocate, a person he had never, nor would ever, meet. Even though the medium was somewhat flawed, it was impossible for Mercal not to be impressed, first, by the young adolescent, and later by the young man who was penning his impressions of everyday events.

As he continued reading, he was moved by a strong desire to meet his deceased client Simeon Gereau. Of course he understood that was not possible, but his reaction indicated how much Simeon's writings and thus, his character, had been conveyed through the flurry of words that graced the tattered pages. What made it more telling was that, lacking ink from time to time, he had penned some entries by dipping the quill into his vein and scratching out the words using his own blood.

He was journeying back in time. It became more and more apparent to his colleagues that unless vitally important, he was not to be disturbed. His entire staff and many in the legal community were aware that the advocate was constructing a case to confront those in the French Army and the entire government if necessary, in an effort to reinstate Simeon Gereau's good name.

After several weeks the advocate had read enough to be able to form a favorable opinion of Simeon; the youth turned young man was in every sense 'Renaissance Man', acquiring skills in carpentry, blacksmithing, and masonry. Since his father was engaged in farming, he also developed an understanding of mechanical equipment and how it worked. He did not pass over the agrarian aspect of his existence, either. Diary entries made during spring seasons demonstrated his understanding of planting and fertilization. He must have read voraciously, since he frequently posed opinions and questions on topics he thought worthy of comment. He recorded incidents where he had annoyed teachers with his probing questions.

It was apparent that Simeon Gereau felt he was ignorant. That realization manifested itself in every aspect of his existence. Mercal compared his client's voracious quest with that of Tsar Peter the Great, another individual who also had an insatiable desire to learn.

A soft rap on the door interrupted his reading.

"It's your wife," his secretary whispered with a smile. Mercal nodded a thank you and drew the receiver to his ear.

"Yes darling, what is it?" He heard Christine sigh.

"Will you be coming home early? I miss you so. I know you are working hard on a very important case but, just tonight, can't you make an exception?"

"I will be there in half an hour. Let's go out to eat. I'll make the reservations. You have been very patient. These last few months have been hard on both of us. I think it's time I pause and take a day or so off. Is there anyone you can recommend I spend my time with?" If there was such a thing, he could feel Christine's smile.

"I might know someone," she flirted, "When can I expect you?"

"I'll be home between seventeen and eighteen." Mercal put the phone down and resumed his reading.

17 August 1915

Thank God! Claire has had the baby without much trouble. I should have been there and I would have been were it not for this damned war. The family wrote me and I received the letter this morning. She had my first son, Jean Pierre, on August 15 at 3. I wish I were by her side. I send my kisses to you Claire, many kisses. If you only knew how much I love you, even more at this very moment. It took just two days for the letter to arrive. That is unusually fast. God and his angels must have been carrying it.

Why am I here? Doesn't the enemy have family? Don't they care about them? Why aren't they home with their loved ones? What dark force has filled them with the insanity to fight and kill innocent people? To what end? It is because of their sickness that I have to be here instead of holding my son, my first son, in my arms. It seems the blood of good men will need to be spilled to stop this madness – what a waste. Those falling into the pit of hell are not content to go by themselves – they want to drag some of us down with them.

Dear Lord - I can't be with Claire right now. You know the situation better than anyone. Please send your angels to comfort and protect her while I do Your will and protect the lives of my French brothers and sisters. Bless me God and bless and protect my new family. There is no one else I can turn to. Have mercy, God, please have mercy on me.

I have to stop now. I'm crying; my tears are blotting the ink.

I love you, Claire.

S.G.

He had had enough. Mercal took out his handkerchief and blew his nose. Doing so cut short the tears that were forming in his eyes. *This god-forsaken world – when is it going to get better?* He muttered. Placing the diary in his inside pocket, he donned his Homberg, put on his coat, and left for an evening with his beloved Christine.

———

The morning sun cast its rays across the dining room table. Its brightness could not have been more appropriate, for Annette Ronda had prepared a special breakfast for husband Jules. As he entered the room and saw it on the table in the glow of the morning sunshine, he was surprised – and pleased. A smiling spouse placed a cup of warm, aromatic coffee beside his plate as the master of the house seated himself.

"What have I done to deserve such attention?" Jules asked, "Or better yet, what am I expected to do as payment for this wonderful repast?" Annette sat down beside him.

"It is my gift to you for not mentioning Simeon for almost a month now. You have come home – the demons that have been plaguing you have taken up residence elsewhere and I am happy for that." Annette placed her head on his shoulder. "Can we go for a walk in the forest? Everything is so beautiful now – please?" Ronda placed his arm around his wife and whispered,

"Of course we can; that is a very good suggestion. But you are correct. It has been some time since I have heard from Mercal. I'll call him when we return." Annette frowned.

The walk Jules had promised his wife did not go as expected. True, everything in the forest was verdant: the leaves were swaying slightly with a soft, warm breeze sliding through them; the sun was bright but not overpowering, the temperature was comfortable. Several birds were warbling; others sang, there was even the occasional hoot from a hidden owl. Still, all this went unnoticed by her spouse. It seemed her mere mention of her husband's deceased comrade had reignited his interest in his quest. It was one of those innocent blunders one makes on occasion that cannot be called back. If there was a way she could have punished herself for her transgression – and that's what it was – she would have.

All that remained was to carry on a very loud one-sided conversation, with Jules grunting affirmations from time to time. During the last month she had succeeded in steering him away from his quest of seeking to obtain justice for his friend Simeon. In one fleeting moment she had thoughtlessly mentioned that name and at that moment resurrected everything she had worked so hard to deflect.

Annette and Jules returned from their walk. As they entered the house, she asked, "Are you going to see him now, or will you go after lunch?"

"I know it has been hard for you. I will go and see him tomorrow. Let's spend the rest of the day together. I love you, my sweet." Husband and wife embraced.

But during the night, Jules changed his mind. He would not be going to see the advocate. Instead, he would return to Saint Germain and attempt to find where the remains of his friend had been buried. The thought of Simeon buried in an unmarked grave was like an open wound. Whenever he thought about it, he experienced pain in his abdomen – he had trouble breathing – he began to shake. If there was one unanswered question in the entire affair that needed resolution, it was this. Contacting the advocate could wait – this question had remained unanswered for too long. Jules Ronda would find his resting place – that was all there was to it.

Found

The plot of ground was like many others, the best locations taken by the families of the wealthy. The rest was occupied by less affluent others. And then there was that piece that few visited and hardly anyone discussed. It was the area of the cemetery where the disenfranchised were interred. These were without family or identity, the embarrassing remnants of the expired who could not pay for their last place of repose. There were no markings of identification. Dates of interment were scratched on the roughly hewn crosses that denoted individual plots, but nothing else. Several bouquets of field flowers were evident. Who placed them there would never be known.

Ronda stood at the entrance and surveyed the crosses. It was as if God had placed a huge stone on his chest – he found himself gasping for breath. Falling to his knees, he asked himself the question, *is it time?* The thought of dying was not foreign to him, but he certainly did not expect it now. Still, he was ready. After a while, the stone was removed as quickly as it had been placed and he was able to breath in a normal fashion again. He rose to his feet. *You are here, Simeon,* he muttered to himself, *was that you calling me?* Walking among the graves, he tried reading some of the dates scratched on the crosses but had no luck. Time, the severe winters, bird droppings and the natural discoloration of the wood due to the passage of time, all had taken their toll. He continued his search. The more determined he became the less cooperative the shards of memorabilia were.

It was getting late. The waning sunlight was the last element to join the fight against his quest. He was beaten. He headed for the café, just coming to the realization that he was very, very thirsty. Had he been less diligent in his search, he might have noticed his behavior was being scrutinized.

He had never realized it before. For the first time he was aware of how the wine slowly flowed across his tongue and down his throat, birthing a small fire of warmth as it disappeared somewhere below. He closed his mouth, trapping the next sip between his tongue and palate. The fluid felt good there, with its flavor sending messages of comfort to its imbiber. His thoughts turned to Simeon. He knew where he was, somewhere within an area perhaps 50 meters square. But that was little comfort. For the moment, there was nothing more he could do. There had to be another way. He decided to find accommodations in Saint Germain, sleep over and try again tomorrow. It made no sense, but he had the strong urge to do just that.

"Looking for an old friend?" Someone asked. Jules turned around. A tall, gaunt man in his late forties stood before him. By his dress he was an artisan or a laborer. The soft tone of his questioning caused Ronda to conclude he might become a friend.

"Yes, I am. He was buried somewhere in that plot about ten years ago. The crosses aren't providing much information. In a little while they won't be giving out any."

"Yes, what you say is true. Will you be leaving now?"

"No, I have not given up. I will try again tomorrow."

"I can see you are not a man who gives in easily. When do you think you will be there?"

"I'm going to spend the morning. If I don't find anything by twelve, I'll go."

"You will be there until twelve? Good luck, then." The man left.

Strange, Ronda thought, *what a pointless encounter.*

Is it a law that all graveyards are misty in the morning? That was the question Jules Ronda posed to himself as he passed through its gates. Making his way to the rear where the unmentionables were, he spotted a man. Coming closer, he recognized it was the same one who was in the café.

"This is a surprise," he said, "I should have known. You were watching me yesterday because the cemetery was your place of employment. That's how you knew I was here."

"I put them all to sleep. Some come with stories – none of them pretty. The rest, no one knows much about them. I say a prayer over each. Who knows what difficulties they had to face." Resting his chin on the end of his shovel he surveyed the cemetery. "They're all here – but who knows their real names? The graves – they're all unmarked.

Criminals, traitors, the poor who have no families – they're all here, sleeping together. I suppose this is their family in a way. God help them." A second digger approached.

"You're wrong," he argued, "I know who they are, every one of them – I keep track. I know the name of each one buried here."

"Do you know where Captain Gereau is?"

"I do."

"Show me."

Leading the way, the second man moved to the corner of the plot. The site was shaded by a large oak tree on the adjacent property. "They don't care where we dig, so I chose this spot. An officer in the French Army should have a nice resting place."

"You know?"

"Don't mock me. I was in the army, too. In fact I was at Soissons when all this happened. They said I was shell-shocked. I couldn't find work anywhere. I nearly starved. Then I met Alfonse, here, and he got me this job. It's not fancy, but it puts food on the table. He got me a few gardening jobs too, to fill in the gaps." He embraced Alfonse. "I love this man."

Ronda stepped forward and shook the man's hand. "Thank you," he said, "You will never know how great a service you have performed today."

"Thank you for serving France. I wish I could also thank your comrade there, but he cannot hear me."

"Don't be so sure," Ronda replied.

———

"You're home," an astonished Annette exclaimed, "How did it go with the advocate?"

"I found Simeon."

"What; where did you go?"

"I went to Saint Germaine en Laye. I felt I had to know where he was, where his remains were. I spent all of one day there and part of the next morning."

"And you found him?"

"I wouldn't have, but for a sympathetic gravedigger who kept track of everyone he buried. He, too, served at Soissons. He put Simeon's grave near a tree so that it would be shaded. He even knew he was an officer. It seems command can't hide everything. The truth just won't allow itself to be buried."

Recalling the resistance he encountered from myriad advocates, the negativism they expressed, the hours and days he spent seeking them out; this one small victory was sweet. To some, the find might have appeared irrelevant, but to Ronda it demonstrated that even the most impenetrable-appearing obstacle can be breached. One needed only to persevere. Though seemingly impossible, he had succeeded in finding the remains of his friend. Now he was certain Simeon's honor would be restored.

"I'm going to see Mercal tomorrow," he said, "I want you to meet him. You can give me your opinion. I think he is genuine. We'll see what you think."

Annette nodded. "When should I be ready?" she asked.

"I want to be there around eleven. That will give us two hours before he takes lunch. It should be enough. I'll send word that we're coming."

"But what if he's busy?"

"He'll make time for us."

———

Someone was knocking on the door. Christine Mercal raced from the sitting room to greet whoever it was. "Pardon," she breathlessly apologized, "The servants are off today." "I know," the man replied.

He was large, plain, not shaven; the kind of person one would send to the butcher or to get the clothes at the tailor, a commoner. Still, there was something onerous about his demeanor. Christine immediately sensed that his visit was meant to intimidate.

"You are the wife of advocate Bernard Mercal?"

"Yes, I am."

"I know."

"What else do you know about my husband? What is the purpose of your visit?"

"May I come in?" the man asked.

"You may not; please state your business."

"Very well; your husband is currently engaged in defending a client whom I shall not name. His involvement places others in jeopardy. His opponents are convinced that he should seek other venues – not this one. Do you understand?"

"You mean perhaps his wife and family may suffer the consequences?"

"I did not say that."

"But that's what you meant." The man did not answer. "Never come here again. It will go badly for you if you do. Tell those who sent you that if they wish to discuss the matter with anyone, it should be my husband. Tell me, how do you feel threatening a woman and her family? Does it make you happy? Do you feel as if you have done well today?"

"I'm only a messenger, Madame."

"That's what they said when they served the *Carte Blanches* and snatched people from their homes in the middle of the night. Were you one of them?" *Touche;* Christine had penetrated that rough exterior. For the first time, he seemed uncomfortable.

"I must go now," he muttered, "I have delivered the message."

"There's a place in hell for men like you," she shouted after him, "Be careful, you're well on the way there now." He turned as if to respond, but then waved his arm in a weak rebuttal as he faded into the distance.

It was at this point that she realized the gravity of the case her husband had accepted. Was there more to come, or was this the initial, and final, thrust? She could only speculate about the question she had posed for herself.

Strategies

The secretary was just as charming as before, warmly greeting Monsieur and Madame Ronda as if she had known them for years. It was her gift, Jules surmised; that was why the advocate hired her. She was the single ray of sunshine in an office where clients came burdened with the threat of punishment as consequences of their behavior. She was the nurse who administered first aid before they saw the doctor. "He will see you in a moment. He's on the telephone right now," she explained apologetically, "he's so busy you know."

There were no other clients. Jules thought that strange, for Bernard Mercal was well known for his vigor in defending the oppressed and those who could not afford legal representation. Before he could finish his thought, the door swung open and he and his wife were invited inside.

"Your office is empty," Jules observed, "That seems strange. The last time I was here it was full."

"It is the cost one assumes when he decides to fight for the principle of a thing. Baron Montesquieu, hanging up there on the wall, and I are in agreement on this point."

"They know you have taken the case."

"Yes, they do, and they are trying to make me change my mind. The only clients I get now are those who are refused by others. Oh, yes, there is an occasional wealthy one who slips by, but they are rare. Adjutant De Voux is sending me a message. It is a mandate. I respond badly to them, you know. Now, do you have anything to tell me? My clerk says you seemed excited when you made the appointment."

"I have found him, that is, where his remains are. Now we can put him to rest in a proper place, one that befits him."

"I would advise against that. The fact that his place of burial is not known to us is a very powerful incentive. What honorable soldier would be buried in anonymity? None; and not one honorable officer in the service of the nation would even consider it. No, we must bide our time. Who else knows of his whereabouts?"

"One of the gravediggers keeps a list of all those that are buried in that section – the one that has no headstones."

"I want to see him – get him here as soon as possible. Is there anyone else?"

"His comrade; he knows."

"Have him come, too – not during the day –and not here. I will arrange a place to meet." Ronda puzzled at the advocate's last remark. He noticed.

"We are being watched. If you look to the left when you leave, you will notice a man reading the paper. From nine to thirteen, it is a short rotund gentleman with a beret. From thirteen to nineteen or whenever I leave, it is a tall thin man with a moustache, no hat. I don't know whether or not you are aware of it, but ours is a serious business. We will be pulling down the pants of some very powerful individuals; they do not intend to have that happen – they are angry. Tread carefully, Monsieur Ronda – you, and Madame – be very mindful of your actions. People are watching."

"How then, shall I be able to contact the gravediggers?"

"One of my men has been following you since you first left my office after giving me the diary. Our adversaries haven't started following you – you're not enough of a big fish yet. That may change soon, especially after I file the brief stating our complaint. For now, I think you are safe. Others have contacted my clerk and tried to get information from her. She is cooperating with them – for a fee, of course – and giving them exactly what I have been telling her to pass on. Right now, the word is that the pressure is beginning to get to me and I have become an angry and unhappy man – unfit to work for. She told them she was considering leaving, but they begged her to stay. They even offered her more money to do so.

Mercal arose. He began to strut back and forth - uncharacteristic for him – "Montesquieu and I have them right where we want them; receiving information that is bogus and building their response on everything she tells them. Of course they are heartened by the knowledge that I may be weakening in my resolve. That also is working in our favor. They may feel the burden to construct a defense may, after all, not be required." He spun around and glanced at the Rondas. "You can help me; will you?"

"You only need to ask," Jules replied.

"Go out and turn left – head down the street so that you pass the newspaper reader. Argue about the fact that I seem to be losing my ardor, how I seem to be stalling. Just don't make it too theatrical – these men are no fools. Speak in loud whispers so one gets the impression you are trying to keep your remarks private. Remember to carry on the conversation long after you pass him. Will you do it?"

"Yes."

—

"Adjutant De Voux will see you now." The aide escorted the man to the door, lightly rapped on it twice and entered. Cap in hand, the man followed. Showing him to a seat, the aide left. One of the cadre of newspaper readers employed by the adjutant to surveil Bernard Marcel's activities, he was the one to have the good fortune to be the bearer of good news. He appeared anxious – perhaps even impatient, a person bursting with information that might bring his employer pleasure – and perhaps a financial reward for the bearer. One could understand his desire to convey what he knew – right away.

"Well, what do you have for me? You sounded very excited when we spoke over the phone."

"I was at my usual post when a couple came out of the building where he had his offices. They were having a heated discussion. The woman said she felt that his interest in the case was waning and that it was a disgrace that army officers got such little respect in peacetime and that during the war everyone respected them but now they didn't. The man argued that perhaps they should seek someone else to represent them but having seen so many that would not take the case, he felt they had to stay with the person they had."

"Did they mention him by name?"

"No, but they spoke about the French Army and the government and how shamefully they acted in the case of this one officer. They seemed very discouraged. I might have followed them, but I was afraid that might give me away."

"Did you get their names?"

"They never mentioned any."

"It might have been a ruse. But then they would have worked very hard to mention names so that you would be sure whom they were discussing. No, I think what you heard is genuine. That is good news." The adjutant opened a desk drawer, took out an envelope and handed it to the man. "Here is a token of my appreciation. You have made me happy. That doesn't happen often. Maintain your surveillance and see if you can add anything to what you have just told me."

The informant left.

So, you are rethinking your position, the adjutant mused, is there a lesson in all of this for you? There may be. Regardless of your skill and your fervor for truth and justice, you may have finally discovered the ultimate truth. Put simply, there are those one never challenges, right or wrong. The cost is too great. Have you learned that yet? I wonder, is it too soon to claim victory, or am I being duped? We shall see – time will tell.

"Cancel any meetings for the rest of the afternoon," He said to his aide, He needed to inform his superior of the latest development. His aide arranged the time and place for a meeting with someone well known in politics but unknown for his affiliation with the adjutant on this matter. Though not discussed publicly, everyone in political life had heard about the allegations and the possible repercussions of the case Advocate Bernard Mercal was preparing to bring to light. It made those who had even the slightest knowledge of the affair very nervous. It might mean the end of a long political career; worse, disgrace and perhaps imprisonment. A tempest was coming and Bernard Mercal was its creator.

⁓

She drew open the drapes and the sun's morning rays gave her nude body a shimmering whiteness. Pale-skinned Annette Ronda was breathtakingly beautiful. Providence had bestowed upon her proper proportion, slender and pleasingly supple legs, breasts of adequate size not overly large or small, raven-black curled and abundant hair, a fetching countenance, dark eyes of seemingly infinite depth; rich, full and enticing lips and, as a final and dramatic aperitif, high cheekbones.

She came down to breakfast as she was. Jules, already well into his morning meal looked up in amazement. His wife noted his lack of response and made one in his stead.

"I am going to the hairdresser's exactly as you see me."

"What is this all about?" Her husband asked.

"I'm tired of being in this legal forest with you. I can't breathe, I can't relax, I have to fight to see my husband, and when I see him, he's taken up with finding justice for Simeon Gereau."

Jules stared at her. Then, in the tone used by those generals who knew they had lost the battle, he asked, "What do you want, Annette?"

"San Raphael, I want to go there. You were there a few months ago. We have friends there. I want to go while the weather is still warm. We can get away from all this. I need some relief - I do, my love, I really do."

Jules embraced his wife. "Put some clothes on; you didn't have to do this. You are so right that I have been dragged down by my quest. I haven't smiled in months and I know you have been doing your best to pull me out of my dark mood. Perhaps you are right; it's time for me to take off my clothes - only not here – in San Raphael. Annette pulled herself tightly to her husband. He felt her breasts flatten as she pulled him as close as she could. It was then the thought came to him: *Why I am I doing all this and ignoring what I have here; my wife, my children, our lives. Am I mad?* It was at that moment that Jules Ronda fully perceived war and its effect on the sanity of all who were drawn into its vortex.

He went to see Mercal.

"We're going to San Raphael. I don't know how long we will be there, but I need to get away from this, Simeon, and the rest. I've come to see whether or not you can spare the diary. I want to take it with me so that we can continue reading it."

"I have anticipated your need, my friend. My clerk has spent weeks making copies – the document is too valuable to risk its being destroyed or stolen. Stop by her desk and she will have a copy for you. I hope your trip accomplishes your objective. You *have* been looking a little haggard lately."

Doing as he was instructed, Ronda received a heavy envelope from the tired but still smiling clerk. He knew why; she had made numerous copies of the diary.

———

It was warm and humid, not the usual combination for evenings this time of year. Bernard Mercal's man sat in a quiet corner of a not-so-popular café, waiting. The person he was to meet was late. He expected that; those who met with him usually had good reason to be cautious. They were the bearers of significant information; pivotal facts that others might deem unwelcome. Ordering another glass of wine, he continued his vigil. Suddenly, someone slowly opened the door leading to the street and entered. Still holding the door open, he surveyed the clientele. Deciding it was safe, he approached the investigator. As he sat down, the man beckoned to the waiter. "What will you have?" he asked.

"Red, I don't care which," he answered, "A large one." The waiter heard and responded.

"What do you want?" the man asked. It was clear he was suspicious, uncertain why he was asked to come to this place. "Am I in trouble? I dig graves - that's all; is there anything wrong with that?"

"I heard you were at Soissons; is that true?"

"Yes, I was; in that terrible place where so many of my friends perished. Yes, I was there."

"Then you know about Captain Gereau."

"I thought he was dead – missing in action they said. That usually means you're either no more or the shells blew you into so many pieces they can't tell who you are. I heard about the captain. Everyone said he was a good officer. I had forgotten about him and that hellhole until one day they brought the remains of someone, 'someone special,' they said. I wrote down in my book where we placed him. I asked about his name. No one would tell me. I didn't give up. 'Give me his name' I pleaded. Finally the priest told it to me. I said 'you must be mistaken.' He was killed in Soissons ten years ago. He told me everything. I was shocked. Then he made me promise not to tell anyone – I swore I wouldn't – on my mother's grave. Then I began thinking about what they did to him, the secret prison, telling his family he was missing; I hated all of it. Now, what do you want?"

"All I can ask of you is for you to keep what you know a secret if you love France, and I know you must, because you risked your life to defend her. Don't tell anyone what you have told me."

The man nodded. "I won't."

"I must ask one more thing of you. I need to borrow the book you keep that shows the plots where all the dead are located. I will return it, but I must make a copy; trust me." The gravedigger reached into his pocket and gave the investigator the book. "I understand your comrade also knows of this. You must convince him to also remain silent. I can't tell you how important it is."

"He's the one who got me this job. He watches over me, makes sure I'm well and don't get the headaches I get from the cannon bursts. He'll do what I ask. He's a gravedigger, but a finer man never lived."

"Another?"

"I never refuse when someone else is paying. On my salary there isn't any extra to buy wine. Can you tell me what this is all about?"

"All I can say is that it is about honor: first, for the brave men who died at Soissons and second, for the officers who were wrongly accused of crimes when they acted responsibly to save their men."

"Go after those responsible – get them – too many of my comrades are buried there. I lived, why me, I don't know, but I did. I have felt guilty ever since."

The investigator reached into his pocket and pressed a handful of bills into the gravedigger's hand.

"What's this?" He asked.

"It's my way of saying thank you. I'm younger than you are. I can live in this place because you and your comrades made it safe for me. Thank you."

The man's gaze followed the investigator as he arose and headed for the door. Opening it and about to leave, he turned and waved adieu.

A New Friend

The wind slid past the open window as the car sped toward its destination. Annette clutched her huge purse tightly, pressing it against her chest. It contained the copy of the diary. Understanding how valuable a document it was, she decided to become its custodian until she and her husband reached San Raphael. On occasion Jules would look over at Annette and smile. He was certain that neither heaven nor hell could wrest the document or the bag from her grasp. Whenever she paused her reading she tucked it away in the shadowy chasms of her enormous purse. So eager to reach their destination, they drove much longer than was prudent. This allowed them to reduce the trip's length by almost one day. They took only two nights' lodging. There, too, the faux-custodian slept with the purse under her pillow. It was almost twelve on the third day when the Ronda's vehicle stopped in front of the Tremaine establishment. Jacques was cleaning the large front window. He dropped his cloth and raced out to greet his old friend.

"Marie, Marie," he shouted, "See who has come." Soon, two couples were vigorously embracing and bussing each another. "Why have you come?" Jacques asked, "Is there something wrong?"

Annette pointed to Jules. "He needs a vacation."

Jules pointed to his temple. "Too much thinking, my brain is wore out."

"Come," Marie invited, "We'll see what we have left in the cupboard; perhaps a few scraps of hard bread and a glass or two of old wine." They entered the *Plus*. No one expected hard bread or old wine.

The Rondas amused themselves while their hosts saw to their clientele at the *Plus*. They strolled through the streets of San Raphael, and when that activity lost its attraction, they returned to the restaurant and took a well-deserved nap – their accelerated travel had finally taken its toll. On this night the restaurant closed at twenty-three – five hours earlier than usual. Once again reunited, the four began to reminisce about old times. All their revelry was cut short when Annette reached into her purse and pulled out the copy of the diary.

"Good," Jacques opined, "Now we can begin where we left off."

"No," Annette parried, "let's move ahead to where he meets Calista – that's the most interesting part. You can catch up on what you missed later. This is a copy – you can keep it as long as you wish." Annette's last salvo seemed to strike home. The offer to let the Tremaines keep the copy and do with it as they wished pleased them. She began to search through the diary for the proper entry.

"I found it," she finally exclaimed.

7 June 1916

> *Often I take a few hours in the afternoon and stroll through the town – just to get away from the men, my responsibilities, and forget about the war. I know the enemy is well positioned on the hill not far away, but for now there is no indication that they are there. All is quiet, and the townsfolk are going about their business as if nothing is wrong. I like to sit at the fountain and watch the passersby, old ladies carrying their shopping bags, young girls laughing and making nuisances of themselves, saying silly things, just being young and funny. Of course there are the men wheeling their wagons, selling fruit or other wares, workmen on their way to or from their jobs, and older people simply sitting in their chairs or walking around slowly, going nowhere in particular and enjoying the warmth of the sunny afternoon and early evening.*

> *Something special happened today. As I was sitting on the rim of the fountain in the square, a young girl approached. I thought she might be eleven or twelve years of age. By the expression on her face I could see she was unhappy. 'You're sitting in my place,' she said. I apologized and moved farther down the rim. She followed. 'Sometimes I sit there, too,' she said. I moved even farther down. 'There, too,' she pointed. I could see I needed to do something – and quickly, so I asked her if there was any place along the fountain Mademoiselle would think*

appropriate for me to sit? She walked over to a spot and pointed. 'There,' she answered. I thanked her and told her that I was grateful for her advice, since soldiers sometimes get very tired and have to rest. I explained that I liked being near the fountain because the light spray from the water was very refreshing. Well, whatever I said changed her mood. She smiled, sat down beside me and began to tell me about her father, her mother and all her experiences since the war began. I was not ready for all that I heard. She said her father was killed in Verdun and was taken to heaven by the angels. Her mother took her own life so that she could be with her husband but God forgave her mortal sin because He understood her desire to be with him in heaven, that Monsieur Dutoit and his wife were her parents now and that they were taking as good a care of her as they could – even if they were a little old.

I am convinced the poor thing is carrying a heavy burden and wants someone to share it with. It appears she has chosen me to fill that need. In her own way she is telling me she wants me to be her friend. Perhaps she is saying this because I am a soldier, or that I remind her of her father, or that she must rid herself of her burden; I don't know which – but I must help her if I can. Such a beautiful young child should not have to bear such dark events.

She reminded me of my own little children. I think I remind her of her father, God rest his soul. Quite calmly Calista – that's her name - told me that Big Bertha had killed him, though she didn't quite understand what that meant. Then she asked me whether 'papa would be in one piece when he was in heaven.' I almost cried when I heard that, but I maintained my composure and, as calmly as I could, told her that in heaven he would be whole.

We talked for some time; she told me that she was a good student in school and that Father Charpentier told her that many times. Madame Dutoit required that Calista keep her room clean and, in addition, every Saturday sweep and wash the stairs. Cutting our conversation short she said she had to go home and help Madame with the kitchen – obviously Calista had other household duties. She asked whether or not I would be returning to the *fountain tomorrow. I said I wasn't sure about tomorrow, but that when I came I would sit in the exact place she prescribed. "Oh, you can sit anywhere, I won't mind," she said as she moved away. God, comfort that poor soul. She has experienced so much tragedy.*

I wish you were here now Claire, you would know how to satisfy Calista's needs.

S.G.

9 June 1916

Today Calista was angry with me. She had come to the fountain yesterday and I was not there. Even after I explained that I had to attend to some military matters, she was irreconcilable. It seems our first meeting had a profound effect on her and she decided that for whatever reason, I was the one she had chosen to be her confidant and that I had to be at the fountain whenever she came. I see now that her need is greater than I thought. Whatever she sees in me it must have resurrected some powerful past thought or friendship she previously cherished. I must be cautious, for I see that if I err, I can damage this child's feelings in a very serious way. I need help. To whom can I turn? She speaks glowingly of Father Charpentier; perhaps he is the one I should seek out.

She asked whether or not I had killed anyone. I told her I hadn't. She asked whether I would be killing anyone here, in Soissons. I replied that I didn't want to, but if someone tried to kill me, I would have to defend myself, wouldn't I? She seemed satisfied with that answer. She wanted to know if we were going to use big cannons. I said that we wouldn't be using the big ones because our troops had to move forward and the big guns couldn't be moved easily. She seemed relieved at that. She asked about my family. I told her that I was married, had a boy and a girl and a very lovely wife name Claire. She asked whether or not Claire would kill herself to be with me if I were killed in battle and went to heaven. I didn't know what to say. Then I told her that we hadn't talked about it yet. She advised we discuss it before I go into battle. I said we would.

Before I left I reminded her that I was in the military and that, at times, I wouldn't be able to get to the fountain and meet her, even though I enjoyed her company very much. At first she seemed annoyed, but then I think she realized I was simply stating a fact; we would both have to live within the confines our lives had placed on us; her duties for Madame Dutoit, and my duties as a soldier. I think she liked that I mentioned enjoying her company.

Claire, I miss you terribly. God protect you and my children.

S.G.

15 June 1916

When I approached the fountain, Calista ran toward me with arms outstretched. Her face was twisted in pain. She embraced me with a strength that was surprising. 'You're all right, you're all right; they didn't get you,' she kept repeating over and over again. I understood. She had lost her father and now she thought she had lost her new friend. I spoke very calmly and steadily, hoping to reduce her anxiety. I explained that I had to make sure some new recruits found their quarters. I also had to introduce them to their comrades. Then I had to test them out to see how they performed. I apologized for not telling her in advance that I could not be present for a few days.

She accepted my apology and told me that she was happy 'they hadn't got me.' I spent the rest of the afternoon listening to her tell me how nice the Dutoits were even though they were old and how nice Madame treated her – except for the time when she got her dress dirty – Calista admitted it was her fault but she couldn't help it. She looked up at me waiting, I think, to ask her why. But, I didn't. Our friendship was young and I didn't want to damage in any way the trust she had already placed in me. After waiting and seeing I wasn't going to ask, she said 'I'll tell you, but you must promise not to laugh or scold me or make fun – do you promise?' I agreed.

Calista and some of her class were headed home after school. One of the students was a very young boy who was escorted to and from school by one of the girls. She always held his hand because he tended to wander off in pursuit of his own interests. On this particular day the conversation in the group became spirited. She forgot herself and let go of her charge. Off he wandered and before she realized where he was, she saw him standing at the rim of a bomb crater. There was some water in the bottom. Too close, the soil gave way. He tumbled down the slope into the water. Frightened, confused, and unable to swim, he started to cry, gasping for air while choking on the water. The rest of the students stood frozen in fear at the top of the crater.

Not so, Calista. She threw her books on the ground and slid down, waded into the water, and rescued the youngster. She was a hero. Everyone reached home safely. But when wet, dirty Calista reached the Dutoit's home, Madame saw her and promptly scolded her for 'looking such a mess.' The girl wasn't even given a chance to explain. She was ordered to go to her room and 'get dressed properly for supper.' Later, Madame called and asked Calista to come down. The boy's mother had come and asked to see her. She thanked her for saving her son's life. Madame Dutoit apologized. She looked at me, waiting for my comment. 'You are very brave,' I told her, 'If it wasn't for you, that little boy might have died. I am very proud of you.' She smiled. 'Now that I know I can trust you, I will tell you my secret; but, not today - perhaps next time.' She ran off. Hers was a happy run.

I am afraid. So great is this burden I have taken on, I live in fear of disappointing her or crushing her hopes for the future. It's this damned war, is there anyone who is not wounded by it?

If you only knew how much I could use your understanding of this girl. I love you. Kiss the children for me.

S.G.

20 June 1916

I have to return to the academy to train more cadets. Command wants to accelerate training to the highest degree possible. To me it's an admission that they sent our battalion to Soissons prematurely. I think that now they will be planning the offensive sometime in the spring of next year. To their disadvantage, they have begun amassing the troops too soon at this location. They have given the Germans ample warning that they will be attacking at this location. The assault, when it comes, will be along a broad front, perhaps three kilometers, perhaps more. Tomorrow I will tell Calista the bad news – that I am going away and we can't meet at the fountain anymore. She will be crushed. I don't know how I can make the news more palatable. God help me that I think of a way to do so.

I love you Claire. Tonight, I blow you a kiss. I love you so.

S.G.

21 June 1916

I told Calista I would be leaving for a short time but I would return as soon as I could. She took the news well. But there was a reason for her unexpected reaction. After we talked for a little while, she said that since I was her friend and she could trust me now, I could meet Gretel. She opened her coat and showed me her doll. It was a ragdoll with a large white face and stringy blond curls for hair. Her eyes were large and black; a large smile was painted across her face. Calista asked if I thought it was silly for girls her age to have dolls for friends. I explained that it was a sign of growing up that youngsters remembered things and toys in particular that gave them pleasure when they were young. All people have keepsakes of one kind or another, and that I was pleased that she had one too. I said I didn't think that she was a child, but a young woman. She jumped up, squealed something I couldn't understand, kissed me and ran off, saying she would be here waiting for me when I returned. Thank you, God for answering my prayer. I did not hurt the child. I might even have helped her.

Good night, my love, I am so tired. My concern for the girl is draining me.

S.G.

24 June 1916

> *I have been back at academy for a few days. The place is a crazy house. We have cadet candidates arriving daily. We have no place to put them so we have placed the burden on the neighboring townspeople. They are billeting the overflow. Some are not happy about it, but they are cooperating. Most of the experienced instructors are gone because they have been moved to the front. So, while I train the cadets, I also give instruction to their instructors on the off-times. I wish LaBarge were here. I wonder what he would have to say about this madness. There is hardly the time to follow up with slow cadets. Everyone is assumed to be proficient without additional practice or further instruction. We are putting out cavalrymen who are not yet proficient. I mentioned this to the commandant. His answer was "Do the best you can."*

Annette interrupted Marie's reading. "Let's pass by that," she advised, "I think what everyone wants to hear is what happened to Calista and all the events that followed. Let's skip some pages and move ahead to that." Since it was the general consensus, the reader began scanning the pages for the appropriate passage.

"Here it is," Marie exclaimed, "Simeon has just returned to Soissons."

10 January 1917

> *I'm back in the barracks at Soissons. I stayed longer at the academy than I anticipated. I was fortunate that I was able to spend the holidays with Claire and the children. It was an unexpected blessing, one I shall never forget. I don't want to die – I must not die. I want the children to have a father – to live their lives with their mother and father, grow old and see my children have their children – my grandchildren. I want to see Claire's hair turn white and mine do the same. This terrible insanity called war, why must it be; why? And then, there is that young child without parents here, at Soissons - I wonder whether Calista has given up expecting to see me again. Tomorrow I will go to the fountain and see if she is there.*

This cold, light snow may keep her away. I wonder whether she has adequate winter clothing. Soissons has changed. What is happening? Command is moving troops in by the hundreds - but I don't see any artillery. They are even bringing a number of those new machines they call tanks. According to what we have been told, the troops are supposed to use them for cover as they move forward. That doesn't make sense – there will be thousands of infantry but less than a dozen tanks – it's impossible, it doesn't make sense. I'm getting a bad feeling about this operation. The strategy hasn't been thought through. In this sector we have a moderate amount of cavalry – but not enough to overrun the enemy with a charge. They would mow us down. From what I am seeing it will be some time before we are fully staffed and ready to launch an attack. Perhaps I'm premature in my concern. I'm not going to think about it anymore. There will be a staff meeting before we attack. I'll learn more then.

I miss you, Claire, I miss you all. Thank you, God, for allowing me to spend the holidays with them, amen.

S.G.

11 January, 2017.

Calista was cross with me. As I approached I saw her sitting there, shivering. When I greeted her she told me she had been waiting for me all this time at the fountain. She complained that sometimes, when it was raining, she would go and stand in the doorway of the bakery. From there, she could see the fountain clearly and know whether I was there or not. On those days when Gretel got thoroughly soaked, she would dry her out by putting her feet in Madame's oven for a few minutes. She didn't like having her doll get wet too many times because she was afraid her eyes would fade. I apologized as humbly as I could, saying I had no choice but to follow orders and do what was required of me.

'That's why they made you a captain; because you are a good soldier. I would never want you to do anything wrong just because of me. We young women understand

about war. We do our duty too. If we must wait, then that is what we must do – even though it is hard at times. I am happy you are back, Simeon, and so is Gretel.' Calista opened her coat and exposed her friend. She waved a warm hello with the doll's arm. We resumed our discussion as if I had never been away. Thank God for that. All my concerns were groundless. I had underestimated the excellent character of my dear friend.

I love you, Claire. Sleep well. Care for our children. God protect you.

S.G.

14 January 1917

I can't see Calista tomorrow; I have too much to do. I will be receiving twelve more cavalrymen. They are new – just out of academy. I will have to train them in the time that is left. I hope we don't mount an assault anytime soon. I can put every day I have to good use.

S.G.

21 January 1917

I spoke to my commander to see if I could go home and see Claire and the family. He denied my request. I think the reason for his decision was that the time for us to engage the enemy is at hand. To make things worse, I have come down with the influenza. About one third of my men did, too. Thanks be to God no one died, but I heard that some of the other units had fatalities. We could never attack now, not with so many being ill. I should have gone to see Claire. On the other hand I might have given the sickness to them. Whatever it is, it makes a person feel terrible – and for a prolonged period. Because I was sick, I couldn't see Calista. When I finally returned, she wouldn't accept the reason for my being away – she thought I went on a secret mission. *No matter what I said, she tried over and over again to convince me that she should be let into my confidence – that she was a woman now, and women can bear knowing the truth. So I lied and said that I was indeed on a very important and secret assignment, that I could not reveal any of the details to her on pain of death. That satisfied her. She also seemed happy that I acknowledged her ascendance into womanhood and that now she could be trusted with secrets. 'You know I'm not a silly little girl anymore,' she chided, 'I'm a woman.'*

Are all women like that? Were you like that at twelve? I love you Claire.

S. G.

16 March 1917

Calista is jubilant; she is so happy about her coming confirmation. It is good to see her so. One could never guess she lost both her parents as a result of this terrible conflict. Soldiers are not the only ones who need courage to survive. At the patisserie, where we meet at times, the baker prepared a special surprise for her to celebrate the event. It was a huge thing, all decorated with several kinds of fruit and crème and sugary flowers. To my surprise, that little girl ate every morsel. I could not have done the same. This was the afternoon where we all forgot about the damned war and found something to be happy about.

For the first time in a long while I will be going to sleep thinking good thoughts. Oh, Claire, if you could only have seen her – she was radiant. This is what we can learn from her: Take the joy of each moment and savor it, and let the rest come as they may. Soon, her time for confirmation will be at hand. That will make her very happy. I think she is worried that if she dies she won't be able to join her parents. This sacrament will solve that problem. She is such an angel, Claire. I only hope our children grow up to be like her.

Sleep well, my love, I blow a kiss for your lips.

S, G.

"We have to stop now," Jules said, "Let's read more tomorrow – that is enough for today."

"You know what's coming, don't you," Jacques asked.

"Tomorrow will be soon enough to hear the rest," was the reply.

"We'll hear what happened tomorrow," Jules remarked as he looked away.

～

Judas

Annoyed, the aide looked up, glanced at Charles Brousseau, smiled, and returned to his duties. The nervous foot-tapping stopped. That pleased the aide.

Sitting for forty-five minutes in to the Adjutant's outer office would make anyone tap their feet, the visitor mused. *What am I doing here, why did he select me? What does he want?*

These were but a few of the myriad questions that were racing through his mind. Well aware that his performance as warden over Jules Ronda and Simeon Gereau was less than exemplary, he mulled over the various 'liberties' he had had taken while holding the position. He wondered whether or not Father Danilou had indeed alerted the authorities as he threatened. Add to his current thinking the fact that he had accused the captain of leading the rebellion at Soissons without any first-hand knowledge. Under his command, Charles a lieutenant, nobleman, braggart, fop, and bungler had much to consider.

He surveyed the wall clock behind the aide's desk; already eleven. He glanced at the aide.

Anticipating the visitor's question he said "He will see you when he is able. He has several phone calls to make. They are very important. I'm sure he will see you as soon as he can."

"Thank you," was all that he could offer in reply. But he was annoyed. *Did the adjutant know I have royal blood? Who does this old war dog think he is?*

One by one the hours came and went. It became fourteen, then fifteen. His patience had worn thin several hours ago. From time to time he inquired about seeing the adjutant. The reply was always the same; that he would be seen when appropriate. Finally on the cusp of screaming obscenities at the aide, he was granted entry.

"He will see you now," the aide informed, "Please follow me." Following in lockstep, he glanced at his watch. It was half-past sixteen.

Adjutant De Voux was still on the phone. While the topic of discussion was never mentioned, the adjutant's tone was solemn. Yes, whatever it was, the visitor concluded, it was serious.

"So, you've come," De Voux said as he placed the phone back on its cradle, "I'm glad you're here. Your nation needs your services." He noticed the expression on his visitor's face. "Don't look so surprised. Did you think I was going to send you back to Saint Germain? That's all over – but sadly, not forgotten. Some just can't let the past be the past. They have to resurrect it for their own purposes. We punished those who mutinied, didn't we? It was your testimony that helped us identify and punish the culprits. You should be proud of that." Brousseau squirmed in his chair. The Adjutant noticed. "What's wrong? You're not going to tell me – not now certainly – that you lied, are you? Of course you aren't. You told the truth, as any good officer should. I know you did." The faltering glance in the adjutant's eyes showed that his gaze lacked the resolve of his words. *So, he lied,* pondered the adjutant; *so what? That terrible incident is past, it is history. Who cares - only that insolent Ronda. He must be stopped, and I have just the right person to do it.*

"As I mentioned, France needs you. Whatever happened back there in Soissons is over. The only one who keeps pursuing the issue is that Jules Ronda. You know him, of course. What are his intentions? The ministry must know if we are to stop him. It's like chess, you see, he moves and we counter. We must know his strategy. That is where you come in. Will you help us? Will you help protect your nation's honor?"

"Don't you mean *your* honor?" he sneered.

"And, what if I let slip that you were the one who informed on your comrades? How do you think that would affect you, your family, and your reputation? Suddenly the hero who recovered from his amnesia after years of wandering would lose his stature. The newspapers would tear you to shreds. What happened to Captain Gereau would seem like a blessing. You would be humiliated. Where would you go to hide?"

He stared at the adjutant. What he said was true enough, but unknown to him his visitor *had* lied. Driven by the fear that he, too, might be identified as one of the principals who initiated the unrest, he implicated someone else, his commanding officer, as one of the instigators. Now, compounding his initial transgression, he was being asked to become a spy and thwart Jules Ronda's efforts to win back honor for his superior. It was too great a burden to bear. But, as in the past, the informer had to deal with the same panic he felt at Soissons. It was his failing. Hidden beneath the pomp, the noble parental lineage, the education, and the affluence, Charles Brousseau was a coward.

"You wouldn't do that to me or my family, would you?" He questioned. The adjutant's gaze was unrelenting. It seemed certain that he would indeed stoop to any measure to achieve his objective. That thought frightened the traitor. He yielded. "To protect my family I will do it. This is a very hard thing you ask of me. I don't know whether or not I will be able to carry it off. I must think further on this."

"No you won't. You will do exactly as I say. You were a soldier once, and not a very good one at that, but you did serve your country. Now you are being drafted into service again. Only this time, you won't be wearing a uniform."

"You have the wrong man. I can't help you. You will have to find someone else."

"Insolence doesn't serve you well; being compliant does. Which shall it be? Call the newspapers now, or wait until you leave."

"Alright, I'll do as you ask."

"My aide will contact you. He will arrange where and when to meet so that you can keep us regularly apprised. That is all."

―――

The knock on the door was soft. Some might have said it had a pleading quality. Claire Gereau had come to see Jules Ronda. She wondered whether he might be able to provide information about her husband's passing. Intuition is the one inexplicable phenomenon attributed to Homo sapiens. No one openly admits it exists, yet many are certain it does. There are many stories of someone taking thought of an event or person, only to find out there was good reason; someone died, or had taken ill, or appeared without reason or warning. Events have been known to follow the same path. Envisioning a happening before it actually takes place is not uncommon. Thus, it did not seem strange that while Simeon Gereau was reported missing in action from the battle at Soissons, his wife Claire firmly believed he was still alive. Without any further proof, she steadfastly held to that belief until several months ago, about the time Jules and Charles recovered from their amnesia and were discovered to be alive. Simeon has passed, she dreamt one night; he is gone. The realization did not cause her grief. She understood that whatever had taken place, he was at peace. Still, she yearned to know the facts of his whereabouts until that time and the circumstances of his existence. Since Ronda was her husband's closest comrade, instinctively she felt that if anyone knew what had happened to him it would be Jules. There was no doubt in her mind that this was the case.

Over the years she had remained essentially unchanged, despite having two lovely children. The passing of time had been kind to her. She heard someone approach.

"May I help you?" The servant asked.

"I wish to see Monsieur Ronda. Is he at home?"

"No, he and Madame are away."

"When do you expect them to return?"

"I can't say Madame; whom shall I say was asking for him"

"Madame Claire Gereau."

"And the purpose of you wanting to see him, what is it?"

"Mention my name; that will be enough."

"Thank you Madame."

"Did you find out anything?" Jean Pierre her son exclaimed as she approached. Nicole, her daughter was not far behind. The children were expecting to find out how their father had died. Until the discovery of Ronda and Brousseau, the matter remained unresolved. Now, there was a glimmer of hope of finding out how father and husband had spent the last moments of his life. But there was a caveat; should Ronda choose to tell them the truth, it might prove unbearable.

"They are away. I will try again next week." Claire patted her son's head. "Don't worry, we will find out about Papa. I promise." That seemed to satisfy everyone. Brother and sister ran off to do something, who knew what?

———

"What; crying again?" Jacques observed, "I know, I feel that way, too. Anyone who reads the last hundred pages of Simeon's diary and doesn't become angry has to have a heart of stone. That shouldn't have happened to him. I thought we were a cultured nation, a people who had feelings, sympathy. It seems we are not – and the death of that child. . ."

"I feel the same, but when she went back to retrieve her Gretel doll in the midst of all that bombardment – I won't be able to sleep tonight, I know it, perhaps not for a week." Marie placed her head on Jacques shoulder. He turned her so that she faced him, and embraced her.

"They say the war is over; is it really? We are still bleeding, but this time no one can see it except us. They think we have come home and all is well; if they only knew."

"I never realized," Marie uttered, as she gazed into her husband's eyes,

"No one does. Those who understand have been there," he replied, "and they will never forget. Only the grave will free them."

"Oh, darling, what can we do?"

"We have done what we could. We have seen Jules and Annette, we have read the diary, and we know now what really happened. It's a good thing that swine Brousseau is not here, I might see to it that he got what he deserved – a good thrashing. More, I would not dare."

"What of Jules? Do you think he will be able to gain justice for Simeon?"

"All vermin are uncomfortable in the sunlight of truth. If he can manage to get heard, then there might be justice. They will try to stop him before that. They will use every device to prevent him from airing his grievance. Of that, I am sure."

Jules visit had lifted Jacques perception of life. Unknowingly he had discarded the role of proprietor and donned the garb of comrade-in-arms to he who was seeking justice. At the moment such a chrysalis had little meaning, but as has been proven many times in the past, should the 'call to arms' come, those who love LaBelle France will respond. For Jacques wife her expression took the form of weeping. For him, it was anger and frustration which at some point evolved into a deep malaise. How could this nation and all it represented allow several individuals to accuse, try, and sentence others in secrecy? Reflecting on that imponderable produced a headache. He had to turn and consider other matters.

Not a word passed between Jules and Annette as their Renault sped along the winding road. He, deep in thought, was reliving the last days of his friend's life. Having once more heard those haunting words written in the diary, he could not escape. Annette, never having taken the time to have read the volume before, was also touched by its contents. Now she too, agreed that a wrong needed to be righted.

He nodded, pointed to a sign alongside the road. She smiled and nodded in response. The vehicle slowed and turned into a driveway. It was fourteen, time for lunch, a welcome respite from pondering weightier matters. The waiter brought the seated couple wine. They had chosen a table at the window. It was a beautiful day and there was no reason not to enjoy it in its fullest. They clinked goblets, wished each other 'bon appetite' and sipped their wine.

"What now?" Annette started, "You have a solicitor. What is next?"

Jules thought about her query. He had not considered the order of events.

"I'll be seeing him when we return. He may need more time to examine the diary. He will also need time to research Simeon's service record; honorable or dishonorable citations, if there are any. Then, we'll have to set a court date. I'm sure there will be a pre-court hearing – that is when they will try to squelch the case. Annette, this may get treacherous – you may be drawn into this."

"Don't worry, I'll be fine."

"If anything happened to you, I. . ." His wife reached across the table and placed her hand on his.

"I know. When we finish and get up to go, I will give you a reward – a kiss, my thank you for your love. I understand you must do this for Simeon. I could not live with myself if you did not. It was why I decided to spend my life with you. You are an honorable man. You are one of that rare and precious phalange of warriors – keepers of the good and decent. My love, I shall, and will be, with you until I am no longer able."

It was an unintended consequence of the tragedy of Simeon Gereau; those who were touched by his travail were inextricably changed. Now the deceased had more defenders than during his incarceration.

Advocate Mercal's office was full. Clients were standing in the halls waiting to see him. It seems Adjutant De Voux's threats to marginalize him had produced the opposite effect. After all, what client wouldn't want to hire an advocate who was not intimidated by the powers-that-be? Such a person would be fearless and unflinching in defense of his client, a most admirable trait. On the other side of the door that led to his office, this reversal was not to his advantage. Simeon Gereau's case required a great deal of study and research; his adversaries would be among the most skilled to be found in the legal profession.

The judge chosen would one of the most esteemed. As the plaintiff's counsel, he would have little room for error. Both the court and the defense would be waiting for the one slip they could use to invalidate their claim. And now this; he was receiving more and more new prospective clients each day. And then it came to him - the adjutant had changed his strategy. Instead of attempting to marginalize the advocate, why not flood him with work? Send legions of clients, all needing representation. In that way he would not be able to devote the required time to the case he was preparing to present before the supreme tribunal. On its face, it was brilliant. It forced the advocate to have a new appreciation for his adversary. He was smarter than the advocate believed. That miscalculation was not to be repeated.

Ronda would be pleased with Mercal's progress. He had hired several young lawyers, the ink still wet on their diplomas. He had investigated their backgrounds and allegiances very carefully. He could not afford to find out at a later date that one of them was a Judas. To the one he thought exceptionally skilled, he assigned the research of Simeon Gereau. Before sending her out however, he explained in full detail the risks and possible consequences of being associated with the case. He gave the newcomer the choice of accepting or rejecting the assignment. Lola Per accepted. The other two fledglings inherited the task of interviewing and evaluating new clients' needs. He also hired a new secretary for each. These, he had evaluated by his personal secretary, the young woman who had been with him since he opened his practice in this office.

Per was thorough in her research. She worked long hours, too long for her employer's liking, but he made no comment. The young woman seemed to enjoy her work, never complaining about the regimen. She understood the gravity of the assignment. She fully intended to complete it in record time and unimpeachable quality.

Early one morning she appeared before her mentor with the goods.

"I will not be available until further notice," he told his secretary. Then he and his researcher opened up the dossier and went through, word by word, what new information she had uncovered. Each time he posed a question or asked for affirmation, his researcher produced ample support for whatever documentation he had before him. It was a rigorous and unrelenting cross-examination of the work and its validity. To the advocate's satisfaction, she survived. In addition, she demonstrated that her work was, without question, beyond recall.

The dossier confirmed what he had already reasoned; that Captain Simeon Gereau was a person of impeccable reputation and unassailable character. His entire existence, as far as could be established, was without blemish. Why then, indict such an individual? Did someone, present at the scene, name him as the perpetrator to himself avoid being accused? It was impossible at this time to validate such a theory. The only way to do so would be to have someone who was there come forward and admit to such a travesty. Such a coup would be unlikely. Pleased with her work, the advocate penned a letter to his client. He was prepared to move forward with the case.

———

The night seemed especially dark, one of those times of the month when the moon visits some distant quadrant in the heavens. It was twenty-three when husband and wife reached home. The servants unloaded the vehicle while the pair sought libation, a late night aperitif.

"A number of persons have tried to contact you," his valet mentioned, "Here are their names."

Jules Ronda thumbed through his jottings. An envelope from Bernard Mercal was among them. Two names were unexpected; Charles Brousseau and Claire Gereau. He would contact them tomorrow. The subject of the advocate's letter was inspiring.

"Annette, Annette, he is ready to proceed. We are going to court."

Sharing his joy, she threw herself into his arms. "I'm so happy for you. You have suffered greatly for your friend. It has been as if you were carrying a large stone." Annette gently stroked her husband's face. "Perhaps we can find justice for Simeon and rid ourselves of this burden. Enough; we deserve to be happy – you deserve it more than I."

The dawn filled the Ronda's bedroom with light. But on this day it seemed more radiant, warmer, and more inviting. As his wife had mentioned, Jules had been burdened. But today it was gone. Whatever happened, wherever the path led, Simeon's travail would be heard. The world would know what *really* happened at Soissons.

He opened the letter from Brousseau. He was requesting to become a part of the effort to redeem Simeon's honor. This incongruity irked Ronda. Why this sudden interest in his charge? He had over a decade at Saint Germain to forge a friendship with Simeon, to treat him honorably, but he did not. Instead he played with his wench Lilly, squandered much of the funds entrusted to him for Jules' and Simeon's maintenance. Had it not been for the priest's intervention, his friend might well have died from malnutrition. Why the sudden change of heart, why now? It did not take long for Ronda to deduce the reason for his former warden's behavior. He was a spy. No doubt someone had enlisted him to determine what tactics Mercal would be employing at court. He needed to contact the solicitor and tell him this. Perhaps some benefit might come of it.

He knew what the widow desired; to find out about her husband. But at this point in time what could he tell her? With the legal battle imminent, how much dare he reveal? His heart ached for the woman. Could she bear hearing about the tribunal, the council, the sentence and his incarceration just miles from where she and the children lived? Still, he needed to provide her with some comfort. It was the least he could do. He owed Simeon that. He decided to meet her, and soon. The advocate could wait. The widow of a hero needed him, and he would not deny her.

Later that week he was knocking on the door of the Gereau house. He did not come unannounced, having sent word previously of his intention. Jean Pierre, Simeon's son, opened the door. Nicole, his daughter, waited a few steps away.

"I am Jules Ronda," he started,

"And my father's very excellent friend," he added, "Nicole, this is Papa's best friend. You know, the one mother has mentioned many times."

The daughter bowed slightly and said "It is my very great pleasure to meet you, sir." Obviously Claire had prepared the children in advance for his arrival. The youngsters ushered him into the parlor where the seated and stately Claire awaited him. The children guided the visitor to a chair.

"At last we meet, dear Jules. It has been a long time – too long." Claire waited for a response. Jules hesitated, not because he was reluctant or apprehensive, but seeing Claire again resurrected the thoughts of the many wonderful times the couples had enjoyed together, loving, sharing, and just being blissful in every moment the terrible conflict allowed. "Is everything alright?" She asked, her expression changing from one of happiness to one of concern.

"I am well. Seeing you after all this time brought to mind all those hours your husband, you, I, and Annette shared together. Whatever happens, nothing can erase those wonderful times from my memory. They were precious – and with a world war all around us."

"Yes, I cherish them, too. I miss Simeon, Jules; I cling to those years we had together. I even accept his having to die, but still unresolved is *how* he died. You were there. You must know. Tell me." Claire turned to the children. "Upstairs with you; Monsieur Ronda and I must talk. After we finish, I will tell you all about your father and how he died a hero." Claire waved her hand and in less time than it takes to tell the two were gone. The widow turned to her friend. "Now, tell me about Simeon."

"Madame, I cherish your husband's friendship more than you can ever imagine. I also cherish yours. He lived an honorable existence. He even cultivated the friendship of a little cherub named Calista. He was like a father to her. He worked so hard to remove the indelible scars that war had placed on her. It gave him great joy when he could make her laugh. Her father had been killed and her anguished mother took her own life. I think you know all this. You desire to know how your husband perished. I will tell you – but not at this time. I beg that you be patient – for just a little while longer. Then I will be able to reveal all."

"I have waited so long. . ."

"Please, trust me."

"Where is he buried?"

Ronda hesitated. "Nearby."

Claire pleaded "Take me to him."

"I will, but please do not ask me anything further until I am ready."

"I will get my coat."

"When you meet, don't ask too many questions. He may become suspicious. Let him talk. I'm sure he'll be so excited about bringing the matter before the court that he'll be bubbling with information. Remember all you can, especially any item that pertains to their strategy at court. We would be most interested in that. Keep in your mind that you *must listen* while he talks. This is not a debate. Consider yourself a scribe – what you recall is most important; what you forget may prove disastrous. Have I made myself clear?"

Adjutant De Voux finally stopped browbeating the thoroughly intimidated Brousseau.

"I understand – yes, I do. I compliment you on choosing me for such an important assignment. I'm sure this is because of my exemplary military record and my service as warden for the accused all these years. I have served my country without complaint all this time. It is only fitting that I should be the one. . ."

"When I saw you in Soissons you were in a hospital bed and only too anxious to lay the blame for the mutiny on your commanding officer whom I have lately found to be an exemplary individual. It is unconscionable that too late have I found this out; and it is too late for me to make amends, for he is no longer with us. Do what you're told, little man. You don't fool me. I know your kind. Go away, you are irritating my gout.

"But I thought. . ."

"Get out," De Voux announced.

As he watched the door close, the adjutant turned away. Now he was alone, subject only to his own scrutiny, not needing to play the game high-ranking military men play when politics are involved. His thoughts drifted back to those days when he and several other field-grade officers were charged with 'cleaning up the mess' at Soissons. Even now, after all this time, his recollections of the details remained vivid, as if someone had etched them in his memory with acid. He saw the faces of those who were ordered to be executed, those who were sent to prison, those who were demoted and finally, the trio: Gereau, Ronda, and Brousseau.

The single reality that had saved them all from the firing squad was that he and Ronda were of noble lineage. The life of the third person was of no consequence. The adjutant wagged his head fiercely, trying to flush away the recurring belief that he had been complicit in causing the deaths and imprisonment of comrade soldiers who had refused to be needlessly slaughtered as the result of deficient strategizing by upper echelon personnel. A cruel fate had chosen him to be one of those who were charged with the untenable task of considering, judging, and passing sentence on bloodied, wounded, and near-dying proud French soldiers.

And now, there was the trial. What would he say in his defense? What could he say? The passing of time had cast a new light on his and his compatriot's actions. For some of those in command of the theater, the matter would be moot; they had already left this life. Nothing decided in the court would have the slightest effect on them or their memory – that was a given; the court would protect them from ridicule. But what would they think of him? How would France judge him? What would they have to say about his denying the rights of the accused, of trying them in secret, of incarcerating them in secret, of appropriating funds *in secret* for their maintenance, of lying to their families by telling them they were missing in action? What could he offer in his defense – nothing.

The path forward was clear. He had to keep the matter from going to trial – no matter the cost.

———

"And you believe that is the reason for his new-found interest in our case? Why?" Advocate Mercal was evaluating the conclusion Jules Ronda had come to about his comrade. In fact, he had already come to the same, but his experience had shown him that what seems to be the case might not always be so. He was simply exploring the possibility of his client entertaining another more onerous intent.

"He is not an honorable man although he makes a good play at it. The man is a scoundrel – in every definition of the word: he is unfaithful to his wife, he is a liar and a deceiver and he is known throughout the mercantile establishments in Paris of being a lavish spender but miserly payer. Only his lineage protects him from the bill collectors – and that, I am told is becoming less and less of a shield. Economically speaking, he is heading for bankruptcy. And I know of no one who will come to his aid."

"This may seem strange to you, but what you have told me is good news. While I have never practiced the art of spying on my opponent, I have become quite skilled in sending false messages – and here, we have at our disposal the ideal messenger. Of course, we will need to be skillful in our dissemination, for the first time they find out the information they receive from him is of no use, they may conclude that we have found them out. Then your comrade Brousseau will be of no further use to us – or them. But, if we jig our fish line a little at a time, we may succeed in having them prepare rebuttals for topics we will not broach. They will be expending treasure and time which will ultimately be of no use to them. Further, it will keep them from strengthening their positions in areas where we *do intend* to attack."

"I can't wait for the gaming to begin."

"But remember, dear friend, many a brilliant gambit has ended in failure because of arrogance, being too sure of the invincibility of one's strategy, and, worst of all, underestimating the skill and intelligence of one's opponent. This is not a game for the faint of heart. We must be cautious; whatever position we assume, it must be on its face, respectful. We are accusing individuals, it is true, but they still represent the government of France, so, by implication, some will interpret our position as accusing the nation. We must vigorously avoid placing any material before the court that fosters that kind of thinking. If our strategy is that slovenly, it may be the bastille for both of us. Again, the gravity of what we will be proposing may have consequences we have not or cannot envision."

"This is your last chance, Lieutenant Jules Ronda. Consider what I have told you, and the possibilities I have mentioned in detail. Do you wish to continue?"

"I see now why you are so highly regarded. Come, shake my hand. Simeon and I always did that before we embarked on a new venture." Never was there a more solid grasp.

———

As the time drew closer for the two sides to appear before a tribunal its date yet to be determined, it was apparent to both that the decisions emanating from the case might require profound changes in the way the military treated its combatants. Matters regarding performance, cowardice, mutiny, and failure to perform in any manner might be referred to authorities and adjudicated in a *public* venue. The accused would have the privilege of a defense, and open trial, and visitation by family.

To the issue at hand, there might be some discussion of compensation for the Gereau family in light of the way the tribunal had accused, judged, and sentenced the defendant based on flimsy evidence and the hearsay of only one individual. Adjutant De Voux, at the center of the controversy, found that he had no place to hide, and no defense that might be reasonable to a jury. What he and his comrades did was simply wrong and beyond any reasonable expectation of exoneration. He squirmed in his seat as he recalled the affair. He envied those compatriots who had passed on; they were beyond humiliation, of a strict and revealing review that would certainly come from the court. His roasting was near. The magistrate would be the one inserting the spit.

In the opposing camp Advocate Mercal decided to include Lola Per in the trial preparation phase. She had smitten him. Her extraordinary presentation and the professional aplomb she exhibited impressive. In addition, she appeared formidable. Not fetching, not unattractive, the tall young woman had an air about her – it was the way she carried herself. She stood erect. After seeing her, one could not deny that she appeared confident, almost threatening. Her demeanor was engaging and warm. She smiled frequently, appropriately; and, if there is such an attribute, professionally. Beyond what could be observed, one felt that an enormous intellectual engine lay behind all of it. It was his admiration for her skill that moved him, not desire. He put his reaction to rest with that convenient conclusion.

One more action was required. He had to inform Lola of the risks; being marginalized professionally after the trial was over, the slurs and remarks she would be receiving as the case droned on. It was only fair that she should be made aware of the pitfalls. Late one afternoon he summoned her to his office. Everyone else had gone home, even those who made it a point to stay a little later in order to impress the boss.

"Yes?" Lola commented as she seated herself across the desk from Bernard. From her manner he surmised she had already anticipated the topic of this meeting. He concluded she was more intuitive than he envisioned.

"Mademoiselle Per, I am considering having you assist me on this case, the one you researched. However, I have some reservations. Would you care to hear them?"

"You are concerned that the trial may have consequences that extend beyond the courtroom, that you and I may be targeted after it is over, that our careers may be over. In your case, you have the means to retire to your estate and choose to grow grapes, or engage in the production of Pate foie, or raise pigs, or some other innocuous venture. But I, not as wealthy, will be left to fend for myself. As an advocate, my career will be non-existent; I may have to roam the streets at night, I may have to become a prostitute, or engage in robbing banks, or some other such folly. Were those your concerns?"

"Here I was concerned that you would be stepping unaware into a lion's cage only to be scarred perhaps forever, but you have already considered the detrimental effects of taking part in such a noteworthy trial. Are you clairvoyant? If so, you will be accompanying me to the racetrack when it opens. And you are right; I can, and may retire after this; they can't hurt me the way they can you. You seem to possess an exceptional flair for this work, something I have not seen in an advocate for decades. You are perceptive. You are determined. I would hate to have you get shipwrecked in your first exposure to trial work. I have been considering this talk between us for weeks. Make no mistake, I would like to have you by my side as an associate, but I fear the cost to you may be too great. Take some time and think about your answer. Whether you decide for or against, it will not change my opinion of you or your work."

"Yes, I will."

"What do you mean?"

"I accept the position of associate counsel."

"But you have not given it any thought."

"I have been thinking of nothing else for a month. I even considered going to bed with you. That is how much I want to be a part of this case." Lola winked. "I will still consider that if it needs to be part of the bargain."

Mercal's face reddened. "I don't want you that way; never have I ever stooped to such measures. I should dismiss you; I will!"

"Forgive me, I made an inappropriate comment. I could never go to bed with you; you are too principled. Most likely you would be discussing Montesquieu's *Spirit of Laws* while you made love to me. You are too good for me."

Mercal laughed. "My, but you are a special one." He paused, "Are you up to this? Don't be flippant about it. This is serious business. Have you considered this carefully? I shouldn't even ask that question – of course you have, it's in your blood."

"When do we start?"

"Hang your coat up on the rack over there. Have you eaten yet? I'll call for delivery."

———

"A Charles Brousseau is here to see you, Monsieur, shall I bring him in?" Ronda's servant inquired.

"Yes, show him in." *There he is*, the master thought, *heading towards me, smiling, and donning his most pleasant manner.*

"It's so good to see you. It's been *so* long since we have talked."

"And what brings you here?"

The visitor became pensive. It was as if he was deliberating on how the world's problems might be solved. Ronda was not fooled for one second. "I have become enlightened; I am repentant. I am trying to make amends for the terrible way I treated you and Simeon at Chateau Germain. It is frightening to think that I was that man, the one who held back rations, who squandered funds intended for his and your upkeep. And yes, there was my affair with that trollop; I am embarrassed about that, too."

Here it comes, Ronda mused.

"I want to make everything right – as much as possible – by helping you with your effort to restore the good name of Simeon Gereau. I want to be by your side, at every meeting, in every deliberation, contribute to every decision – I want Simeon's honor restored. Will you let me do this? Please, I beg of you, help me to erase the terrible things I have done by participating in this process. I know I have no right to ask. I know that you do not like me – and for good reason, mind you. I understand why you despise me. But after all, you are a Christian, and a good one. Isn't it your belief to forgive once repentance is shown by the sinner? I am asking for forgiveness, Jules – I am *begging* for it!"

Well done, Ronda mused, *I could not have done better. But I won't answer you just yet. First, I will strike a pose, so. Then, I shall curl my fingers around my chin, as if I were deep in thought. After that, I shall cover my face with my hands, as if I am examining my innermost self, so. Then, I shall be silent for several moments, like this. Now, I will turn and face you. I will smile and say,*

"You can help, Charles, you can help us clear our comrade Simeon Gereau's name."

"Really? Oh, that makes me so happy. I can't tell you how I feel; I think I can fly, yes, I am so happy I feel I can fly."

"Not in here, please, the ceilings are not that high."

He took out his watch and glanced at it. "Look at the time – I must run. I will be in touch later in the week. Please let me know when the first meeting is. I don't want to miss even one." The servant escorted him out.

You play Judas well. I almost believed you. "James," he called, "Come." The servant appeared. "Follow him; find out what appointment is so important that he can't stay with me and learn all he can about saving our comrade's honor."

The brothel was located on the cusp of the commercial district. In one way of thinking, it, too, was a kind of commerce – of flesh. Brousseau ran up the steps so swiftly he stumbled. James, a short distance away, had difficulty containing himself. Upon his return, he sought out his master and prepared to tell him what he had found.

"It's a brothel, isn't it? He's gone to a brothel"

"How did you know?" The servant asked, surprised.

"It's his behavior James, as long as I've known him he's always been like this. He's the Charles Brousseau I've always known. There has been no repentance."

A happier Charles Brousseau told the adjutant's aide "Tell the adjutant I have engaged the enemy and infiltrated his lines. Tell him I did it very skillfully. I completely fooled our opponent."

The next day Ronda met with Mercal and said "The fish is hooked."

—

At Last

S ad; a grown woman kneeling over a grave, scooping up bits of dirt in her hand and then letting them fall back to the ground through her open fingers. It was as close as Claire Gereau could get to her beloved husband. "Oh Simeon, at last I have found you. You have been so near to me all these years, but no one told me where you were. I could have come and brought you flowers; forgive me, forgive me." The tears cascaded down her cheeks and wet the soil beneath her. Only her sobbing broke the sweet silence of early morning. Jules Ronda, the one who had taken pity on her and escorted her here, could only stand a few paces to the rear and remain respectfully silent. But inwardly he was proud of himself. He had assisted in helping Simeon and Claire meet once again, even under these tragic circumstances. Now she could visit her beloved as often as she wished. The mystery concerning his whereabouts had been solved. But Ronda did not tell her the rest. She would be hearing all about it soon enough. Once the legal proceeding began, the newspapers would be publishing every detail, every opinion, every reflection concerning the treatment and incarceration of Captain Simeon Gereau. Rather than have her read about it with no warning, he had decided to meet with her the night before the trial and prepare her for what was to come. Claire's question brought him back from his musings. "When they buried him here, why was I not told?"

Ronda helped the widow to her feet. "There is more, Claire, and I will reveal all of it to you – at the proper time. You recall I asked that you trust me. Now I ask once more; trust me to tell you when the proper time comes. We are friends. On my honor I will never deny you."

"I have never questioned your honor. Of the many men I have known, you are one of the few I trust implicitly."

Ronda kissed her hand. "Thank you. All of this is hard enough for all of us; let us not make it any more difficult."

He escorted Claire out of the cemetery.

"Did you find out about Papa?" Young Jean Pierre asked, "He must have been on a secret mission, that's why we never heard anything about him."

Nicole interceded, saying "Please tell us Mama, please."

"I have found where your father is buried. For the time being, I cannot take you there."

"Why not," the daughter inquired, "We could offer prayers and ask God to forgive his sins. We should go."

"What you say is true, dear, but we must wait. I cannot tell you why, but we must bide our time."

"Does he have a special place where heroes are buried?" Jean Pierre could not contain himself. He was a young child when last he had seen his father; Nicole, a baby. All they could cling to were Claire's stories about him, how wonderful and kind he was, and how he must certainly have died performing some act of heroism. It was the gift she had given her children; a father of unblemished honor and great stature, ripped from them by that terrible occurrence named war.

"I know," she said, "Let us get dressed tomorrow and go to church. We will all pray for Papa. Isn't that a good idea? We can even start tonight when we do our evening prayers."

"That is the best idea you ever had, Mama," Nicole replied, "I'm going to bed early so I can start then."

Jean Pierre ran toward the stairs. "Beat you up to bed." The girl glanced at her mother and frowned.

———

At the end of a long day a comfortable chair and a glass of wine completes it in proper fashion. But for Lola Per it was simply the beginning of the second phase of her very busy existence. The advocate had supplied her with a copy of Simeon Gereau's diary. Annotating a section, he suggested she read and familiarize herself with its author's incisive observations. The young advocate was ambitious. It was not by mistake that she chose to interview for Bernard Mercal. At school she had heard of this practitioner who was both skilled and fearless. Some in the profession had no use for him; they actually despised him.

But many, both young and old, wished they could be like him. All they lacked was his courage, its attainment not available for course study at the school. Historically, testicular or estrogenic fortitude were wonderful qualities, but rare. Working with him became her main objective. She would not consider any other mentor. And when she had achieved her goal, fortune smiled on her once again. She was given the task of researching Simeon Gereau, the subject of the most important trial case of the decade, perhaps the century. She used every ounce of energy she could command to produce a dossier of as high a quality possible. In addition, she worked equally hard to frame a series of questions challenging the validity of each item in her research.

Thus, when her employer sought to advertise the weaknesses in her report, there were none. She had already investigated, found and corrected them herself. If the solicitor needed support through the tedious and demanding elements of the trial, he had unwittingly supplied himself with a person of gargantuan skill. He would not only be shielded, he would be protected by a towering wall.

Now, let us see what this saint of a man has to say for himself, Lola mused, *it should be interesting.* She removed the marker Mercal had added, and began to read.

April 1917

Why are they doing this? Everyone knows we are preparing an assault. They are making such a fuss about it that even those in China must know. Certainly the Germans entrenched on the hill must have seen and heard the unrestricted clatter and clamor our trucks and machines are making. Shouldn't we be quieter, hide our movements, and not advertise our intent? I can't understand our utter disregard for secrecy. Even Calista knows something is about to happen – and she's only a child. I haven't seen any artillery. They must be bringing up the big guns later; what else would provide cover for advancing troops? I hope all the noise doesn't make the enemy too jittery. Next Sunday is Calista's confirmation. It's going to be a wonderful day. She is so happy about it. I want it to be a special day for her. She has suffered so because of this war. So, please, God, grant her this one day of happiness, with many more to follow. Please, God, for her sake, and the rest of the children, too. We are ready. After church, my company will lead the parade to Saint Waast church on the other side of the river where we will have a celebratory lunch. The farmers say Sunday will be sunny and warm for this time of the year. I only hope they are right. Enough tragedy has burdened Calista's life. She deserves better.

I love you, Claire. You and the children sleep well.

S.G.

April, 1917

Today I railed at my comrades. It was the first time. I inspected their horses' tack and found them dirty. I told them I wanted everything perfect for the parade. What would all those lovely children think if they found out that we couldn't even keep our gear clean? I told them to shine the brass, soap and clean the leather because I would be holding inspection at eighteen. They were not happy about that but I didn't care. This is for Calista. It has to be perfect. Everyone in town has come to life. This confirmation mass will make them forget about the war, the lack of food, the death and dying of their comrades, sons, and daughters. People are baking and sewing and stitching lovely things for the children.

They are tearing up cloth remnants and sewing new clothes. I saw a farmer washing his horse and combing its mane. As I passed by, he waved. Weeks ago I saw the same man; he looked as if he were going to a funeral. The lights in the Patisserie are on until late. Francois is baking all of the bread and cakes for Saint Waast; their bakery was destroyed last year by artillery. Everyone's spirits has been elevated. It is a good thing that will happen soon. It is a blessing, this confirmation.

Can you know how deeply I love you? I hope so. Sleep well, my Claire.

S.G.

Lola skipped a few pages in order to get to Sunday.

April 1917

Calista had Monsieur Dutoit escort her over to my billet. She wanted to be sure I understood how grateful she was for all my help and that she never could have gotten to this point in her life without me. Of course, this was in no way meant to diminish the help Monsieur and Madame had provided. She said that tomorrow she would add in her confirmation prayer the names of her father and mother, the Dutoits, and me, because she felt that God had provided another father for her while her real father was in heaven with her mother.

She bowed, and left. Monsieur Dutoit was smiling. So was I.

I hope that all goes well tomorrow. I still can't put aside my concern about the enemy forces on top of the hill. Should they decide to do something, we would be at their mercy. I keep asking myself; how can they? There will be my company of cavalry at the front followed by wagons filled with civilians.

Why would they ever think we were attacking with such a motley force? I worry too much. They are smarter than that.

It touched my heart that Calista felt she needed to see me this evening. I love her as my own.

S. G.

April 1917

I am confined to quarters. The worst has happened. Calista, my lovely Calista is dead – and it is my fault. They started to shell our parade as soon as we crossed the bridge. Didn't they see all the civilians? Didn't they see the wagon with the children in their confirmation dresses and suits? The first salvo destroyed a wagon carrying some of the grandfathers and grandmothers. All my men dispersed among the civilians and guided them to safety while trying to quell the panic. I looked for Calista. I found her in a ditch. Her dress was covered with mud. Everything was exploding all around us. I tucked her under my arm and headed for my horse. She wriggled out and ran back to the ditch. Her doll Gretel was there. After she found it she came back. 'I knew you would come to save me,' she said, 'I knew it.' I spurred my horse and galloped toward the bridge. We were almost there when – and that is all I remember. I awoke in the hospital. Jules was at my side. He told me I had been unconscious for two days. I asked about Calista. He told me she died in his arms.

I will never forgive myself. She is dead because of me, of my pride, of my arrogance. I wanted everything to be perfect; how? By having my unit march ahead of everyone? If my company would not have been there, they would not have shelled the group. Oh Calista, I would give my life to redeem yours. What have I done, what have I done? Now you are with your parents in heaven and it's my fault. God, oh God forgive me. How will I be able to live with this? And now we are preparing to fight, to make the assault on that barren hill.

There is no cover. The German artillery has registration on all the key points: the road intersections, the narrow winding parts of the road, and each major street in Saint Waast. Our troops will be slaughtered. I must stop it. There has been enough bloodletting. Perhaps in this way I can make amends for her death. I must get out of this bed but I can't. My head keeps spinning. I must get dressed. Damn my head; the room is still spinning. I must lie down. Later, this evening, perhaps. I must get up and take command, if only to save my comrades from utter annihilation. I can't let them go up that hill. If I'm ordered to do so, then I will lead the charge. It will be a fitting way for me to die. I don't deserve to live after what I did to Calista. God forgive me.

Claire I love you. Keep the children safe.

S.G.

And this is the man the tribunal sentenced to spend the rest of his life in prison? Lola opined, *how could they?* Simeon's scribblings deeply moved the young woman. She marked the page. The court would certainly have to hear the passages she had just read. She was beginning to comprehend the value that needed to be placed on this person's life and the enormous implications it placed on the correct resolution of this case. No freethinking Frenchman would stoop to exact such a burden on another human being, especially one with such an honorable background. It would take utter desperation, a state approaching temporary insanity or panic to seize upon such an alternative. And, if those actions were to be suddenly revealed in a court of law, how much more desperate would perpetrators become in their attempt to hide it?

It came to her in a flash; *I may be in danger.*

Someone knocked on the door. Per glanced at her watch; twenty past twenty. *Not too late, but who would be calling at this hour,* she reasoned. "Yes, who is it?"

"I'm a friend of Jules Ronda – I served with him. Simeon Gereau was my commanding officer."

"How did you find out where I live?"

"Your employer told me."

"He never gives out anyone's address without consulting them. What is your name?"

"Charles Brousseau."

"How did you find out where I live?"

"I followed you. I understand you will be working on Simeon's case. I want to help."

"If you really want to help, you will leave this instant and never come here again."

"But I want to help." Per moved away from the door. She went to her bedroom. She returned.

"I am armed. Now will you leave?"

"As you wish – I only wanted to help." She heard his grumbling become fainter and fainter as he departed.

———

"What information should we give him?" Ronda asked, "He's not that smart. We can fill his mind with all sorts of tales; he won't even know the difference."

"No, but those who sent him will. We have to convey information that seems real, so much so, that it will not be questioned."

Advocate Per burst into her employer's office. "A person named Charles Brousseau paid me a visit last night. Who is he? I was ready

119

call the police if he didn't leave. I told him I was armed. He must have decided it would be better to leave than be shot." She paused. "Of course I wouldn't, but I did threaten him with the alternative. Is he dangerous?"

"He is the opposition's spy. He served with Jules here, and Simeon. We have a strong feeling that he is the one who accused Simeon of telling the troops not to engage the enemy – to save his own neck. He's worse than a coward. Did you tell him anything?"

"I told him to leave, that's all."

Mercal glanced at Ronda. "It seems Providence may have provided a perfect conduit to feed our spy the information he requires." He turned to Per. "Can you control your displeasure of this worm and be friendlier? You would be the perfect person to feed him all the trash we want the other side to consume. Will you consider it?"

"Is he dangerous?" She asked.

"Only if he is drunk or in a brothel," Ronda remarked, "He is bravest when there is no danger. If any appears, he is nowhere to be found."

"Then I'll do it. He gets one hour - only one, of my time and, no more than twice a week. You see, I am working on a very important case, one which I'm sure he will be interested in."

"Let's get back to the matter at hand. Did you start to read the diary?"

"Yes, and I had a great deal of difficulty with it. It makes my heart heavy just to read it. He has touched my heart. How could all of this have happened to such a good man?"

"We will make it right, won't we, Jules?" Mercal added.

"You are the advocate, I am the client. I want justice."

"And you shall have it, on my honor," He insisted.

"And mine," Per echoed.

And so the net was set. Lola Per would appear more disposed to answer his inquiries since he was so concerned about the need to seek justice for his dear departed commanding officer. She wondered how she might arrange to meet him again without appearing anxious.

That was all taken care of. Leaving the building after an arduous day, a man approached.

"Forgive me, but I need to apologize. I am Charles Brousseau and I was the assassin who stood outside your door the other night. I just had to meet you and tell you how sorry I am for invading your privacy.

It's just that I want to help you and whoever the advocate is to restore Simeon's good name. I still want to help. Am I wrong in asking you again?"

He seems so sincere, Per mused, *but I'll not say yes just yet. I must not appear too willing.* "I understand. I will give it some thought. Let's meet here tomorrow, say, at nineteen. I'll give you my answer then."

Thank you, thank you," said the spy.

A wolf in sheep's clothing, she mused.

———

"You could have seemed a little less anxious. Even my clerk would have suspected something by the way you approached her; how did she seem after she met you the second time?"

"After she saw who I was, she appeared calmer, *Mon Adjutant,* I believe I convinced her that I wasn't a threat."

"And did you convince her that you weren't a spy? What about that? She is no fool. All the reports about her say the same thing – she is formidable and not anyone's fool. Hmm; if she thought you were a spy, she would have jumped at the chance to engage your cooperation. That way, she could have used you to provide us with false information. No, she didn't do that; she decided to wait. Hmm; perhaps she is going to confer with Mercal about letting you into the inner circle. That would be the proper thing to do. A young associate would most likely do that."

"What do you think? Will she let me in?"

"Yes, I do. I believe you will be all right. Even with all of your blundering ways you have managed to get behind enemy lines."

———

"Are you all right?" The customer asked, "The two of you seem different lately. Is one of you ill, is it a family matter? Just what is wrong?" He was not the only one who saw the changes in Marie and Jacques; half the neighborhood had taken notice. They were concerned about their friends the proprietors.

"It's nothing," the owner replied.

"Don't tell me it's nothing. I'm your friend; I've known you since you opened this café. For God sake, be honest with me. Can I help? Do you need money? What is it?" Jacques pulled up a chair and sat down.

"It's a long story – a very long story. You need not know all the details. It's a legal matter – it doesn't concern us directly, but in a way it does – in a way it concerns every one of us. If you knew what it was you would see why Marie and I are so upset. It's something we want be a part of, yet we can't. We're here and the trial will be in Paris. We won't know anything about it – how it's going, what the results are until it's all over. But we don't want that. We want to be there."

"Well, why didn't you mention this before? I have the answer. You should have asked me sooner. Right now, the way you two are, you will lose all your customers by the first of the year. No one wants to be in a place where the owners are sourpusses. And you two are certainly that these days. Tell your customers something very important has happened and that you have to go away for a time. Close the place up. That way, everyone will be praying for you and just waiting for you to come back to show you how much they love you and Marie. Go, for God's sake. If whatever this is means that much to you, then go. You will never forgive yourself if you don't."

Jacques turned away and shouted, "Marie, Marie!"

—

Having bravely borne the isolation as her husband Jules pursued his quest, the appearance of Jacques and Marie Tremaine was an unexpected gift. Annette Ronda did not hide her joy in seeing them. And to have them stay for an extended period was even more exhilarating. The pair came unannounced, their letter reaching Annette the day after they arrived. It didn't matter. Whatever the circumstance, they were welcome – always. Their bags unpacked, a short nap later they met with Annette to discuss how Simeon's case was progressing.

They explained they could stay away no longer. They needed to be a part of the effort to regain honor for their departed comrade. Since Annette was not privy to the case's progress, the conversation soon turned to reminiscing about past times and the pleasant episodes the two couples shared. The war now seemed distant, a nightmare once dreamed but now placed in its proper place and scope; a sad episode survived but better forgotten.

The only overarching reality left from it was regaining the good name of their friend. Thus, it was not difficult to leave that issue for some other time and not wile away the precious hours lamenting over past injustices. It was far more enjoyable to engage the memory in recalling the good times. It is accepted as one of the myriad of human failings: to remember pleasant things and put aside all else.

Dinner was served and the three sat down to dine. Jacques questioning glance drew the appropriate reply.

"Jules seldom gets home this early. He and those legal people are always discussing or ironing out one detail or another. He usually gets home at twenty-one, sometimes later."

"It must be hard for you," Marie offered.

"Yes, it is, but we are nearing the end to all this business. Jules has borne this burden long enough. Soon, he and I will be free. Claire too, will finally be able to put all of her unknowing to rest. It will be good for everyone. Just a little longer, a little longer. Be brave, that's what I tell myself every morning. Jules is the most courageous man I know. He awakens every day ready to carry the fight forward. We have breakfast, he kisses me and then he is off. His stride is firm and his walk that of someone determined. And I must be that brave woman he expects to be waiting for him when he gets home." Annette stiffened. "And, I am."

Marie placed her hand over Annette's. Her message was unspoken, but clear. Her host replied with a knowing smile.

"We are here to help."

"In any way we can, Jacques added, "The *Plus* is closed until further notice. All of our customers have an idea why we closed the café, but they are not privy to the details. We have kept that from them. It will be exciting to bring good news upon our return. We are hoping for that." He seemed pleased with himself. He felt the sudden surge that many feel when they become involved in performing some benevolence; such as keeping Annette's spirits high.

The closing of the front door signaled Jules' arrival. "Mmm; whatever it is, it smells good." Entering the dining room he was surprised to see his two friends.

"Isn't it wonderful," Marie opined, "They have come to support us." The host slid into his chair. A servant raced from the room to retrieve a serving for his master.

Jacques poured wine and brought it to his friend. "This should help. You look tired, my friend. Is this pace too much for you? Perhaps slowing down a bit may prove beneficial."

Ronda ignored the comment. "We are close. Soon we will be ready to go to trial. We have amassed a mountain of evidence, some of which will prove very damaging to our opponents. I am going to love watching them squirm."

"When will it begin?" Marie questioned.

"There is nothing firm yet. We have been requested to go to a preliminary hearing next week. We should have a good sense of what we will be facing at trial after that meeting. We expect the worst. But we are prepared for it."

For the moment silence was the order of the day. Ronda consumed his meal with the gusto of one who desperately needed nourishment. Three goblets of wine helped lubricate the passageway that led to his digestive machinery. The rest watched the warrior for truth feed himself. When it was over, the discussion resumed.

"They may try to subvert you, you know," Jacques opined, "infiltrate with someone you know, get some information about how you intend to present your case."

"They already have," their host answered, "But we have that under control."

"Who is it?" Marie asked.

"It's a secret. I can't divulge that information."

"Is it someone we know?" She continued, "Why can't you tell us?"

"Spies lose their value once they are exposed. This person is valuable. We can convey false information to our opponents through him. They will be preparing to defend against topics we will not be mentioning."

"Him; then it is a man! Do we know him? We must; I'll bet we all know him. Who is he Jules; tell us, please." Marie could barely contain herself.

Ronda arose. "I'm exhausted. Please excuse me. I need some rest."

"PLEASE!" She persisted. Ronda raised his hand. Marie fell silent.

"Get a good rest my friend, you have earned it." Jacques called after him.

———

He could hardly contain himself. Having rushed all the way to the rendezvous, he had run out of breath and could hardly convey what he had learned to the aide.

"Calm down, take a few deep breaths, that's it. I can wait until you restore your normal breathing. There, you're looking better already. The blue is subsiding. A few more minutes and you'll be all right." The aide wagged his head. *Who does he think he is?* He mused. *At his age, running that fast could make him faint. What he has must be really important for him to take such a chance. It had better be. De Voux needs all the ammunition he can get. His defense is weak. If I had the money, I would be betting his side will lose.*

Brousseau stared at the aide. He took a deep breath, then another, and, another. Finally, he was ready.

"Tell the adjutant that they have contacted the officer in charge of the tanks, you know, the four that were blown up by the artillery at Soissons. They expect he's going to say the infantry didn't have a chance of taking that hill. The assault should have been cut off – at least until we moved our own artillery up to give them cover."

"Who is he? Do you know where he lives? How can we contact him?"

"I didn't get any of that. They are very secretive. I have good relations with the junior lawyer Lola Per. I have to pry the information out of her - she's not that talkative. Oh yes, they're also trying to find the officer in charge of the artillery battalion. It seems he has the same opinion as the tank officer. They let it slip that he's from Metz – all those artillerists come from that region. Try there. Someone must know him."

"It's been over ten years – finding him will not be easy."

"You have plenty of personnel. Are you telling me you can't find one man even after ten years? You wouldn't make a very good officer. I just told my people to do it and it was done. They didn't whine about how hard it would be." Not happy, the aide left.

But the information he had received was in no way what Lola Per had discussed with the spy. She had simply *alluded* to the possibility that others, who did not engage in the assault, might have had doubts about the wisdom of ordering troops up a long hill heavily defended with automatic weapons and artillery, and without any benefit of defilade. She never mentioned tanks or artillery, or, for that matter, the mess steward. Brousseau, already well known for his flights of reasoning simply put two and ninety-two together and called it two and two. During armed conflict, such erroneous claptrap would, when discovered, mean prison or a firing squad for the raconteur. Here, the storyteller was safe. In their zeal to upstage Mercal and Ronda, De Voux's team welcomed any scrap of information, even unverified, to examine and evaluate. The stakes were high. They dared not discard even the most inconsequential bit of information they received.

"You had him followed?" Lola asked Mercal.

"He reported to De Voux's aide. God only knows what he said. What did *you* tell him?"

"I created the unsubstantiated possibility that perhaps there were other officers, not at Soissons, who questioned the wisdom of making the assault. I gave him nothing further. He kept asking about the tank commanders, the artillery council, those who were second in command, the infantry officers – everyone he could think of. I imagine the wheels in his brain were turning faster and faster. Fortunately he left before they exploded." Per laughed. "He is such an arrogant fool. I don't think I have ever met anyone like him."

"This fool, as you call him, denied food to Gereau, pilfered money specifically earmarked for his and Ronda's care. He spent the money on some woman he encountered. Only interference by a priest forced him to relent. That, Lola, is your arrogant fool." Mercal's eyes were ablaze with rage. She had never seen him like this. Lesson learned; this was the advocate everyone talked about, the one whose passion for justice could not be assuaged. This was the man she respected and, perhaps, loved.

"Do you always get like this?" She asked.

"Take warning, this is a side of me you don't want directed at you."

"All right," she said demurely, "I'll be good." Mercal smiled, wagged his head and waved Lola Per to get back to her desk.

―

"Is this where he is?" Jean Pierre asked, "Not a very good place for father," he complained.

"Over there, under that tree. Be careful, don't bend the flower stalks."

"He'll like these, Nicole added, I picked them myself."

"Come, let us kneel." Claire suggested. The trio then offered prayers: one, for Simeon's soul and that he should be forgiven his sins, two, that the family had finally found his remains so they could give homage, and, three, which only Marie said to herself, that soon her husband's honor would be restored through the efforts of his friend Jules Ronda and the advocate he had retained. The daughter placed the flowers on the mound and then made a cross in the dirt with two of her fingers. The son noticed and did the same.

"Papa, we love you," Claire exclaimed, "Now we can be with you again."

The grief of family for a loved one is one of the unforeseen and seldom discussed effects of war. After the flag waving and the much repeated hatred for the opponent fades into the sands of time, what is left is the reality of families having to bear for life the inconsolable loss of a loved one. No matter how bravely one carries the burden, the inescapable reality is that it could all have been avoided were there no conflict. That, too, is seldom, or never, discussed.

"Let's sit, on that bench over there," the boy pointed, "That way we can be with Papa a little while longer." The weather being favorable and the breeze warm and soothing, the three remained close to the gravesite the entire afternoon and into the early evening. Claire saw that the extended respite improved the children's mood and their acceptance of what was.

"Mama, how did you meet Papa?" the girl ventured, "You don't have to tell me if you don't want to." The question was perfect for the occasion. What better way to remember a loved one than relive his life.

"Your father was a wonderful person. His father owned a farm and he worked on it after school. He learned or taught himself all the skills necessary to farm and even some others. He could work with wood, know when and how to plant certain seeds at the proper season, even make metal things as a blacksmith would. Everyone admired that he had learned all these things at such an early age."

"And what about you, Mama, how did Papa meet you?" She repeated. The boy moved closer to hear more clearly.

"When it came to girls, Papa was not so good at that. He and I were in many classes together, but we hardly spoke. I tried to encourage him by smiling, but every time I did, it was as if someone hit him with a stone – he stopped whatever he was doing and stared at me. But I wouldn't give up – I kept smiling."

"Yes, yes?" Her son intervened.

"One day, as I was walking to class, he approached. I could see he was very nervous, so I smiled and greeted him with a hello. I can't remember what else I said, but my goal was to calm him. Finally, he took a deep breath and said in a very soft voice 'Claire I want to be with you but I don't know how. Please help me.' I said I would. And that is how it all began." Both children seemed pleased.

"That was nice," Nicole opined. A grinning Jean Pierre nodded.

Claire glanced at the sky. "I'm getting hungry. Is anyone else?" Both children nodded. "Let's hurry, it's getting dark."

Pacing, pacing, pacing; when is he going to stop? The aide mused. *I told him everything that idiot told me. Why is he angry? What could he have expected from that imbecile? After all, he was the one who betrayed his commanding officer. What honor is there in him? I wouldn't trust him with feeding my horse. I think the adjutant finally realizes with whom he is dealing. He bet on a dead horse. I wonder what he will do now. He's stopped. Here it comes – I can feel it; he's going to start screaming at me.*

"Where are you? I can't see you. Why is it so black? I can't see – I can't see!" The aide approached. The adjutant made his way to his chair by touch. He had lost his sight. His complexion had turned sallow. He was sweating – hints of ashen gray appeared near his lips. The aide raced out of the room screaming for help and shouting for someone to get a doctor. By the time he returned with one, the adjutant was on the floor - unconscious, but alive. More medical personnel arrived and, racing through the city at high speed, reached the hospital in quick time. Not young, but not that old, De Voux was not able to accommodate the strain that the case involving the honor of Simeon Gereau placed on him. Worry, lack of sleep, frequent chest pains, and horrendous headaches had taken their toll. The adjutant was a very sick man.

His aide visited him the very next day. Concern and fear were etched in the young soldier's face.

"Don't worry, I'm going to live," his boss offered, "You're not going to get off that easily."

"Thank you sir, that is wonderful," was his reply.

"Have we received a date for the hearing?"

"No sir. Perhaps someone else should take over. You are not well."

"I am in charge. I will remain in charge. Pass the word: De Voux is still in charge."

"Yes sir." The aide left – hastily.

He was alone now, left without distraction, stripped of his rank, his authority and his power; able to confront his naked humanity and the reality that he was mortal. At such a time, a certain clarity emerges; gone are the follies of life with all their fantasies. Life and its ending seems very near. The void, the path all see as the chasm between life and death, manifests itself in frightening nearness. De Voux was not the first atheist to turn religious.

A new perspective entered his thinking. For the first time he saw the Soissons event in a different light. He was not a commander restoring order to a frightened cadre of soldiers. At last, he perceived their reality; certain death from a withering crossfire of automatic weapons and accurately tuned artillery. It was as if, for the first time, he was standing in the same field and experiencing the horror they felt. The crushing insight of those moments caused him discomfort, even panic. His breathing became more labored, he began to sweat profusely, A pale blue spread across his lips. About to lose consciousness he shouted "Nurse, Nurse!"

The adjutant was approaching the void.

After an intense effort by medical personnel his life was spared and he resumed consciousness. He could not understand having been spared. He knew now that if he had succeeded in passing, Hades would be his destination. He understood; he had earned it. He began to weep; no one but he could fathom the reason for it. Was it guilt, was it the remorse he felt for those he had ordered to the firing squad, was it his flippant acceptance of that scoundrel Brousseau's accusation of his commanding officer? Was it the distaste he felt when the tribunal held for the three was conducted in utter secrecy? There were other instances De Voux might have recalled where he had misbehaved, but none were more profound than his behavior at Soissons. He pulled the chord and the tiny bell tinkled. The nurse came.

"I am leaving," he announced.

"But sir, you can't, you are not well."

"If you want me to get better then let me out of here. What I am going to do when I am gone will do much more to make me feel better than anything you or your doctors can do."

"Please sir. . ."

"Don't 'please' me – get me my trousers."

Once fully dressed, he started for the door. He was a man on a mission. He had solved the Soissons dilemma. He knew what needed to be done. Suddenly everything was spinning. With considerable difficulty, the nurse eased the large man's slide to the floor. In his last waking moment he pleaded with the Almighty "Let me live, let me live. I have to finish this – please let me live."

———

Someone once said, 'the mills of God grind slowly, but exceeding fine.' The time was approaching when this saying would be tested. Advocate Mercal received by messenger a letter designating the date and hour of the hearing in question. The date might have been sooner, but the court explained that a significant witness in the defendant's case had been ill and that the extension was granted for his benefit. He knew who that was. He called Lola in from her office.

"Here it is. We are going to a hearing on this date." He handed her the letter. "Are you ready?"

"I have been ready for two weeks. If we feel we need them, I have twenty witnesses, all soldiers both whole and wounded, one blind. They will all testify to what happened there. I have several retired field grade officers who will attest to the futility of making the assault at that time and under those conditions. Those still in service have refused to testify. I can understand that. They would have paid a heavy price for doing so."

"Well done."

"I refuse to ask Claire Gereau to testify or have anything to do with this hearing. She does not need this. She has been through enough. I hope we can reduce her exposure to the public and spare her all the details of what happened to her husband. As disgusting as it is and her right to know, I don't want to encumber her life any more. Still, I'm afraid the press will not relent."

"You are a good person, Per, I compliment myself daily for having chosen you."

Per moved forward and kissed her boss on the cheek. "Respectfully," she added, and left.

Mercal, realizing the gravity of this encounter and how it might prove to be the only chance for vindication, went to the extreme; he closed his offices until further notice and notified his staff that they should expect to be on call twenty four hours a day until the date of the hearing. Their tasks would be on an as-required basis and executed with the greatest of haste. Errors would not be tolerated. He designated Lola Per as the person responsible for all staff assignments.

The advocate felt obliged to visit De Voux at the hospital. While such activities were not in the best interest of his client, still, he had the need.

"So, you're here. What do you want?" The adjutant was defensive.

"Forget if you can that I am an advocate and your opponent. Let us have an understanding; no discussions regarding the case."

"Agreed; now, what do you want?"

"I see an aging warrior who is not well. It concerns me." Mercal paused. "How are you, brother?"

"No one has ever said that to me – called me brother. Are you trying to compromise me?"

"You are an old war horse. Twenty years ago rolling a loaded wagon over your chest wouldn't have drawn even a whimper out of you. Now you're lying in this bed as if you are a four year old child – and most likely as weak as one." He drew nearer. "How are you, brother?"

"Are you trying to be humane? Everyone knows you can't be – for God sake you're an advocate. Everyone knows they have no soul."

"I thought we agreed to talk of things other than the case. I will leave if that will make you feel any better." The advocate was sincere. Finally, the patient realized that.

"I almost died last week – twice. I've never been a religious man. That was for other people – the more stupid ones. I always felt that, especially if you believe you are one of the smart ones. Now, I'm not so sure. No one tells you how dying might feel. Being close to it changes the way a person thinks. It has changed me." De Voux leaned forward.

"I'm not the same person I was. I know what life is and I have had a glimpse of what it's like not to have it. Live, that's what I'm going to do; every second, every moment - to hell with making my pension larger, to hell with lauding all our generals, our politicians and our supporters. I have life – and I'm going to cherish every second I have left."

The advocate nodded but remained silent.

"They say I can leave this place on Wednesday. I'm going to march out of here and never come back. If they want me I'll be in some bistro or near a beach or in some countryside eating fresh plums or cherries or something. I'm going to grow fat, fat as I can. Maybe I'll find some nice skinny lady to get fat with me."

Mercal couldn't hold back his laughter.

De Voux joined in. "That's what life is all about," he said, "I'll see you at the hearing."

$$\sim$$

"I spoke to him."

"You spoke to whom?" Lola Per questioned.

"I went to the hospital to see De Voux."

"What made you do that? You know how the magistrate will respond if he finds out."

"I couldn't stop myself. I appreciated his conundrum before, but this time I was afraid for him, that he might die. The strain of all this pending litigation is wearing on him. That was what burst the dam. They said he claimed he couldn't see and then collapsed. He's a scoundrel, Lola, but he's served France for many years – and honorably. All this is too much for him. I think he will retire – if he survives."

"How will you proceed now?"

"What is done is done. He can bring it up to the magistrate if he wishes or let it pass. I'm at his mercy. It may color the magistrate's opinion of me but it won't hurt our case. Even if he dismisses me, you will be able to take over. And you will do well. That, I know."

"Should we get back to work?"

"I see you also are clairvoyant. Is that Brousseau fellow still bothering you?"

"He is my limpet – you know, that fish that clings to sharks and eats the scraps. He is waiting for me every day when I leave, hoping to get another scrap of information."

"How do you respond?"

"Once a week I give him something. More often might seem suspicious. It's fun."

Her employer watched as she marched out of his office. He had already conceded that Lola Per was a person with spirit. Then, those notions returned: yes, he was happily married, yes, he desired Lola and, yes, it was impossible under the present circumstances, impossible perhaps, forever. Still, the thought kept returning, inserting itself into his stream of consciousness. Their continuing proximity was a negative. Eating together, at times being so close they could touch one another, laughing at each other's humor, noticing the tiny incongruities in her dress, appearance, and physical features; this made it more and more difficult for advocate Bernard Mercal to maintain decorum. But he fought the good fight; he held his ground.

Lola, in a different galaxy, was not constrained by any of the obstacles that held her employer hostage. From her first interview with him she was taken with the total persona: dedication, a soft and intimate way of communicating, and the little flash that raced across his pupils from time to time. She was ready for a full-blown encounter, and the rising tension associated with the approaching hearing only sharpened her expectations. It was not the sex alone that drove her, but the intimacy with this wonderful being.

She was not unaware of the circumstances that surrounded her situation. She did not minimize the dangers and consequences of her dilemma while expanding the intensity of her desire to overshadow the lawful requirements posed on him by marriage and his prominence in the legal community. The rumor of an affair at this juncture would be devastating to the Gereau case. How could an unprincipled person appear before the magistrate and speak of principle? Still, all was not lost. Perhaps, after all this was over, then there might be time. The young female advocate was irrationally, unreservedly, illogically in love. She might as well have been in her teens.

The Shedding of Light

"Please sign here," The valet took the package and brought it inside. Since his master had not yet come down for breakfast, he placed it on the table near his plate where he was certain to see it. Then he withdrew to the kitchen to continue preparing the morning meal. It was not unusual for Magistrate Fournier to receive documents - it happened all the time. Involved in matters of importance meant having to digest a great deal of written material from scores of documents. Valet Antoine often joked about how the practice of document carrying was the only regimen he needed to strengthen his biceps.

"Antoine, what's this?" Fournier called as he seated himself at the table.

"It arrived early this morning," was the reply, "It has no return address. Were you expecting something confidential?"

"No – I wonder what this might be." Carefully tearing off the protective wrapping, he came upon the cover of the mysterious document; it had no writing on it. Turning to the first page, he read

29 April, 1902

My name is Simeon Gereau and this is my twelfth birthday, Tuesday, the 29th day of April of the year of our Lord, 1902. I am starting this diary because I am sure I will become famous, perhaps a pilot, or fireman, or village postmaster, even a president of some great company. I might find I am brilliant and become a doctor, teacher, scientist, even a religious person like Jesus our Saviour, but that is not likely. The stiff white collar the priests wear is not for me. I will never become a politician because Papa says they are dreadful people, dishonest and not to be trusted. It is nighttime now and I am in bed and supposed to be sleeping, but I have lit a candle and am writing down my thoughts and events of the day, as all famous people have done. . . . . .

Mercal, he sent it, Fournier mused, *he knows the rules – he shouldn't have.* Was the advocate trying to bias the magistrate? He thought not. Instead, he reasoned that the bizarre and very unusual circumstances of this case had ignited, to an even greater degree, his passion to see justice done – and that was the reason for taking the bold action he had – sending the magistrate a document he had no right to see before the opening of the case in court.

"Bring coffee into the study,' he ordered, "I have some reading I must do." The valet bowed slightly and withdrew.

He found the opening pages entertaining and touching; a youth intent on recording the events of his early life, certain that he was headed for some momentous appointment with fate; that nothing in God's earth could keep him from his objective. It was a wonderful gambit through another's life. Fournier found it difficult not to begin drawing parallels with the events of his own youth.

But this was not the reason he was reading the document. He turned the pages and arrived at the section he was interested in.

The entry was just before the assault from Soissons was launched.

I don't understand. They are not bringing up the heavy artillery – not even the field guns. When I asked the orderly why they hadn't, they said the word from command was that we were going to surprise them. How could that be? We have been moving troops and trucks filled with supplies and weapons around here for weeks. How could there be a surprise? Everyone within five kilometers knows that we are planning an attack. And look at the terrain - there is not a spot of defilade to hide behind. The two or three kilometers of uphill terrain to enemy positions provides no cover – a chicken couldn't find a place to hide. I'm going up to command and ask them – beg them, to start a barrage to soften up the enemy positions and provide cover for our men. It's the only way they can ever hope to gain the ground they need to overrun the enemy positions.

Just what does command think they are doing?

Fournier turned a few pages ahead.

The attack starts early tomorrow. My company will attempt to charge up the hill and neutralize the automatic weapons. I don't know how we will fare. They have clear shots at our horses and men while we have to try to weave back and forth to avoid being downed. Folly, that's what it is, but we will try. If only we had a creeping barrage to keep them pinned down - that would help. But we don't – it's to be a surprise. It isn't any surprise! The infantry will be slaughtered. I can't see them gaining any ground. It's true we have many soldiers, but to automatic weapons that means nothing. That's enough for tonight. I must rest. Tomorrow – who knows what it will bring? It may be my last.

I love you, Claire. Take care of the children. God, please protect them.

S.G.

The magistrate turned the page, then others.

There are mounds of dead on the battlefield, all ours. Our cavalry assault was mowed down the moment it started. We lost nine horses in less than a minute. Half of our company was wounded or dead in the first fifteen minutes. Two horsemen got within ten meters of a gun position but were killed before they could do any damage. Most of us never advanced farther than sixty meters. The infantry did worse. As soon as they left the cover of the village buildings and proceeded onto open ground, they were mowed down like the ducks in a shooting gallery. My horse was shot out from under me, but thankfully we weren't going fast, so when it fell, I dismounted and was not injured. A bullet glanced of my scabbard. My leg still aches from it.

Our Frenchmen are dying by the hundreds. This is a bad assault. We must stop it before we lose more men. Tomorrow, if they form up again for the attack, they will have to climb over their own dead. And when they get to the top of the heap, the enemy will make them join their comrades.

I love you, Claire. God bless you, Jean Pierre, and Nicole.

Fournier read on. The assault deteriorated. No ground was gained. There were many more casualties, many more dead. Captain Gereau's cavalry company was almost totally destroyed. Only he, Lieutenant Ronda, Lieutenant Brousseau and several others survived.

And then, there was the page that mattered – the one that had caused an even further tragedy to be perpetrated.

The soldiers are unhappy – they are grumbling – they are talking about not forming up to carry forward the assault. I'm going to go to command and request they halt the attack. We are not gaining ground and the cost in personnel is too high. We gain 50 meters in the morning and then in the afternoon they drive us back. They lose some soldiers, we lose 1000. We cannot sustain this. It must stop. I'm going to go round and tell them to stay still until I speak to command. I hope they change their minds about this attack.

I love you, Claire.

S.G.

Fournier had had enough. He tabbed those pages he had read and put the document down. *But what effect did the death of Calista have on him?* He mused. He turned ahead to those entries that Captain Gereau made while incarcerated in Chateau Germain. He found that these were the most agonizing times for him. He blamed himself for her death.

It was your confirmation day. How beautiful you looked. I wish your father and mother were alive to see you. They are probably looking down upon you from heaven. I loved you Calista as if you were my own daughter. Nicole, my own, would have loved to have you for an older sister. I think Jean Pierre would have liked you, too. Do you know that I thought about bringing you home when all this was over? I did, you know. I wanted to make this day so wonderful for you. That was why I had my new cavalry unit polish their leather saddles and all their tack – so that they could lead the procession across the bridge to your celebration dinner. It was a mistake. When they saw our horses they thought it was an attack. They shelled us. But, how could they? Didn't they see all the children? Didn't they see all of the elderly: the priest? I shouldn't have put our men out front. It was my fault.

And now, you visit me every night as I cry for your soul and my sin, for having taken your life. You tell me that God has forgiven me and you have forgiven me. But I can't forgive myself – I can't, I can't. This is the place for me – it's the hell I have created for myself –God forgive me – God forgive me.

I wish you were here Claire, God help me.

S.G.

Fournier read on. Gereau's agony was affecting him. Antoine came into the study. He looked surprised.

"You haven't eaten any of your supper. Do you desire something else?"

Fournier shook his head. "I must finish this," He said softly, "I must finish." As Antoine left, the magistrate turned to the next page. Eventually, he came to the last page. Cold and wet, is hands were trembling.

Calista will be coming for me tonight. She will be taking me to heaven with her. For those who may ever read this, they might think that I have gone mad. It is not so. I only dream of Calista when I sleep. She comes of her own accord; I do not summon her in my dreams. Would an insane person long to see his wife and children? Would an insane person long to be freed from this dungeon and resume his life, the one before he was imprisoned here? Would a madman long to see justice, to be vindicated, to be brought before a tribunal in public view so that he could defend himself? No, he would not.

> *I am not mad, but I might have become so, were it not for the valiant effort of my good friend, Jules. He has visited me every day, sometimes all day – even into the night, when he saw my spirit falling. One time, he stayed with me all night – until dawn; he on one side of the door and I on the other. We spoke of intimate things, those anecdotes that only a priest might hear - under the protection of the confessional. I learned he was not perfect, and I confessed to him that I was not, either. . . .*

As the magistrate continued to read, the words of the condemned man drew him deeper and deeper into understanding the web of corruption and malfeasance that had been perpetrated. He read one more paragraph and then had to stop. He could bear no more.

Mercal did not err. He was right to send the diary. The magistrate *needed* to see the entire horizon; the decisions, their consequences, the twisting and turning to hide them, the innocent souls that suffered because of them, the hiding behind the law, the military code, the subverting of common decency, the secrecy - he needed to be exposed to all of it. Fournier placed the diary on the desk. He was tired. The clock on the mantle indicated the hour was two.

<hr/>

The court reset the time for the hearing. Rumor had it that the adjutant was recuperating, but not as swiftly as expected. Mercal, concerned, considered visiting him again, but decided against it. Not a particularly godly man, still, he offered up a brief request. He wondered whether or not God would laugh at his plea, the first in many decades. The rigors encountered while attending Catholic school had unintentionally convinced him to become un-religious. De Voux's illness opened a door closed for many years. Perhaps coming events might open the door even further.

He reopened his offices. The junior advocates could handle incoming clients while he, Per, and two secretaries continued preparation for the hearing. So far, the press had not heard of the hearing or the matter to be aired. As a rule, they focused only on cases when they came to trial. Since so many options were available both to defendant and plaintiff at the hearing level, they felt it unproductive to send someone to report on 'each time someone stepped on someone's toe.'

For now, Claire Gereau and her family were safe. Mercal was grateful for that. Of all the events that had transpired in the immediate past, that fact gave him the most satisfaction. Although he had never known Simeon Gereau, he felt he was his friend and sparing his family was one appropriate way to honor him.

He also envisioned how bringing the case before the court might have a telling effect, more telling than the shells that rained down on the citizens of Soissons that April day, and more telling than what happened to those poor souls who refused to take up their arms and fight another day in those fields piled high with their comrades' bodies. The advocate was beginning to understand how God's justice worked; at its own pace and not mankind's.

Someone knocked. "Come," he said.

Lola handed Mercal an envelope. "It came by messenger," she mentioned, and left. He opened it. Adjutant DeVoux had sent a short note.

Monsieur Advocate,

> *Do not be concerned. No one knows about our meeting, and I shall not tell anyone. I am convinced you came much the same way I would have when I visited one of my wounded comrades. It was my way of honoring their sacrifice. I am certain now that you did the same. I appreciate your gesture. I shall not forget.*

> *De Voux*

He tore up the note. What kind of a world is this, he mused, when a person can be honorable to the extreme at one moment and so despicable the next? For the second time in recent history, his thoughts drifted back to his youth. He was perusing a statue of the crucified Jesus. He didn't know what to make of the scene. At first, it terrified him. Later, he became calm. He understood something about what he had seen, but could not decipher what it was. He remained for several minutes gazing intently at the crucified figure. Suddenly he had the urge to leave. He understood. What it was, he could not say, but deep within his soul he had come to grips with a truth he could not yet fathom, but was at peace with it.

It was at that moment he realized that his visit with De Voux was an act of mercy, of reconciliation, of what Jesus might have done. The incongruity of his sentiments unsettled him. He visited the adjutant with the best of intentions. A little later in the day, he toyed with the idea of seducing Lola Per. He well knew that a person could be bad and good depending on the circumstances. Now he saw himself as the principal player in life's drama, subject to all the erratic fluctuations of positive and negative urges.

Mercal donned his coat, snapped his Homberg on his head and headed for home. He had frightened himself.

⁓

The morning came too soon. Husband Bernard was still entwined with Christine, and undoing himself was the last thing he wanted to do. It was his wife that sweetly suggested they arise and greet the morning sun. She softened their untying by offering her love a sumptuous breakfast and fresh coffee. At first, Bernard resisted, but then, as all men who love their wives do, he acquiesced. An appreciative Christine bussed him tenderly on his cheek and left to make good her promise. *This is good,* he mused, still using the bedcover to shield himself from the ever-brightening morning sun, *this is good.* Still, the thought of Lola Per lingered in the recesses of his consciousness. *Is this how it starts,* he wondered, *is this how adultery starts?* He had never given the matter much thought, having sown his seeds freely during his youth. He eventually met his wife and they married. Thirty eight was considered old by some, about right by others, the majority of those being male.

A smiling spouse served breakfast and a happy husband consumed it. As he kissed his wife and left, a thought crossed his mind. He wondered whether Lola would be wearing that purple dress.

On the way to the office he found a seat in an obscure corner away from other passengers. The train ride to Paris was always uneventful and smooth. He never had any trouble concentrating because many had the same idea as he: while aboard, use the travel time efficiently to get some work done. But on this day he could not. He rode all the way to Paris staring out of the window and thinking of Lola. It was the wrong thing to do and he knew it, but he made no effort to correct his malfeasance; that was what he called it. Clients who came to him to discuss such matters left in better spirits when they understood their sexual transgressions rose only to the level of 'malfeasance.'

But that term was for them, not him. He fully understood the implications of infidelity from every perspective. He did not want to injure Christine; yet, he refused to dismiss the desire to seduce Lola. She, single, was free to engage. Further, she indicated in a playful manner that he was attractive. Many use flattery to gain their ends, but Lola was not one of them. That was why her effect on other barristers in the court room was like that of a hammer hitting a nail; sharp, decisive, direct. It was clear she was attracted to Bernard. She made no effort to hide her feelings.

Many noticed the change in Lola Per. At times she seemed preoccupied. Junior personnel seeking her advice had to wait a few moments until she 'came down from her cloud.' That was the question, and it was the common topic among the subordinates. Of course, not one person would dare ask her about it, even though the suspense was growing. Eventually one the oldest male advocates, an ancient twenty-six, deduced the answer. Lola Per was in love – to whom and for how long was yet to be determined, but without any question, that was her malady. The problem solved, the cadre could now resume work at the required fever pitch. Per did not tolerate dawdling or daydreaming from staff.

The young investigator was correct. Lola was in in love; infatuated would be a term that better described her condition. Perhaps it might blossom into love at some point, but at this moment Lola desired Bernard. The thought permeated every vacant space in her stream of consciousness. How it began, what made it flourish was subject to interpretation. But whatever the cause, it had become a raging desire in this aggressive woman of intellect and purpose. Bernard Mercal was doomed. When and where, how and by whose initiative, were irrelevant. The matter was settled. They were going to bed.

The following days grew into weeks and then a month. After several delays, the date was finally set for the hearing. Having been restored by skilled physicians, superlative nursing, and God's mercy, De Voux was able and eager to attend.

Jean Baptiste Fournier possessed one the finest legal minds in the French judiciary. His legal opinions were internationally acclaimed, some causing a great deal of controversy in those nations where administering justice was 'sensitive' to other biases. Many denied the truths he espoused because they had already subverted or ignored them. Still, his opinions existed and anyone who could fathom their clarity and high moral purpose was the better for it.

Tall and thin, he carried himself with a certain air of daring dignity. It was not arrogance; it was commitment. The jurist was consumed by his quest for justice. Chiseled features coupled with dark piercing eyes and an unmanageable white crop only enhanced one's realization that here was someone who not only understood the parameters of justice, but *was indeed* just.

The adjutant had strongly suggested that this jurist preside over the case. As the time for its resolution approached, he became more and more unsettled. Fournier's verdict would be final. No jurist of any consequence would dare challenge him. He began to question whether his choice was prudent. De Voux had ridden into the valley of Cannai as the Romans had. He could only hope that his outcome would be different. His concern was: would Fournier act as Hannibal had and destroy his enemy, or, would he cooperate?

On the day of the hearing, Bernard Mercal, Lola Per, and Jules Ronda approached the courthouse. The skies were gray. A light early morning mist had dampened its granite steps. They glistened as the sun's rays found weaknesses in the dark vapor that dominated the heavens. Given several hours, Old Sol would reign once again.

The mood of the day drained any positive aspirations the team might have had. Perhaps the brightly lit interior of the courthouse would offer respite. But Mercal could not escape reading the hearings' portent into the weather of the day. Captain Simeon Gereau's life, and the injustice imposed on him, had cast a dark cloud over the nation's system of justice. But today light, fairness, and truth, would return. What happened inside would wash away the blemishes of the past and resurrect jurisprudence as it was meant to be administered.

Behind the plaintiff's group De Voux, advocate Colonel Alfonse Beriot, and assistant advocate Henri Flanget traced their opponents' steps up the wide stair. All were silent. Such a condition was not surprising. The tenor of the day discouraged flights of fancy or other happy outbursts.

The long, extravagant valleys of stone and bronze artifacts inside served well their purpose. Moods of both parties changed for the better, leaving sadness and gloom to seek other victims who dared to venture out.

The room where the hearing was to occur was Spartan. The wooden seats, obviously made by well-disciplined gifted craftsmen, shone from the many coats of varnish laid upon them. The table tops likewise evidenced an equal level of effort and care. The judge's bench, the focal point of the proceedings, was the master touch. It exuded the perfume of justice. Even with the seat empty, one could not escape the sense that this was the place where grievances and their injustices could be set aright.

A person in uniform entered. He announced the coming of the judge. All rose. He entered. All sat. Opening the folder he brought with him, he spent several moments perusing its contents and then glanced, first at the plaintiff, and then the defense.

"Is all that I have read correct? A person tried and sentenced in secret and relegated to confinement without anyone being informed of his whereabouts? Not his family, his friends, or anyone? And this happened with the full knowledge of a number of high ranking officers and most likely government officials?"

The judge stared at the defense. "HOW CAN YOU DO THAT?"

Counselor Beriot arose and responded "It was war and some of the troops mutinied. Order had to be restored. There was only one way to do that: execute a few, send some to jail, and reprimand the rest."

Counsel's reply caused the judge to scowl. His face reddened. "I sentenced a man to death. Last week, he was to be executed. I allowed his wife to spend his last night on earth with him. He was a criminal. He murdered seven people after robbing them. He admitted his guilt. He confessed to a priest. Everyone knew of his crime. Everyone knew where he was jailed. It was announced when he would die. Do you take my point?"

"Word of the troops' mutiny might have gotten to our enemies. They would have surely attacked. It was done to save France. We had no other choice. It was war. Terrible things are done in war. It is not the way anyone behaves during peacetime. We had to act. And we did." Beriot stood erect. He was proud of what had been done.

"I understand that part, but why keep the disposition of Gereau, Ronda and Brousseau from their families? That had nothing to do with your enemy finding out about their sentences."

Beriot fidgeted; he was uncomfortable. "It's complicated."

"I'm waiting."

De Voux arose and raised his hand. "May I speak?" The judge nodded.

"Lieutenant Brousseau was the one who accused them. He even admitted being a part of it. We could have executed the captain alright, but the other two, we couldn't do that to them – they were of royal blood. And, we couldn't tell their families what we were going to do to them – that would have ended our careers. So, instead of executing the three, we decided to put them away for a while – that is, until Captain Gereau died. Then we could make up some story about finding the two; amnesia, or something like that. They would return to their families, we would have done our job and all would be resolved. At the time, it seemed the right thing to do."

Judge Fournier shook his head. He motioned to De Voux. He sat down.

Counselor for the plaintiff asked to be recognized. Fournier recognized his request.

"Many injustices are perpetrated in war. We know that. But this. . ."

The judge raised his hand. Mercal stopped speaking.

"I have reviewed the briefs submitted by the plaintiff and defense. In my entire career both as a magistrate and an advocate I have never seen a complaint such as this. It brings to light every tenet of jurisprudence army officials and their superiors have ignored to hide the terrible injustice they have committed. Why? Only God knows. I cannot imagine what that might be."

Fournier turned his attention to Mercal.

"Your statement is not required at this time. A trial date will be set. I shall require the press to attend. You will have your say then."

Beriot, indignant, rose to challenge the decision. "We believe it would be in the nation's best interest to have this adjudicated without fanfare. In the interest of France, we. . ."

Fournier stared at him. "And if I don't do as you wish, will you try me in secret, too?"

The advocate's face reddened. Mercal understood, as did Per. Ronda looked skyward and muttered something. He crossed himself.

The hearing was over.

―⌒―

Elated, Ronda, Mercal, and Per took their leave. Subdued, so did Beriot and De Voux. Outside, Old Sol, bright and shining signaled the transition to a glorious afternoon. Bernard Mercal was correct in his prognostication: today, justice did prevail. But both sides understood this victory was pyrrhic. While it was evident that Judge Fournier did not agree with what had happened to Captain Gereau, there remained those valid arguments concerning military discipline, some distant justification for cloaking what had happened, keeping knowledge of it from the enemy, and maintaining some semblance of order within the military. All these views begged the single, albeit alarming, query: can soldiers refuse to engage the enemy when it is evident that the order to do so is blatantly and unreservedly wrong? Many elements of tradition and deportment were entwined in the seemingly straightforward dispatching of the individual's rights. Guilty or innocent the accused was mistreated – horrendously.

"We navigated that easily – I was surprised," Mercal quipped, "It couldn't have gone any better."

"This is only the opening salvo," Per replied, "I'm sure we will hear much more about the traditions of the military, following orders whether or not they seem right or wrong, the establishment and blind acceptance of commands issued from superior officers and how it must be maintained no matter the cost."

"Hmm. . . You would make a good commander, Per, you have the right attitude."

"I didn't say I believed any of it, did I?"

"I was teasing; perhaps I overstepped my bounds."

"Speaking of overstepping. . ." Per turned abruptly and kissed her employer. "One day that will only be the beginning." She walked away. Mercal watched her as she crossed the street, turned the corner, and went out of sight. He felt a tightening in his chest. Thoughts, desires, and phantasms surged through his consciousness. Eventually they all melded into one question: *How can I do this to Christine?* Though he posed the question, he felt no guilt.

Jules could not contain himself when he told Annette. He embraced her, lifted her off her feet and twirled. "The judge is on our side. He sees our point. In fact, in his own way, he scolded them. Simeon would be proud. Finally, finally, he will get his day in court."

"It is only because of you, my love. It is your work that has brought this to fruition. Oh, how I do love you." Annette kissed her husband. It was long, long, and tender. Jules picked her up and carried her up the stairs. What better time?

Fournier spent the rest of his day poring over the documents provided by both plaintiff and defense. From time to time he would wag his head in disbelief. *How could this have happened*, he thought time and time again, *what fiendish impulse ruled these men*? He could deduce no answer, at least none that could fall within the bounds of civilized behavior. He had seen and tried cases, many, where actions were taken that could not be justified as coming from sane men. The perpetrators had to be demented, or worse.

But standing before him were those accused, persons who seemed to be calm, reasonable people. What event or circumstance had turned them? What flaw in their character caused them to act so heinously? In a multitude of cases the answer was always the same: war; that insane macabre dance called for by politicians, generals and fanatics. It signaled the frustration of all frustrations, the one whose only response could be brute force. Protocols of decency were extinguished, empathy ceased to exist, vengeance replaced both.

And now, this travesty of justice; in its own way more grotesque than all the others. Many die in battle, but even unto, and beyond death they possess their identities; a piece of cloth, a wallet, a ring, a scrap of paper once a letter. They provide a memory of the fallen. But in this case, no such designation was afforded the accused. Thought dead, he endured a life of incarceration without anyone knowing that he still existed. Fournier had never heard of such a sentence, nor could he fathom the reason for it. Under different circumstances, all the reasons given by the defense would be taken to have some validity, but not here.

Were Simeon Gereau alive, he would have marveled at the impressive array of individuals who came to plead for and against his case.

Adjutant De Voux, born into a military household, had a grandfather and father who achieved the rank of General. Several of his uncles achieved field-grade rank: Major or Colonel. The child experienced a never-ending exposure to battle, tactics, and strategy. The array of his toys could be identified in four categories: soldiers, weapons of war, vehicles of the same, and battle flags identifying friend or foe. Unlike his progeny, the youngster had no desire to extend the family's military lineage. Alas, he longed to be an engineer. Building things and seeing them built excited him. On a regular basis Madame De Voux would go out searching for him when he did not appear for supper. She knew where to look. All she had to know was where the nearest building was being raised or the location of the trenches where new sewer or water lines were being laid. The problem became more complex when several projects were simultaneously under construction. But clever Madame solved that, too. The answer was simple: go to the one that was the most active. That would be where her boy would be; mesmerized by every movement the workers and the equipment were making.

"Time for supper," she would plead, knowing the sacrifice he was making to leave. But he would obey, for Henri De Voux was a good boy. As time passed, familial ambition trumped his meanderings. He had less time to seek out the new projects, for 'father' was spending more and more time with him, acquainting the boy with the military side of life. He endured the harangues as best he could. Afterward, he would feign exhaustion and retire to his room. Late into the night he would draw sketches of the projects he had seen, first in their present stage of completion and then as they would finally appear. Fortunately for him, father was more and more often required to spend his time away from home. While Madame was unhappy, Henri was not sad about it.

Not an athlete by any measure, he grew up to become a portly young adult. Whisked away to military school at eighteen, he quickly mastered the subjects given and also surprisingly, the politics. This enabled the cleverer, but not necessarily the more competent, to rise more rapidly in the ranks. The question will always remain how a military cadet, exposed to military training, of which physical endurance is a component, could have matriculated successfully while still exhibiting such obvious avoirdupois. As mentioned, the youth was skilled at politics.

A graduate of the officers' school at twenty-three, auburn-haired, gray-eyed Lieutenant Henri Bonaparte De Voux was ready for duty. Of medium height, and an impressive Roman nose with bushy eyebrows and sharp angular features, the well-fed officer nevertheless presented a favorable image.

He hoped he would be assigned near some significant construction project. While that was not the case, his office assignment was a comfortable compromise. He could leave several times a week stating he was needed here or there and would be gone for the rest of the day. No one dared challenge his excuses. His father was a General.

Henri loved his work – especially the times when he was out of the office and at the construction projects.

His influence grew: he assumed command of his section. First, he took command of the entire floor; second, the unit and finally, the entire building. Now Adjutant, he could come and go as he pleased. The world had become his plaything.

Then, the incident at Soissons occurred. Soldiers refused to form up for battle. Everyone at echelon was talking about it. Something had to be done - someone had to go there and restore order. Of all people he was chosen to lead a small cadre of officers to 'clean up the mess and restore order.' Proud but uncertain of his new assignment, he had no idea what corrective action might be needed or how 'cleaning up the mess' would be accomplished. He could not understand the reason for being chosen. Those officers who desired a military career and intended to rise in rank had refused the assignment because of its sensitive nature. It was one of those damned-if-you-do-and-damned-if-you-don't missions. The adjutant was sent because he would be missed the least were events to turn onerous.

When finally he came to understand that, it was too late. His superiors' ruthlessness disturbed him. He was hopelessly ensnared with no way out. Now he had to see it through. The other officers assigned as support were of the same ilk. Aides to Generals, aides de camp, translators; they knew little of war or tactics or what combat entailed. But they were the ones charged with restoring order. They were given Carte Blanche – power to mandate any punishment they saw fit. Another disturbing aspect was that no legal person was assigned to answer questions regarding lawful or unlawful behavior should they be asked. De Voux did not know it, but not even one advocate would agree to go to Soissons. They considered it a fatal career move.

Thus, the adjutant and his cadre, acting as judge and jury, pronounced sentence on scores of soldiers, without any semblance of jurisprudence, any hint of defense offered for the accused. Even the Inquisition was better than this – there, mock trials were held.

Soon, at the trial, all this behavior would be discussed openly, and the entire world would hear of it. For him, there was no safe harbor – even mercy seemed out of the question.

~

Colonel Alfonse Beriot, born of privilege, wealth, and education, had risen in prominence because of his father, mother and their well-to-do relatives. He had not the smallest reservoir of skill, ambition or intellect. Many were the days when his parents sojourned at the headmaster's or dean's offices and begged them not to expel their son. Their pleas would have been in vein, but for the enormous influence their families had in the community. Biting their lip and no doubt cursing under their breath, Alfonse was allowed to remain in school. It was not mercy, or hope of better performance that prompted their decisions. It was fear of being discharged.

A face as repulsive as a disfigured burl on a Willow tree, a voice that reminded one of a squealing pig, and a manner more irreverent than a drunken seaman recently returned from a long voyage, he was still able to take his place among his fellow advocates. This was the result of his wealthy and influential family lineage. No one cared to be near him, or hear him, or see him. Still, decorum mandated he be treated respectfully. He received few referrals and thus, little business. His private law practice on the brink of collapse, his parents once again came to his aid and arranged a post for him within the military tribunal – a lifelong assignment with little chance for dismissal. He was greeted by his peers as one would greet Bubonic Plague; his reputation preceded him.

Now his superiors were 'rewarding' him for his mediocre performance by appointing him chief counsel for 'The De Voux Case.' No punishment could be more appropriate. The case and its presentation before the court were fraught with pitfalls, the greatest being maintaining the image that the Military was a noble and principled force, ready and able to defend France to the utmost, the present affliction being an absurd and ill-advised misappropriation of authority. The French Army would never have done to Captain Simeon Gereau what it had, except that there were other, more important considerations. That would be the position taken by counsel in defense of Adjutant De Voux *et al.*

The strategy proposed by the advocate was shallow, indefensible, and burlesque-like; no one, in command of their senses would have ever proposed what the adjutant and his cadre of officers had done was in any way reasonable – or lawful, but the advocate was sure he could convince the judge it was. The jury was another matter. Still, he decided to gamble because of the imperious attitude he had in all his dealings. Wealthy parents and their influence had falsely imbued him with the belief he could do no wrong. No matter how heavy the load, he could slip from under it, because of the *gravitas* his parents carried.

Diametrically opposed to the maneuverings of the Defense, Bernard Mercal was an advocate of different stripe. Reared by an educated and principled father and mother who both had a high regard for the law, as a youth he blossomed under their tutelage. Even when his beliefs set him apart from the rest of his friends, he found no difficulty in clearly defining the limits of what he would or would not do. Thus, when all the silly and, at times, dangerous flights of fancy his friends decided to perpetrate, he was not to be found. Having a few good friends and being scorned by the rest did not deter him from being his own person. He was destined someday to be a person who would be noticed and admired. He had chosen engineering as his career. Quite happy to be in the world of building things, he looked forward to when he would be assigned large projects; bridges, perhaps long tunnels through huge mountains. He could hardly wait to complete his education.

Then, it all changed.

Someone absconded with the bank's funds. Gone were the hard-earned savings of his parents. Even when the scoundrel was arrested and tried, he did not reveal the whereabouts of his ill-gotten gains. Why, Bernard questioned, did the authorities not pursue the matter further: investigate the perpetrator's friends, investigate whether or not he had bank accounts in other banks, question his girlfriend and see whether or not she had suddenly acquired a large sum of money. All of these avenues of inquiry were apparent to Bernard – but not it seemed, to the authorities.

Their savings gone, Bernard's father had no choice but to remain employed. Fortunately he was in good health and could continue in his profession. His mother courageously accepted the family's fate, forced to dismiss any thoughts of a comfortable life in their last years together.

Bernard, angry, abandoned his desire to be an engineer. His parents, and how many untold more, needed an advocate, someone who would fight their fight, and win! They could not find one. His outrage drove him to excel, to be the best, attempt to be better than the best. He graduated first in his class at the university. His intellect had a part, but it was his revulsion of what he had experienced that drove him to the top. Striving to make a success of his burgeoning law practice, he could not escape the anguish he experienced in seeing his now very old father dressing, kissing 'Mama,' and, with great effort, leaving for work. It was the sentence some scoundrel had imposed on his family. Bernard Mercal's rage seemed never-ending. That was why his reputation as an advocate spread so quickly; he never gave up. His losses could be counted on two fingers.

Time, the perfect balm, soothed his anger. The tightness in his stomach subsided. His respiration slowed. He found he was able to relax from time to time. Beloved Christine aided greatly in his recuperation. He had confronted his rage. He was able to set it aside. Once again he found meaning in his life. With the passing of his father and mother, Bernard Mercal was free to move on.

The rage resurfaced. Captain Simeon Gereau's circumstances had resurrected it. All the injustice he felt because of his parents' situation now embellished the case before him. This time he would not be denied.

Mercal's comrade-in-arms was the indomitable Lola Per. She had her own dragons to slay. Taken on a picnic by her loving uncle, she soon found herself fighting, and then biting him as he attempted to 'hug' her. Her dress shredded, she ran all the way home and told her mother. She did not believe Lola. Thus, uncle was always close by, always attempting to get nearer, ever nearer to the young girl. One day, Lola decided to allow her admirer to approach. The day was sunny and they, alone, were in the woods near a babbling brook. Lola chose the rendezvous because of the noise the brook made. Fourteen now, Lola had had enough of uncle's advances.

The place where the ambush was to happen was an escarpment that rose over ten feet above the brook. Lola coquettishly ran up the incline toward its highest part. There, she waited for him. As he approached, she faced the brook. In order to 'hug' Lola, uncle would have his back to the edge of the escarpment. As he approached and prepared to engage, Lola placed her hands on his belt – and pushed.

The hard rock bed of the brook and the large, round rocks that lined its edge did their work. Uncle had broken both legs and a shoulder. The doctor opined that he would never completely recover. His constant companions would be two canes, not Lola as he had intended. The girl visited him. She apologized for the accidental push. She explained she was simply funning and that she NEVER intended that this horrible event would ever have occurred.

When Uncle asked her to come closer, she stared at him and said, "Shall we go to the stream again?" The invalid understood.

Much like her mentor Mercal, Per also was capable of rage. But for her, much of it lay with the fact that, as a woman, she was not considered an equal. Being a female in a profession that was almost entirely male, she had to remain professional while ignoring suggestive remarks and an occasional slap on her derriere by a bolder assailant who soon learned how vulnerable one's groin can be. Thus, word spread swiftly about the new female advocate who expected to be treated in a professional manner.

Her only Waterloo was that she had fallen in love with her mentor. Some would call it infatuation, but were one to understand Lola Per and the way she approached her existence, they would have understood that it was love and not the other. She desired him. She wanted him to father her children were she to decide to have any. She envisioned vacations on the Riviera, skiing, dancing, dining, and making love with him. These thoughts were always there, sometimes at the forefront, sometimes in the background, but they never left her consciousness. Lola Per was seriously, hopelessly, in love.

Reality Beckons

Night enveloped Paris like a silent cloak, unnoticed by those who were working in the offices of Advocate Bernard Mercal; neither were the radiant rays nor the many-hued clouds that depicted an unforgettably beautiful sunset, its ever changing hues sliding across the floor, chairs and desks of the outer rooms. In the deeper bowels of the establishment little of the changing light marking the passing of the day were allowed to enter, for this was a place of toil, of deliberation; appreciation for other things held no sway. Still toiling were its principal and his chief assistant, Lola Per. But on this night the mood of the two was unlike other times. Bernard could not stop thinking about his colleague, and she, waiting while working, was anticipating his approach. Tension in the office was palpable.

"Enough that is enough! Let's get something to eat. *The Gendarme* is still open." Lola nodded, rose from her chair and put on her coat. Bernard moved to assist, but was too late. They exchanged glances. Each believed they knew what was about to transpire. The short walk to the bistro was made in silence. Before entering, Lola scanned the stars in the sky and smiled, even though the streetlamps blotted out all but the brightest. Bernard, never taking his eyes from her, wondered what she was thinking.

The Gendarme's dimly-lit ambiance was appropriate for the occasion; it seemed as if they had entered a dark cave, endlessly descending, making their way down, down, ever deeper, finally arriving at a level place punctuated by a semicircle of candled, round tables. All faced a curved row of footlights that revealed a crimson curtain. The time for performances had passed long ago and now the curtain served as a shroud that signaled the end of the night's performances.

The advocate had come not to be entertained, nor to eat. A dark-haired, dark-eyed, smiling waiter with a black and meticulously incised moustache took their order. Bernard was very nervous. Lola thought his behavior comical but said nothing. *Imagine,* she thought to herself, *here is a person well established in his profession, well regarded by almost everyone except his opponents, a family man with an adorable and faithful wife, far removed from any hint of scandal or treachery, behaving the way a twelve-year-old school boy would as he tried to speak to the girl he had feelings for.* Lola enjoyed watching Bernard squirm, even though the matter before them she knew to be serious. Wine was served before the meal. Bernard took a gulp and began.

"You know I am married – happily married. Your coming into my life has changed that. . . Lola. I want to propose that. . ."

She interrupted. "Let's wait until the trial is over. I want what you want, too. Unlike you, I have no ties. The thought of infidelity or cheating has no hold on me. You have to deal with those issues, I don't. Perhaps husband-stealing might be something that might stop someone, but I don't care about that. I'll be plain; I want to go to bed with you. Ever since I saw you I decided that's what I wanted to do. I could love you, but we will see whether that's possible or not. If it happens you also fall in love with me, you will have to deal with the issues that follow our interlude. But we must wait. The press will be following our every move, our every statement, where we eat, how much time we spend at the office, and all the rest. How can we defend Simeon Gereau's honor if we don't show any ourselves? I will leave the discussion of honor or dishonor for another time."

Lola leaned forward.

"This will be the most famous case of the decade, I'm sure of it. It will establish me, a young *woman* advocate as a formidable presence in the profession of law. I am not going to let my superior's ardor, whom I love I think, let that bright future run afoul." Lola reached across the table and grasped Bernard's hand. "We can wait."

He emptied his goblet. "I knew you were formidable, but I never expected this. You have a will of steel. You have such perfect control of yourself. Don't you ever stray outside your fortress for some fun? Don't you ever make an intentional mistake?"

"I have plans for myself. I will achieve them. They may include you. But if not you, then someone else, someone who I choose, not someone who chooses me. Whatever comes, whatever happens, I will be the one who controls - only I."

"I'm not sure I would want to be with someone like that. Christine and I always shared; we have always come to a mutual understanding about everything." There was a pleading tone to Bernard's remarks.

"Why do you desire me? It is not because we mutually agree on everything. You want me because I am a challenge. You won't push me into bed. I will go and lay down of my own accord. And, if I decide not to, teams of galloping horses will not make me. That is what you want; that is why you want me. There is no compromise, only challenge; victory or defeat. You are in a different game. If it is too much for you, then withdraw. If not, keep hold of yourself until after the trial."

The waiter approached. He brought the entrees and departed.

"Are you a religious man?"

"I am, to some extent, yes."

"What will you tell the priest at your next confession?"

"I haven't been to confession in years."

"How will you equate my intrusion to your allegiance to your wife? After all, you promised God you would be faithful and take care of her for the rest of your life."

Bernard squirmed. "Are *you* religious?"

"No. I left those burdens to my father and my mother. After he left with another woman and we had to struggle to survive, my belief in God evaporated. All I could see was my mother working herself to an early death trying to care for her children. She needed God's help, but He was nowhere to be found."

"Are you uncomfortable with the thought that I would be betraying my wife?"

"No; life is life. It has no bounds other than the ones we set ourselves. I am free of most of them. Those that are important to me have to do with my career. The rest are optional."

"You are a cold one."

"You recall that you were the one who suggested our involvement. Who, then, is the colder, you or I?"

"You use the wrong word. I am insensitive. You are cold."

"When you bed me, you will see which one of us is the colder."

157

Outside, Bernard and Lola bid farewell, they did not kiss or embrace. It was not proper to do so.

—

"You heard him - we can't win. I will be vilified and condemned. Not only will my career be over, I will return to my family a national disgrace." Adjutant De Voux's impressions were correct. Magistrate Fournier's remarks made it clear how he felt about the entire affair.

"I can see you don't understand how the game is played," Advocate Beriot advised, "He is protecting himself. Of course he will seem angry at what was done. After all, he is an employee of the state. He has to be careful of how he proceeds in this matter. This is a prominent case. How he rules will be recorded in the annals of jurisprudence, to be used over and over by others in the future. He will be setting a precedent." A smile followed. "And, he wants to keep his job." It was a different Advocate Beriot who was strutting around in De Voux's office. In court, he was red-faced, frustrated and disarmed. Here, he had returned to form, imperious and confident.

"What can we do?"

"Don't worry. I know a few judges who are good friends of mine. Perhaps they may be able to soften Fournier's opinion about Soissons and what happened there. Also, we will surveil Mercal and Per. We will know where they are and what they are doing at every moment. The press will be made aware of any misstep, any malfeasance. If we can't beat them in court, then we will beat them by any means available."

"That's despicable."

"It's the game we play at this level."

"If you did this in the military, I would personally see to it that you were shot"

"Careful, my dear adjutant, after they find out what you have done, they still might shoot *you*."

—

"Is there another one?" Mercal asked Per, "Is there a new one shadowing you?"

"Yes, there is. But this one is not very good at it. They keep changing employees. They think I won't notice. Are they that stupid?"

"Desperate is a terrible place to be. Many times it results in making irrational decisions. They heard how the magistrate reacted when he read the briefs. They have to find a way to counteract that. That is why they are shadowing us. They are looking for any weakness, any way to make our case less credible."

"Then I should feel good about myself, shouldn't I?"

"That was what the boy said before he fell into the river after believing he could walk atop the bridge railing from beginning to end. Until that last step he was feeling much the same way you do. If you keep your nose up too high, Lola, you too, might fall."

She fell silent, realizing only too well what her mentor had said was true. She made a mental note to be more cautious.

"The wine was excellent, the cuisine exemplary. Now, tell me why you really wanted to have lunch." Fournier was no fool. He had not seen his colleague Chief Magistrate Arnos Clemand in months. Three days ago he called Fournier and invited him to lunch. The reason was apparent.

"You must be aware that I and many of your colleagues have the greatest respect for the significant decisions you have handed down over the years. I would never question any of them."

"Thank you."

"But this Soissons – Simeon Gereau's case, do you have to hear it? Can't someone else take it over? You know, of course, that it will be riddled with controversy - and perhaps animosity. You will be retiring in a few years. Do you really need this? I would be happy to take it over for you."

Fournier leaned forward and whispered "Arnos, you are the fourth magistrate who has offered to relieve me of this case. I am touched by the compassion all of you have shown for my advancing years. I will give you the same answer I gave them: no, no, no! Thank you for a very excellent lunch – I believe I already mentioned that." Fournier rose and left. Clemand closed his mouth; it had fallen open without him realizing it.

"No luck? You're the fourth, you know. I give him credit; he will not be swayed. Thank you for trying." Beriot put the phone back into its cradle. His attempt to surreptitiously remove Fournier from the bench had failed. He would still be making his arguments before the most renowned and well known jurist in France. *Think, think,* he commanded himself, *there must be something I can do. If I can't remove him, then perhaps I can stain the reputations of Mercal and Per. Let me see, who would be the most vulnerable; which of them most newsworthy?*

———

Lola Per was exhausted. The long hours and protracted concentration had taken their toll. She left the building barely aware of what she was doing or where she might be going. Suddenly she found her portfolio and the documents in it flying into the air. Someone had run into her. Excusing herself, she quickly knelt to collect the fallen material. The perpetrator, a handsome, dark-haired man, knelt down beside her to help. Apologizing profusely, he continued doing so until his victim agreed to let him buy her a glass of wine as a peace offering. He appeared truly sorry for his clumsiness.

At the cafe, Lola began probing. *Who is this person? What is his intent?* But whoever he was, he began asking questions before she did. It seemed he was as anxious as she to find out more about the person sitting across the table.

"What is your name?" he asked, "I can't drink with someone whose name I don't even know."

"I am called Nicole; and yours?"

"Alfonse, but everyone calls me Fazzi. How does that sound? Is that satisfactory? Does that answer your question?"

"You really didn't bump into me by accident, did you? I've had men do the same before. Do I excite you? Are you a gigolo? Just what is your game?" Lola waited. "Well?"

"I'm a messenger. Sometimes I deliver packages to clients in that building. And what do I see coming out? I see this very attractive woman. She is almost always alone, and looking very serious. I ask myself, 'Why is she so serious? Is there no joy in her life? No lover?' Then I feel sad – for her, of course. But now I feel satisfaction, because I have made a part of her day happy. Will you let me keep making your days happy – will you?"

He reached across the table and tenderly grasped her hand. She did not pull it away.

"I will think on it. Give me a few days. Then I will let you know. Is that satisfactory?"

Fazzi nodded.

Lola looked past her admirer, out into the street. Bernard was passing by. He saw her but did not wave. The expression on his face changed. It made her wonder. Was it jealousy, displeasure, or what? She made a mental note to speak to him about it as soon as she came in tomorrow. Noticing the change in her expression, Fazzi turned and looked out into the street. Bernard Mercal had already passed from view. When he turned back, she was smiling. Whatever or whomever she had seen was gone. Gone too, was her expression of surprise.

"I must go. Thank you for the wine and the pleasant time, but, really, I must go."

"May I escort you home?"

"That would not be appropriate. Perhaps when I get to know you better and we established some form of trust. . ."

"I understand. May I see you again, tomorrow?"

"That would be too soon. Perhaps next week might be better, providing you allow me to keep the notes in my valise."

Fazzi laughed. "Alright, next time I will."

Outside on the street once again, Lola turned right; Fazzi, left. *Is he another spy,* she thought, *I hope not; he's cute.*

Bernard was already at work when Lola entered. He looked up, smiled and then returned to his reading. Lola thought his smile sincere, not sardonic or mocking. She considered mentioning seeing him last evening, but decided to wait and see whether he would broach the subject later.

As the day wore on, it became apparent that her meeting with Fazzi would not become a subject for discourse. Still, the expression she saw on her mentor's face and the effect it had on her would not go away. She had to know why he looked at her like that. She left her desk and entered his office.

"Bernard, do you have a moment?" She asked as she shut the door behind her. He tabbed the page he had been reading, closed the book, and gazed at her.

"Yes, Lola, what can I do for you?"

"You saw me last evening in that bistro having a glass of wine with a young gentleman, didn't you?"

"Yes, I did."

"Were you angry?"

"No, I was not."

"Then what was the reason for that look on your face? Were you jealous, did you feel betrayed? Why did you look at me like that?"

"How did you happen to meet such a handsome man? Do you mind telling me?"

"Why? Don't you think I'm capable of finding a handsome man? I'm not ugly, you know. I'm rather attractive."

"How did you meet?"

"Well, if you must know, I was leaving the office and he bumped into me and knocked all my papers onto the ground. He couldn't apologize enough. I suppose he felt guilty, so he offered to buy me a glass of wine, that's all."

"Will you be seeing him again?"

"He wants to. I'm considering it."

"See him as often as he wishes. I encourage you to do so."

"What? Now you are getting into my affairs? How dare you? I didn't tell him my name. I told him it was Nicole."

"That was very clever, but not clever enough. You recall I told you about the dangers we might be facing when we accepted this case."

"I do."

"Your handsome suitor is Alfonse De Fazone, Beriot's top investigator. He has been watching you for some time: when you get in, what time you leave, whether or not you take lunch out or remain in office, where you live, how long it takes you to get here, and every aspect of your behavior he can glean from remote surveillance - without letting on that he has been doing so."

"How could you know so much about his movements?"

"It is because *my* investigators have been surveilling *him*."

"You never mentioned this to me"

"This is one of those situations when the less one knows the better. I could not take the risk of having you searching out everyone who approached you hoping you would encounter this person. In my defense, I never expected him to approach you. Now that he has, we may be able to use it to our advantage. Fazzi, however, is not like Brousseau. This time, you will not be dealing with an ingrate. He is skilled, he knows how to move, and when. If he suspects, even for one moment, that you are aware of his true identity, he will try to seduce you; he will lure you into a situation that will bring discredit on you and us. The press, everyone in France and all of Europe will know of your transgression. Only the Buddhist monks of Nepal will not have heard, and that is because there are no newspapers there."

"When I agreed to participate in this case I never expected anything like this. I thought that this time, I might have met someone attractive. I was aware of a possible spy scenario and I played it that way. Still, I was hoping I could be wrong."

"My offer stands; if you feel this is too much for you and you want to be assigned elsewhere, I will honor your request without ever thinking the less of you. Give it some thought. You can give me your answer tomorrow." Mercal yawned, "I'm tired. It has been a tedious time for all of us. Go home; I will do the same. We can discuss this further tomorrow."

Was her glance one of gratitude, dismay, or partly both? He could not decide. Lola gathered up her coat and brief, and left. A few minutes later, her mentor followed.

~

"Have you found out anything?" Beriot asked his investigator.

"I've just become acquainted, I need a little more time," he answered. "She has chosen to call herself Nicole. She's a clever one; always on the defensive. I'm going to have fun extracting information from her."

"Don't have too much; we need as much as we can get as soon as possible. The trial date is approaching. We must be ready." Beriot stopped what he was doing and stared at his employee "Do you understand?"

"She asked for a week to decide whether we should continue."

"Make it faster. You are skilled at this – do something," said the annoyed advocate. While he realized law and tradition were markedly in favor of the sentencing of Simeon Gereau, he had no defense for De Voux and the others keeping what they had done secret. That one act of malfeasance could overturn his bold premise; that no matter what action they elected to take, the French government through its military was above reproach when they strove to quell the mutinous behavior of the soldiers at Soissons. His argument was well founded; it sounded logical – but in this instance, there was no doubt other elements of law had been disregarded.

"She's beautiful, you know; fascinating, too," Fazzi opined, "I could see myself involved with her for some time. I might even fall in love."

Beriot waved his hand dismissively. "You couldn't love Joan of Arc. You'll never love anyone. All you're after is – well, you know what. The only reason I keep you on is that you are good at what you do. All the rest, I despise."

"Oh, so now you hate me, is that it?"

"I would never invite you to my home. People like you belong elsewhere. I won't say where, but you know what I am saying."

"Remember, it's *you* that is hiring *me*. I do the work you command but you are the murderer; I am the knife. I don't like you either, but the money is good so I swallow my pride. Make no mistake, monsieur high-sounding advocate, I do what I have to do to survive, even associate with hypocrites like you."

Beriot was speechless. De Fazone had torn away his thin layer of respectability. Before he could mount a reply, the investigator had walked through the door and escaped his wrath.

~

The late afternoon was warm. Old Sol, low on the horizon, still maintained his dominance over the day. An occasional breeze, cooler than others preceding it, signaled he would soon be losing his grip over the radiant heavens.

As he approached the advocate's office, Brousseau spotted someone talking to Lola. Devious to his core, he immediately identified him as a rival. *He too,* he reasoned, *must be a hireling, most likely engaged by De Voux to perform as I have. Does that mean I am deficient? Is this man my replacement? No; I will never allow that. I will try harder; I shall outmaneuver this foppish, handsome man who is so obviously trying to charm his target.* He followed them. *They are stopping; they are entering a café. What are they doing in there? Why did she respond so favorably? Are they going to have an affair? They are coming out. She is leaving. He is going the other way. Now is my chance. No, wait; she might think I've been following her. I'll wait until tomorrow.*

The next day the former lieutenant was on the mark early. Pacing impatiently, he was pleased to find only himself waiting for Lola. He took pride in the fact that he had arrived before his rival. *And, when that gigolo sees Lola talking to me, he will know that there is someone else, not just him, who is involved in catering to her needs; someone very adept and skilled, someone like me.* So involved was he with his fantasies, he nearly missed Lola. Fortunately, being a man of the world, the odor of perfume caused him to turn around, an automatic reaction for someone of his considerable skill in bedding many of the gender of the opposite sex.

"Hello," he cooed, "It's *so* good to see you again."

Lola cast a suspicious glance at him. "Are you well?" She asked, "You seem rather friendly today, a bit too friendly. It's not like you."

"I apologize. I don't know why I acted that way. Please forgive me."

"What do you want?" Her tone was harsh.

"Is there any way I can help? You know how well I thought of Simeon. I just want to help. Please forgive my clumsiness. I am new to this line of work – I mean line of thought."

"I understand how you want to help. At this point, I'm not sure there is any more you can do. Did you find that individual I mentioned? I have not heard anything about him from you. Did you find him?"

Brousseau was silent. Finally, he replied. "No, I couldn't find him. It seems he never existed. No one there had heard of him. Was the name you gave me correct?"

"Well, that just shows you – my people found him. He's here in Paris. We are questioning him right now." It was a lie, as fallacious as the name she gave him. But her answer served to put to rest any thoughts he might have had of him being duped.

"It seems your people are better than mine. Is there any other way I might help?"

"For now, no, there is no way you can be of service. But don't be discouraged. We are looking for some others. Perhaps you might help us find them. Come next week." *Dangle the hook and keep the fish interested,* Lola thought, *don't let him get away.*

Her last remark seemed to breathe life into the man. "I'll see you next week. Are you sure there isn't something more I can do for you?"

"I know how anxious you are to help. You must have respected Captain Gereau greatly. Please be patient. When I find something you can help us with, you can be sure it will be you I will ask."

Brousseau moved away with a spring in his step he had not shown before.

What a fool, Lola Per observed.

~

"Come," the Chief Magistrate replied to the knock on his door.
Magistrate Fournier entered.
"Please be seated."
"Thank you."
"You know why you are here, of course. Everyone in the legal community knows about the Captain Gereau case. I am wondering how much the government will have to threaten you to get you to rule in their favor."

Fournier turned his head and glanced out of the window. "Soon it will be spring. There will be vegetables to plant. Do you know I have forgotten where my overalls are? I suppose it's a sign of an aging mind. But I will find them, even if I can't recall where I put them." He turned and stared at his questioner. "I may be getting old, but I still remember how the law should be administered. What happened at Soissons was wrong – no – it was egregious. What those men did to those three soldiers catapulted French Law back to the ethics of the Inquisition. What do you want me to do, say that the government has the right to keep prisoners incommunicado *for years* while their families believe they are dead? And then, bury them like some beast or farm animal, without flowers, without family, without a proper funeral ceremony at a church. The men who did this are beasts. I am not."

"You were three years behind me at the Sorbonne, and then at law school, but already you were getting into trouble with your professors. You simply would not accept how the practice of law was conducted. *You* were interested in justice, not accommodation. I admired you for that, but because of your intractableness I am sitting in this chair and you are not. You have paid a heavy price. Do you want that to change? For once, do you want to take advantage of what I can offer you – a seat – equal in authority to mine. It's yours. I can elevate you today – in an hour – just step down from this case. Will you do that?"

"I could. But then it would grate at me. Night after night, I would think of how I failed those men. Either I would go mad or commit suicide. I could not live with the knowledge that I would have broken my oath – to uphold the law, to defend those who needed it most, to keep French jurisprudence bright and fair and true." Fournier sighed once, then once more. "Tonight I shall sleep well. I will not step aside. I will hear the case. I will consider every aspect - strength - weakness, and I will deliver a verdict. Perhaps in another life I shall sit in your seat, but not this one. I have a more important mission – and you know what that is."

The Chief Magistrate arose. He approached as Fournier prepared to leave. "I wish you well, my friend. You *are* a just man. I think I always knew that. But understand you are placing yourself in danger. Your search for truth may take you farther than is prudent." The Chief Magistrate watched in silence as the door closed.

———

Thud, thud, thud, thud; the secretary employed in the office on the floor below Adjutant Henri De Voux's office was leaving for lunch. She had never done this before, but the adjutant's incessant pacing placed sanity ahead of the economic advantage of eating her lunch at her desk. His never-ending pacing had unnerved her. The receptionist in the front office smiled as the secretary passed by. It was a knowing smile. Everyone on the floor was talking about it. When would he stop? What worry could be so great that it would produce such a reaction? How long would this go one? He had already been hospitalized. Was this the beginning of another episode? No one knew the answers to these questions, but the general feeling among the personnel was that something big was afoot and a response would soon be in the offing.

The victim secretary prayed fervently that it would rather be sooner than later.

He was concerned. Why shouldn't he be? The more he thought of what happened at Soissons the more he realized what a travesty it had been. He could not recall what he thought about at the time; his reasons for doing what he did, his justification for doing so. The only emotion he could recall was the fright, the fear he felt if he did not succeed. It drove his decisions, his commands and his willingness to allow certain events, events he knew were wrong and unjust. But he allowed them because he was obsessed with not failing. That emotion overrode every other attempt to arrive at a reasonable solution to the so-called mutiny. He could not fathom standing before his superiors and tell them he had failed.

Over the years reason had returned. De Voux's understanding of what he had allowed disgusted him. He began to hate himself. He became his own worst enemy. He became intransigent; every order needed to be followed to the letter; there was no latitude for error. His world became total compliance or dismissal. His subordinates respected him. Fear dominated that respect.

And now this; the entire affair would be resurrected for the world to see, to judge, to condemn. He sat down; his calves were aching. How long had he been pacing back and forth? He could not recall. Now his feet hurt; his heart had been aching for months. That was why he was sent to the hospital. Would he be going there again? He didn't care. He wanted this over. Even death might be desirable if it would stop the unrelenting flow of time. He considered taking his own life. That would stop everything. He decided he wouldn't; that would be the coward's way out.

He rang for his aide. "Get me Beriot. I want him here – today." A swift 'yes sir' and he was gone to do the adjutant's bidding. De Voux's office was on the top floor of the building, away from all the clamor and activity of administration. The large windows set behind his desk revealed a panoramic view of the Paris he loved; the Eiffel Tower in the distance, the Louvre, the Champs Elysees - not all visible from his perch, but very real to him. Today the sun seemed to be shining more brilliantly than on other days. Its brightness improved his mood. Perhaps everything wasn't as bad as he had assessed; there might still be a way to salvage his predicament. He leaned back in his chair. The sun's rays warmed his legs, then his hips, and finally, the upper part of his body. It was comforting; God's way of tucking him into bed as his mother had with his large woolly blanket too many years ago.

He fell asleep.

Folly

He glanced at his watch for the tenth time. *She might not be coming,* he thought. *Lawyers sometimes work late when they find some new item they think might prove to be an advantage.* Still, he decided that whatever the case, he would wait.

Just turning the corner, *he* came into view. The rival took a path to intercept *him.* The lieutenant raised his hand and Fazzi came to a halt.

"I don't know who you're working for but leave her alone, she's mine." Brousseau tried very hard to appear fierce, determined. It didn't fit. He awaited a reply. He had hoped it would be acquiescence.

Fazzi pointed. "The asylum is that way, sir. It's only a few minutes' walk. I'm sure they will be able to help you there." As he tried to pass, his opponent blocked his way. As he tried to pass on the other side, again his way was blocked.

"Are you her lover?" He asked, "If that's the case, then I apologize."

"Let's dispense with the charade. I'm working for De Voux, ADJUTANT De Voux. Are you working for him, too?" An amateur to the core, he had given away the reason for his seeing Lola while being totally unaware of the identity of his rival.

"I deliver messages to firms in this building, that's all. If the 'her' you are talking about is Lola Per, then, yes, I met her. We had a drink together, what of it? But, if you are courting her, then I must warn you, you have a rival; me. I hope you understand. I think I love her."

Dumbfounded, Brousseau was speechless. Fazzi's ploy of 'I'm innocent – what's going on here' had worked countless times because, through its use, it disarmed the opponent.

"So, you're telling me you have fallen in love with her?"

"I'm not sure how she feels about me, but I know how I feel about her. I love her. What about you?"

"I'm just trying to get some information from her. There is a big trial coming up and I'm sort of the spy for the opponent," Brousseau winked, "You know what I mean."

"I would never have guessed you were a spy."

"Yes, I am pretty good at it, aren't I?"

"I would have never guessed. Let's work this out like gentlemen. You have to get your spying in and I want to see her regularly. What do you say you take Tuesday and Thursday and I take Monday, Wednesday and Friday? How does that sound? You get your job done and I get my courting in."

Brousseau took a moment to give the proposal some thought. He never took much time to give anything 'some thought.' "That sounds good to me. Then she won't suspect I'm trying to pry information from her – it will be a little more informal. Yes, I think that will work."

"Well, since today is Wednesday. . ."

"I understand. I'll be on my way."

—

"I'm here. What do you want?" Beriot seemed as impatient as De Voux. Their positions resembled that of two pugilists circling each other searching for a weak point.

"Have you devised a way we can avoid taking this mess to court and preventing the press from knowing about it? I don't want to become the whipping boy for Soissons."

"But you *are,* my dear adjutant, you are. When you made that decision to keep your doings secret, you left behind the military code, the code of jurisprudence, and any shred of decency. I will be hard pressed to save you, no matter what the press says. And, I can, not because of what you have done, but because I am very, *very* skilled at what I do."

"I have regretted what I did every day since this again came to light. I need release; I need to clear this terrible episode from my mind."

"I am not a priest. Absolution is not one of my tools When you were there, you were a grown man, not some young officer drooling with ambition doing whatever he could to further his career. You should have known better. But, if someone were to ask me, I would say that you were weak. You yielded to what you thought was expected of you. To put it plainly, you prostituted yourself."

"How dare you! I have served France for almost four decades. I have seen battle – not personally, but I have seen its results. I have had friends die from their wounds. How dare you call me out like that?

"I was testing you. That is what the other side will be saying. It's good that you were indignant, angry. Don't forget to show those same emotions during the trial. It will be very convincing to the jury."

"Oh, so now you are testing me? Perhaps I should have done the same before I retained you. You didn't sound so skilled when Fournier had you before him the last time. He whipped you pretty good."

"Losing a skirmish is not losing the battle. I have a few surprises for our famous jurist. He will come 'round, I assure you." De Voux noticed the glint in Beriot's eyes. It served to calm him down.

"Tell me what they are."

"Their effect lies in their secrecy. I won't let you ruin that. I think you understand." The adjutant nodded.

"Oh yes, before I forget, call off that imbecile you have spying on Lola Per. He told everything to my man, how he was spying on her with this big court case coming up – all of that. Save yourself further embarrassment. If the press ever finds out about him, you won't be able to avoid being called a fool – or worse. It may even jeopardize the effect my surprises will have."

"He's a stupid, arrogant and self-aggrandizing man. He thinks so well of himself. They say he's on the brink of bankruptcy. But to hear him tell it, he's the wealthiest nobleman in Paris – and the most respected. The brothels enjoy his presence. I'm told he spends lavishly and tosses 100 franc notes around as if they were confetti. Where he gets them, I will never know. My people have spoken to those who provide goods for his home. They haven't been paid in months, *many* months. They even stopped deliveries. I don't know what his wife is going to do. Her hairdresser will not do her hair without payment in advance. But he doesn't care. As long as the women of the night keep inviting him, he will keep coming. There, it's all cash. Still, I wonder where he gets it."

"And this is the man you trusted with obtaining information from Lola Per? It seems your ability to choose well may be faulted.'"

"It's the pressure."

"The same way it was in Soissons?"

De Voux stared at Beriot. "You should leave now - immediately."
As the advocate closed the door, the adjutant muttered "Bastard."

—

The courier smiled as he entered the office. It was his way. He handed the official-looking document to the secretary, smiled again, and left. It was addressed 'Advocate Bernard Mercal.' As soon as she read who the recipient was, she left her desk and moved briskly toward her employer's office. Tapping on his door lightly, she entered, approached, and handed him the document. She turned to leave.

"Stay," he commanded. Opening and reading the first page of the document's contents, he said "Get Mademoiselle Per, please."

As she came through the door, Mercal looked up and announced "Two weeks, the trial begins on Monday two weeks from now."

"I'm frightened," Per replied.

"Why do you feel that way?"

"We have spent so much time preparing. We are sure of ourselves, of our position. Now the time has come for all our work to be scrutinized by the court, and by our opponents. What if we missed something? What if we failed to comprehend our opponents thrust? We'll lose - and become the laughing stock of the legal community. This is a high profile case; people will be talking about us for many years to come – we may even set a new legal precedent – or we may fail terribly. Too much of what I have worked so hard for is at risk. That is why I am afraid."

"Perhaps now you understand why I chose you to be on this case. It is exactly that sensitivity, that clarity of perception that is essential for this case. You are new to this field of battle, I am not. It is not the protocol, but the outcome that matters. True justice transcends everything. Even if we were to lose this case, thousands, even several thousand people will have read and heard about Simeon Gereau and how that honorable man died; how unjust was his punishment, his incarceration, and the sentence that was passed on him. Win or lose, we will have shed light on the matter for all to see, for all to judge. And that it why we are here, to shout, to scream loudly and long for those whose voice has been taken from them. The moment we step into that court we will have already won.

His words were just the stimulus she needed.

~

It seemed much larger than she remembered. Standing there, foreboding, yet in some mysterious way freeing, the marble columns were a phalanx of silent guardians, offering their mass as a shield from the darker forces in the world. The sturdy doors, made of brass and copper, further insured that justice would remain inside and not be corrupted by the legions of the impure surrounding it. All sorts of complaints were heard here, from the frivolous to those of grave consequence. Whether of lowly birth or noble, within its walls the offended might hope for justice. All who came stopped for a moment to pay homage to an eternal truth - humankind possessed certain inalienable rights and no one, not even the powerful, could usurp them. Without fear of malice, the plaintiff could state his grievance, and, when the time came, the defendant could refute his allegations.

Now that same grey edifice awaited Bernard Mercal, Lola Per, Adjutant De Voux, Advocate Beriot et al; ready once more to dispense justice within its walls, ready for the jury to digest the evidence, mitigating circumstances, and the theater, an unfortunate element in all trials. The advocates' ploys and maneuvers would be utilized at every turn, their appetite for victory insatiable, hungry to defend and win, without regard to which premise was just and which was not.

The trial begins.

First to present his case is the defendant. This is a change from the normal protocol.

"I call Captain Jean Magrid. He is the officer in charge of scheduling cases involving the French Code of Military Justice," Advocate Beriot explained.

"How long have you served in your present capacity?"

"Twelve years."

"And what are your duties?"

"I oversee those court-martial proceedings where soldiers have been accused of breaking the code and are being tried for their crimes: desertion, striking an officer, stealing, cowardice, rape; you know, things like that."

"So you try only serious crimes?"

"Overstaying leave and other petty crimes are handled by the commanders of the units."

"And how many cases have you tried for desertion or refusing to obey the lawful order of a superior officer?"

"I have tried five for refusing to obey, none for desertion."

"And what were the sentences given for desertion?"

"We have never had one, but if we did, the punishment for desertion would be execution; for disobeying an order, it would be demotion with imprisonment."

"And what about spreading word among the troops not to fight, in effect disobeying an order from the officer in charge to stand and fight – how would that be punished?"

The witness stared at the advocate. "I have never heard of such a thing. I don't know whether the code covers an instance like that. Disobeying an officer, the punishment is clear for that, but enticing others to also disobey, I think that goes beyond the code. It is a matter for a court martial to decide."

"Can you think of a name for such transgression?"

"Treason comes to mind, but I am not an expert in those situations. You would have to consult a higher authority."

"I have no more questions for this witness." Advocate Beriot took his seat.

Advocate Mercal arose to question the witness. "You say you 'never have heard of such a thing.' Is that true, that you *never ever* heard of such a thing?"

The witness became uncomfortable. He squirmed in his chair. He avoided looking directly at the advocate.

"Remember that you are under oath. After all, you are an officer in the French Army; no one has to tell you what honor and truth mean. Are you ready to answer?"

"Many years ago I heard some rumors – you know, stories about a mutiny – I don't know, somewhere in the north – it was in 1917 I think, yes that's when it was. Some soldiers refused to form up for battle – that's all I know."

"Can you recall where this *rumor* of mutiny occurred?"

"I think it was in the north – oh yes, I said that – somewhere along the Aisne River I think – where, where, - I'm thinking – give me a moment – yes, I know – it was Soissons, I'm sure of it, Soissons."

"You said April 1917 in Soissons, is that correct?" The witness nodded. "I believe you must be mistaken. Perhaps you are suffering from loss of memory. Were you ever in battle?"

"Yes, I served during the earliest part of the war. I was there when the enemy entered France from Holland. I was early wounded and had to be taken back to Paris for surgery. I almost lost my leg."

"And that is the reason you have trouble remembering?"

Magrid sat up straighter in his chair. "Sir, I have a perfect memory. Ask me anything."

"For some reason you recall this rumor remarkably well. How many cases do you handle yearly?"

"Routinely we handle about two hundred. One year it was three hundred."

"And I'm sure you can recall the salient arguments for most?"

"I pride myself on that – yes."

"Then why did you call this mutiny a rumor?"

Magrid sat silently as the advocate went to his desk and returned with a sheet of paper.

"I have here a document dated April 16, 1917. It requests your presence at 'The City of Soissons to oversee a very important legal matter.' Is that the rumor you mentioned before? It wasn't a rumor was it? You didn't go, did you?"

Mercal retrieved another sheet of paper. "Here is your reply. Citing a 'heavy workload,' you declined to go. Tell me, Captain Magrid, why did you refuse? Were you aware or did your colleagues tell you not to go because it might be a career-ender? Was that why you didn't go? Remember you are under oath."

"Why should I go? No one else wanted to - they all had heard about the mess out there." He glanced at De Voux. "And look who they sent to oversee it, someone who spent most of his career in office work."

"So you had your reasons for not going. I understand that. Did you hear any more about what happened – how the mess was resolved?"

"Not a word. The rumors were flying – some said three were executed – others said a dozen were sent to an island prison – there was a rumor that twenty were executed – the stories were all over the place. I didn't believe any of them. And frankly, I didn't care. I was just happy that I had nothing to do with that."

"I appreciate your candor, Captain Magrid."

Mercal turned and slowly strolled in a tight circle. He placed his forefinger on his lip. "Tell me, Captain, have you ever heard of a Chateau Germain?"

"No, - no, I don't think so." His change of pallor betrayed him.

Mercal crooked his finger. A clerk rolled a cart laden with papers to a location directly in front of the witness. "Shall I read these," he asked, "or will you reconsider your answer?"

"Where did you get those? They are confidential."

"Not any more. Of course you know what they are. Your signature is on every sheet."

Magrid nodded. He lowered his chin to his chest. He was sweating.

"These are invoices for food – to be delivered to Chateau Germain – hundreds of them. I would say about ten years' worth – and signed by you. Is that correct?"

The captain nodded.

"You knew what they were for, didn't you?" The witness did not answer. "Didn't you?" Again, he did not answer. "Come now, don't try my patience. If you lie, you well know what the consequences are going to be. I would hate to imprison one who has served our country so well."

"Those three soldiers I said were executed – well, they weren't - they were missing in action. That was the official answer if anyone asked why they couldn't be found. But I had no part in it. I just requisitioned the food and signed for the expenditure."

"Were you aware that relatives were not informed that they were alive but told that they were missing in action and presumed dead?"

"No, I wasn't. My God, who would ever do that? That's despicable. I heard that no one ever visited them. I concluded the family must have been ashamed of what they had done." Magrid turned his gaze to the adjutant. The expression on his face signaled disgust. De Voux turned away.

"You realize you may have culpability in this matter."

"Why? I didn't do anything. All I did was sign for the expenditures, that's all."

"And you kept secret the incarceration of three men at an unauthorized location while being held incommunicado. Really, Captain Magrid, do you really expect the jury to believe you knew *nothing* about the entire affair – a man of your expertise and understanding?"

The witness glanced at the jury. Their expressions appeared as chiseled granite.

"Thank you Captain, I have no further questions." He turned to the magistrate. "I reserve the right to recall the witness should I require further testimony."

"So ordered; call your next witness."

Beriot beckoned "I call Charles Brousseau to the stand. The lieutenant was at Soissons during the time of the. . . err. . . err. . . incident."

"Call it what it was – a mutiny." Mercal added.

Magistrate Fournier stared at him. The advocate melted back into his seat.

"You are Charles Brousseau," Beriot began, "and you were at Soissons during those days of April 1917 when French troops refused to form up for battle, disregarding the lawful command of superior officers?"

"I was." The witness turned and smiled at the jury. He tweaked his moustache and winked at a particularly fetching female member.

"And it was you who reported the offending leaders of the revolt to the investigating officers?"

Ronda started to rise from his seat but Mercal restrained him. "Hold back. We'll get our chance," he whispered.

"Which soldier or soldiers did you identify? I might add here, that, at the time, you were lying gravely wounded in a hospital bed while you were being questioned."

"A flesh wound to his foot," Ronda whispered to Lola Per. "No surprise," she whispered back.

"I identified Captain Simeon Gereau and Lieutenant Jules Ronda. I also admit briefly taking part in the action myself."

"What?" Beriot looked surprised. "You took part in the mutiny?"

Brousseau puffed out his chest a little. "I did, and I'm proud of it. After the third day of the assault everyone knew the enemy had the entire field covered by crossfire. We lost hundreds of men during the first day. God only knows how many we would have lost during the following days."

Beriot turned to the magistrate. "This is new testimony. I had no idea these were the opinions of the witness."

"He is *your* witness," the magistrate replied, "You should have questioned him more completely. Do you have any further questions?" The advocate shook his head. "Advocate Mercal?"

"Your advocate mentioned you were gravely wounded. Is that so?"

"I don't know how gravely it was, but yes, I was wounded."

"Where exactly, were you wounded?"

"My foot." The lieutenant bent over and pointed to the edge of his right foot, just below the instep.

"That doesn't seem very serious. Couldn't they have bandaged you up and sent you out to continue commanding your men?"

"They were afraid of infection."

"By your own testimony 'hundreds of men were dying.' Didn't you feel an obligation to help save them?"

"I told you, they were afraid of infection."

"When were you wounded, that is, what day were you wounded?"

"Yes, I was, on the very first day of the assault, the first hour."

"It seems you had bad luck, being taken away from your men so soon."

"Yes, it was. I regret that."

"I take it you would rather have been with your men."

Brousseau lowered his head. "Yes, that's true."

Lola Per came forward and handed Mercal a sheet of paper. "How long were you in the hospital Lieutenant?"

"Seven days."

"That's a long time for fighting an infection, wouldn't you say?"

"I don't know anything about those things. I leave all that to the doctors."

"Were you a good patient?"

"I never gave them any trouble, if that's what you mean."

"I disagree. I think you were a terrible patient, and perhaps a very clever one, at that."

"What do you mean?"

"The doctor's report; I have it here in my hand. Shall I read it? Have you seen it?"

"No, but go ahead."

Mercal began: "The lieutenant was wounded within the first hour of battle, shot in the foot. These types of wounds are common. Soldiers shoot themselves in the foot or hand so that they can leave the battlefield. I am not sure this is what happened to this officer. But his behavior during the next several days led me to believe this was the case. Asked to leave his bed and return to active duty or at least return to the bivouac, he refused. We needed the beds for the hundreds of the severely wounded that required immediate attention. Day after day he was requested to give up his bed for the more critical cases but time after time he would not do so.

He only agreed to leave the day after word came that the troops refused to engage the enemy. Two aides carried him in a stretcher to his cot. Words cannot describe how I feel about this patient. I am considering reporting him for cowardice before the enemy."

The advocate glanced at the witness, only to find him staring back.

"So, you say you took part in the mutiny? How exactly did that happen? Did you hobble out of bed and go around telling the troops not to form up? How, exactly, did you make contact with Captain Gereau and Lieutenant Ronda? You didn't. You were shitting in your pants in that bed, hoping you could hide there until the fighting subsided – the surgeon should have reported you."

"The witness jumped to his feet. "I consider that an insult!"

"SIT DOWN. Carrying on about how innocent you were is pointless."

"Is that all? May I go?"

"You are not excused. If you can be patient, Advocate Per has a few more questions."

Brousseau slumped back into his chair.

Per smiled. "Do you know me? Have you ever spoken to me?"

"Why, yes, I recall we met on the street outside your office, quite by accident, of course."

"Didn't you tell me that you wanted to help us with this case, that you felt Captain Gereau was unjustly dealt with?"

"Yes, I said that."

"Were you also sentenced to Chateau Germain?"

"Well, not actually sentenced, I was put there to take charge."

"Oh, so you were free to leave any time you wanted?"

"Well, not exactly – I had my responsibilities."

"You mean like keeping that young woman at your side both day and night?"

"No."

"Like pilfering the food money Captain Magrid sent you so that you could buy wine and presents for her while she serviced you?"

"I've had enough of this." Brousseau started to get up.

"SIT DOWN, or I will have those guards over there seat you. There is more."

"Is it true that you identified Captain Gereau and Lieutenant Ronda as leaders of the rebellion? And that you told this to Adjutant De Voux and his staff?"

"I did. I felt it was my duty."

"That is very admirable. But how did you come to know this? After all, you said you were in hospital during the entire assault. You also said you helped them. How did you do that? Your counselor indicated that you were gravely wounded by that self-inflicted shot in your foot." Per turned and faced the jury. "Tell me, how did you do all those things?"

"I object to this. . ."

"No more charades Lieutenant, it's time to be truthful."

"Is that all?"

"Just one more question, if you please. Who directed you to spy on us while we were preparing our case for this trial?"

There were murmurs among the jurists.

"What? What did you say? I never did any such thing."

"Our detectives made note that you entered the building where Adjutant De Voux has his office. Do you know anyone else there?"

"Why, yes I do, as a matter of fact."

"Could you please tell us their name so that we can confirm that?"

"I don't know her name."

"You don't? You visited that building twenty times since having met me. And you *don't* know *her name?*"

"She is a private person."

"Adjutant De Voux's secretary recalls your waiting in the anti-room to see the Adjutant on numerous occasions. Shall I call the secretary in to testify to that? There was no woman, was there?"

He wagged his head and looked at the ceiling. "All right, all right, so I did spy on you. I had to do something – he threatened to expose me. I couldn't have that – I have noble blood."

"I can certainly see that. Just to be clear, who was it that commissioned you to spy on me?"

The witness looked at the adjutant and pointed

"Let it be recorded that Lieutenant Brousseau identified Adjutant De Voux."

"Is that all?"

"Just one last question, if I may. Adjutant De Voux threatened to expose you – why – for what?"

"I won't say."

"You are in a court of law."

"I won't say, I told you!"

Per glanced at the magistrate. "I withdraw the question. The witness may step down. I reserve the right to question him at a later time."

The magistrate nodded. "The witness may step down." He glanced at Beriot.

"Our next witness is Alfonse Duchard." A large man stepped forward and took the witness seat. It was obvious from his physique, movement, and clothing that he engaged in manual labor and was of the working class. "State your name and occupation."

"Alfonse Duchard – I am a gravedigger."

"You tend the graveyard where one Captain Simeon Gereau is interred?"

"What does interred mean?"

"You know, buried – where the captain is buried."

"Yes, I am."

"Do you remember when – and how - he was buried?"

"Oh, yes I do. It was very impressive – all those soldiers – and then they fired those shots into the sky. I never saw anything like it."

"And when was that?"

"It was a long time ago. I can't recall exactly – but I remember the ceremony. It was very impressive."

"It was an honorable ceremony for one of our fallen." Beriot turned and stated that he was finished with the witness.

Mercal stepped forward. The witness was nervous. That was not unusual; most called to testify are uncomfortable with having to appear. But the advocate suspected there might have been another reason in play. "Sir, Could you step away from the chair?" Duchard did as he was asked. "Those are very nice shoes. You don't dig graves in those, do you?"

"Oh no, not these; I bought these special for the trial."

"And how much did they cost?"

"They cost me 80 Francs."

"How long have you had them?"

"I bought them last Tuesday."

"What do they pay you for your work?"

"I get seven Francs a week and two Francs extra for each grave I dig." There was an inaudible but visual reaction from the jurors.

"I have no further questions for this witness. I reserve the right to recall him."

The magistrate nodded. "The witness is excused. I think that is enough for today. Court will begin at ten tomorrow." Magistrate Fournier gaveled the close of court.

———

Mercal threw his coat over the chair. "That scoundrel bought off the gravedigger. Saying they buried Gereau in a potters' field with full military honors; what a travesty to even suggest that."

"Perhaps we can use that to our advantage if we can discredit the gravedigger's testimony and Beriot's inference that Gereau was given a proper burial."

"How so?"

"The gravedigger has a friend, remember what Ronda mentioned? Perhaps he can be used to extract the truth. If we can establish that Beriot was involved in getting him to perjure himself, then we have him, the advocate, that is."

"Yes, that's it. "Good thinking."

An angry Jules Ronda burst through the door with the secretary running behind and mentioning over and over that he couldn't enter. "Full military honors - what nonsense. There were only three people at the interment – two gravediggers and Father Danilou. Simeon's coffin was burlap, so old it was rotting. Brousseau even complained about the cost of the wagon that was used to bring the body to the cemetery."

"Can we get Father Danilou to testify?" Mercal questioned.

"If you have a direct line to Heaven you can. He passed away some time ago."

"Then we have to contact the second gravedigger."

"Why is Beriot going to these extremes to make his case," Lola asked.

"Because he feels his case is doomed to failure. If he wins, the public will be outraged; if he loses it will be the military and the government who will be incensed. I suspect those in charge want to be rid of him. This is a very well-planned and structured assassination – of reputation, of course. I suspect if he wins, he will be able to retain his position. If he loses, he may have to join the gravediggers for employment. I bet anything they expect him to lose."

"We have another surprise if we need it," Mercal posited.

"You are willing to put her on the stand?" A surprised Per asked.

"I will, if I have to."

"Who is that?" Ronda asked.

"Lily." The advocate answered.

"I remember; she was Warden Brousseau's 'entertainment' at the Chateau. He spent some of Simeon's food money buying her little trinkets to keep her happy – that is, until I told Father Danilou about it."

"I never heard of that part of the story," Lola Per added.

"They didn't incarcerate Charles and me because we were of noble lineage – it would have raised questions. So they sentenced us both to the Chateau, me as guard and he as warden, our sentences to be as long as Simeon lived. Upon his death, we would be freed."

She rolled her eyes. "What insanity; I can't believe what you just told me actually occurred. It's the most horrible thing I have ever heard."

"Oh it happened, and no one would have ever known if I hadn't survived. Brousseau would never have mentioned it."

"I think I'll take a ride tomorrow – to Saint Germain. I wonder where I might find Lily," Per asked.

"She will be at the nearest café – or with the richest wayward person."

"Why do you speak so unkindly of her?"

"She was complicit; first, by taking advantage of the situation, and second, by remaining silent about the theft of the money. She was aware, *believe me*, she was aware of the entire scheme – she may even have encouraged it."

"I disagree; she doesn't have the mental capacity to conjure up such an operation. She may be greedy, but she is not smart.

"So, we disagree - now I *must* find her." Per stated.

———

"You are drinking too much," Gravedigger number two Nicholas Parreri, cautioned, "All you did was to tell a few lies – that's no big thing. He smiled. "I've heard you lie before – many times before, like that story you told me about the woman you met in Reims. Now that was a *real* lie."

"I shouldn't have done it. What I should have said was how I felt when we buried him. 'How can you bury a soldier like this? Don't you have any feelings?' His family didn't even attend the funeral. It was just us and the priest. That's what I should have said, not help them cover their asses."

"So go back and tell them the truth."

"Do you know what they do to you if they found out you lied? The advocate told me; they put you in jail. I'm stuck – I don't know what to do. I want to make it right but I don't know how." He waved to the waitress. "Bring some more."

"Don't torture yourself like this. It's not worth it. Go back and throw yourself on the mercy of the court. You're a good man - you're a veteran – why, you've even been wounded. All that stands for something. Tell them that bastard of an advocate made you do it."

"You're right I should, but I don't know if I have the courage."

"I'm your friend – I got you this job. Do you think I would do something to harm you? On my mother's grave, I wouldn't. Go back and do it. If you don't, you will be regretting it for the rest of your life – you owe it to the captain."

"All right, I'll do it – but how? Who can I see who will help? Oh, I don't know. I want to; perhaps it's too late."

A man sitting at the bar overheard the entire conversation. Turning his seat so that he faced the two, he whispered "Perhaps I can help." He was one of Bernard Mercal's investigators.

—

Saturday was a bright, sunny day. The train to Saint Germaine En Laye carried half the passengers it would have if it had been a workday. She was aware that the town was the birthplace of Claude Debussy. If she had time, she planned to visit 38 Rue du Pain. As the train sped on, Lola Per wondered what kind of person she would find. Would Lily be a prostitute, a wayward wife, or one of the tens of thousands who had sacrificed their husbands to the war and, because of their grief, lost their way?

The polished leather briefcase of a man sitting across the aisle caught the sun's rays and for an instant reflected the beam directly at Per. The momentary blindness brought her back to the moment. The incident caused her to consider Simeon Gereau's circumstance;

surviving almost a decade without ever seeing the sun or the blue sky even for a moment. The reflection happened again, but this time she greeted the burst of sunlight. After what she had come to know, it was more than welcome.

The train slowed as it approached the station. Placards alongside the tracks advertised Saint Germain En Laye. The flight of stairs that ascended to the street level seemed unusually wide. There were no hand rails along its center. Lola chose to climb it using the handrails conveniently placed on each side.

It was ten, too early for a prostitute to be advertising her wares, and much too early for the cafes to be encouraging any form of fraternization. *Where might Lily be,* she pondered. *I could inquire at the church over there. That might be a good place to start. It's not too far,* she calculated, *the priest may know her. I'll look there first.*

She passed by a woman selling flowers. The bouquets were exceptional. As her gaze slid along the array, she stopped. A small sign near one end of the cart proclaimed the owner's name; FLOWERS BY LILY. Lola caught her breath. *Could this be that easy?* Might Providence have interceded and placed the object of Lola's journey at the top of the stairs leading up from the station?

She approached the woman. A light shawl draped over her shoulders protected her from the chill of the morning breeze, the day still awaiting the full force of the sun's warming rays. Saturday was an odd time for sellers of flowers to be hawking their wares. At this hour, those using the train would be going to elsewhere, not returning home. She would be more successful much later in the day.

Lily smiled at her potential customer. "Beau jour, isn't it a beautiful day? Some flowers would help brighten up the office, wouldn't they? May I choose a bouquet for you?"

Lola paused. *How shall I broach the subject,* she pondered - *what to say, what to say?* Finally, an answer surfaced. "Charles sent me."

"Which Charles; I know many men by that name. Does he live in Saint Germaine en Laye?"

"Charles Brousseau."

Lily turned away, suddenly seeing a need to tend to the bouquets. "I have not heard that name for some time. Is he well?"

"You have heard about the trial?"

"Who hasn't? I follow it every day in the papers. The press is really making a big thing of it, aren't they?" Lily faced Lola. "What does

Charles want now? That scoundrel – he married me. For a while after Father Danilou passed, it was wonderful. We even had a baby. She died from the influenza. After that, he changed. One day he came home and said he was going to receive a lot of money. I asked from whom? He said that was none of my business and that he was leaving me. He never told me about his other wife – or his mistresses." She wagged her head. That liar – that cheat – that thief. I should have known that anyone who steals food money to buy trinkets for his whore – yes, that's what I was until we married – cannot be trusted. Why didn't I see this before?"

Lola reached out and touched Lily on the shoulder. "It was because you trusted him – because you loved him."

Lily wept.

"Where can we sit and talk? Put your wagon aside. I will pay for the sales you lose by being closed. And I will buy your dinner if our talk lasts that long. I need to know what you know."

"Who are you?"

"I am one of the advocates who are defending the memory of Captain Gereau. Can you help us?"

"Oh, that poor man, I feel sorry for him. Charles mistreated him so. He was his prisoner. That guard Ronda was his only friend, the only one he saw during all that time he was in the chateau."

"You seem to know a great deal. Can you tell me more?"

Lily swung the doors closed on the cart and pushed it up against the wall of a building. "No one will bother that until I come back. I leave it there all the time. Let's go. I have a great deal to tell you. I've been holding it inside for all these years. Now I can let it out. It will be good for me."

The pair headed toward the church. It was not where Lily wanted to go. She had something better in mind; a café she could never afford to frequent.

———

"What do we do now?" A disturbed Adjutant De Voux commented, "He made Magrid look like a fool. No one would ever believe that he was not complicit in the Saint Germain incarceration. Even I wouldn't; and that Brousseau – what a piece of work he is. And he's of noble blood? Who would ever believe that after what he said today? He's a coward, that's what he is – and a liar to boot. Did you see what he did? He winked at one of the jurors. I'm sure that went over well. And, as if that weren't enough, you called a gravedigger to testify. Who would ever believe what he said – a full military burial in a potters' field? My God, Beriot; are you that inept? I could have done better myself."

"We'll see. Monday I am going to call you to the stand; and you had better be good. Your reputation hangs in the balance. Depending on how well you do, I'll decide who I will call next. Should you do badly, then we are finished, I mean *really* finished. After all, you *were* the one who was in charge. When you speak, defend yourself – tell them about the war, the tension you felt, the need to keep order among the troops, and for God's sake, DO NOT mention Brousseau, Ronda or Gereau! Talk about the glory of France, the pride of the French army, its victories, its noble intent of protecting the nation – you know, lay it on as thick as you can. I want the jury to hear the national anthem while you are speaking. I want them to think of heroes and the waving of the flag." Beriot paused. "It's all we have."

He sat down and placed both hands over his face. "A thought has just come to me."

"What is it?"

"I know why I was given this assignment."

"And I know why I was sent to Soissons."

Both men stared at each other.

Nothing further needed to be said.

—

It was late. The last train from Saint Germain en Laye left at twenty-three and Lola Per almost missed it. She was exhausted. Listening to Lily recall memories of her sad affair with her lover and former husband was almost more than she could bear. It seemed the poor soul had been waiting for someone, anyone, to come and ask her about that time in her life so that she could unburden herself and let the truth be known. Those years, the ones when he was warden, having authority over Gereau and Ronda while amusing himself with her, were seared in her memory. The experience brought to light one glaring fact; that Charles Brousseau was a monster. His utter disregard for the lives of those other than his own was primal. Everyone, everything that was not for his pleasure or use was expendable. His dark side was his secret weapon and only those who were very close or unfortunate enough to be one of his victims were aware of it.

Lily did bring to light something that even surprised Lola: there was a conspiracy – between Brouuseau and others, a person or persons she had never met. He controlled the purse strings; he was the one who dictated the amount allotted for use in the chateau. The remainder, deposited in several bank accounts, was presumably shared by Charles and others. While Lily had no idea who they might be, Lola had a strong inclination as to the identity of one of them.

She could hardly wait to see Bernard and disclose what she had discovered.

The morning mist hung over the streets of Paris as Lola entered the office. She was surprised to see one of the investigators already there. He, too, had a key.

"Good news?" She asked.

"The news is very good, very good indeed." He replied.

She continued on; there was much to do before Bernard would be appearing. She wanted to confirm her suspicions before proposing anything to him. Proud of her discovery, she immediately set to work. First, she made several calls to close friends who worked in the banking community. Realizing her intentions, they were eager to give her the information she requested. The next communique was directed to the four well-known luxury car dealers in Paris. Reluctant at first, Lola eventually 'persuaded' them to provide the information she needed. In addition, one of the dealers in question also gifted her with the address where a certain luxury machine was delivered. The tax bureau closed the circle by naming its owner.

It was as she suspected.

Bernard Mercal came in later than usual. He had stayed up the entire night considering his alternatives. He understood that his case was strong, but he felt he needed more. He wanted to totally discredit those involved; he wanted to show that their intentions were not honorable as they would have everyone believe, but instead were based on greed and personal gain. He desired to vindicate not only Gereau, but in some way, his parents. Illogical as the desire was, it existed. In his mind it would make right not only this travesty, but the former one that had escaped justice.

"You look tired," Lola observed, "Didn't you get any sleep last night?"

"The saying is 'never get personally involved.' In this instance, that's not happening. I am, and deeply."

"Perhaps *this* will allow you to sleep a little better." Per placed several documents on his desk. "Now you know the secret of the chateau and all it meant, not only to the three victims, but to a number of others."

The advocate glanced at the first page. As he read on, his eyes widened; he straightened. In an instant he was immersed in digesting the information it offered. He turned his attention to the next, and then the next. It took several minutes. Not wishing to miss one word, he returned again and again to previous pages to scrutinize them again. He glanced at Lola Per.

"Last night I tried to develop a strategy which would show how despicable these men were in what they did. I could not find the evidence to do so. You, Lola, have provided not only what I needed, but you have uncovered just how ruthless these men were. They are even more monstrous than I could ever have imagined."

"How shall we hang them, high or low?"

Someone knocked on the door and opened it a crack. It was the investigator. Mercal motioned him in.

"I found the other gravedigger. While I was sitting at the bar, I overheard him and his friend, the one who gave testimony, talking. It seems the fellow, poor soul, was suffering. His conscience was bothering him because he lied about the burial. He felt he dishonored the memory of the deceased. I have a written account of what they said, signed by both. He is willing to take the stand again and this time, tell the truth." The investigator placed a large envelope on the advacate's desk.

"Well done." Mercal turned to Per.

"Shall I?" She asked.

Her superior nodded.

"You have a new assignment. As soon as possible, I need the bank records of these accounts; dates, deposits, signatures of the depositors." She handed the man the documents. "This is to be done quietly and in a highly confidential manner. No one is to know how you came to have this information." The investigator nodded, picked up the documents and left.

Mercal produced his watch. "We are going to be late. Fournier will be angry."

Snap, The Trap Closes

Entering hastily and avoiding the magistrate's piercing gaze, Mercal and Per took their seats. Fournier took out his watch, surveyed its face, shook his head and placed the piece back into its nest. "May I assume we are all ready?" Silence was the reply.

"Does the defense have any more witnesses to call?"

Beriot nodded. "I have two more. The first, I call Lieutenant Pierre Gouget, retired. He was an aide to those in command of French forces at Soissons in April, 1917." The witness took his seat.

"What was the situation at Soissons during the time in question?"

"The Germans were well entrenched along the Chemin de Dames, a road about 3 kilometers up the hill from Soissons and the Aisne River."

"And what was the French situation?"

"Our troops were encamped on the west side of the Aisne in, and around Soissons."

"When did the preemptive bombardment start of the enemy's positions?"

"There was none."

"And why was that, Lieutenant?"

"The commander wanted to attack and surprise the enemy."

"Was that a good strategy?"

"Absolutely – it was early in the year. The enemy would never have anticipated such a bold move while the ground was still wet and the possibility of snow still existed."

"Did all the junior officers agree with this strategy?"

"At the meeting where the strategy was announced and orders were being issued to troop commanders, several objected to beginning the assault without first shelling the enemy positions."

"And what reasons did they give?"

"That moving thousands of troops into Soissons and along the Aisne River had already alerted the enemy as to our intentions, that the surprise was *no surprise at all* – that lives would be lost if there was no softening of enemy positions."

"What resulted from these complaints?"

"We went ahead as planned."

"Was that a good idea?"

"It's not for me to say. When I'm given an order, I follow it. That's the way the system works."

"You are correct, lieutenant, that *is the way* the system works. It's the only way an army can work, following orders – one more question, please. What would happen if someone disagreed so strongly that they refused to obey?"

"They would be shot."

"I am finished with this witness."

Bernard Mercal stepped forward. "Where were you stationed at the time of the assault? Were you on the front lines? Were you in the infantry, artillery, tanks?"

"No, I was in support."

"And where were you stationed exactly?"

"I was sent to Reims to direct the traffic of arms and equipment for those engaged in the assault."

"Then you were not present at any of the meetings you mentioned, is that correct?"

"That is correct – but I heard about them."

"A few hours after they occurred, the next day, a week later, perhaps?"

"Well, no, I heard about them when a friend of mine stopped by the office. He was one of those who were wounded in the assault. He was one of those who got off with just a hand wound."

"Self – inflicted?"

The lieutenant smiled. "I couldn't say."

"What did he have to say about what he saw? I heard that our troops almost overran the German positions before they were driven back."

"Whoever told you that? It was a massacre, plain and simple – our men were being mowed down before they advanced a mere fifty meters. I heard that by the fourth day of the assault, our troops had

192

to climb over the piles of their own dead in order to advance. I don't blame them for. . ."

"Would you care to finish your statement?" Mercal suggested.

"I have already said too much."

"I think the jury understands what you meant. Thank you. That will be all."

"I call Colonel Hugo Ramilleaux to bear witness. He is in charge of all military expenditures not related to active military assignments – those that have to do with administrative functions," Beriot announced.

The colonel seated himself.

"You are in charge of approving expenditures including those expended by Lieutenant Charles Brousseau at Saint Germain for the period in question?"

"I don't *approve* them per se, I review them to see whether or not they seem to be in order. Once they pass through my section, *then* they are approved for disbursement."

"So your section is the last one to determine whether or not any sum of money is justified or not. What happens if you find a sum is not?"

"We do a complete review. We send out personnel to investigate, to question, to examine, and to find out just what the reason is for so great a disbursement."

"And, for the sake of argument, let's say you find out the sum is exorbitant, then what do you do?"

"We send the paper work and our findings to the Chief Magistrate's office. His people go over our findings, and advise the Chief Magistrate. He has the final word on the matter."

"And his people found nothing inappropriate with the sum of money being allocated for Saint Germain?"

"They did not."

"How many reviews come under your scrutiny?"

"Almost all that are not what we call 'regular' expenditures like food for the troops, uniforms, maintenance of equipment costs and the like – regular military expenses we call them."

"How many – please give me a number."

"I would say between seven and eight hundred – some years, a thousand – it depends on what is happening in the military."

"Did you review the Saint Germain expenditure *every* year?"

"No, we stopped challenging the amount after the second year. The Chief Magistrate's office suggested we do that."

"Why?"

"I don't know. I suppose they felt the amount was justified and that looking it over every year was a waste of time."

"Do you feel they were correct in doing so?"

"They have some of the best accountants and lawyers in the nation. I would never question their judgement."

"So, let us be clear, the expenditures at Saint Germain were justified?"

"According to them; yes."

"And what about you; certainly, you must be sure, too."

"I can't say that, sir."

"Are you questioning their decisions?"

"As I said, they have the best people."

"Then you agree with them."

"I can't say that, sir."

"ARE YOU QUESTIONING THEIR COMPETENCE?"

"I can't say that, sir," Ramilleaux replied.

"THEN YOU AGREE WITH THEM!"

"I can't say that, sir."

Magistrate Fournier intervened. "I think the witness has made his position clear."

"*YOUR* WITNESS," a frustrated Beriot announced.

Mercal stepped forward. "I appreciate your candor, colonel. Not many would have the nerve to question the decisions of their superiors and say so. It is quite obvious that you do, but refrain from saying so openly because you want to keep your job. I understand your reticence."

The colonel did not reply.

"You mentioned that you processed somewhere between seven hundred and a thousand questionable accounts a year. How many did you see fit to forward to the Chief Magistrate's section for review?"

"I think we forwarded about eighty."

"Why were there so many?"

"The army has a budget. Let's say the government provides an increase of two percent this year. That means that ongoing operations, whatever they may be, are more or less bound by that increase. Of course there are extenuating circumstances in some cases and, after reviewing them, sometimes an increase greater than the standard is allowed."

"Has the Saint Germain budget been over the standard increase allowed?"

"Yes, it has."

"How long has it been over the standard increase?"

"It has never met the criteria."

"And, how far above the criteria has it been?"

"It has exceeded the allowed amount regularly by 800 percent. Once, it was 950 percent."

"Have there been other disbursements that have had the same excessive spending?"

"Yes."

"How many were there?"

"This year, there are 39."

"Have you followed protocol and sent all of them to the Chief Magistrate's section?"

"We have."

"How many have had their increases approved?"

"All of them."

"How do you feel about that?"

"Some were so exorbitant that we broke protocol and suggested outright that they be denied."

"And, were they?"

"We received a letter advising us not to prejudge anything we submitted to them. They stated they were quite able to make the determinations without our help."

The jury was whispering among themselves. The revelations were unexpected, and shocking.

"That is all I have for this witness."

But before the witness stepped down, Magistrate Fournier cleared his throat – rather loudly. Mercal looked up. If one could discern a message in the magistrate's eyes, it would be *don't let him get away – continue your cross examination – I want to hear more.*

"Colonel, would you mind remaining; I have a few more questions."

He sat down once more. He appeared puzzled, but not anxious.

"The thought just came to me – why would someone like the Chief Magistrate have any say in funding the military? That seems strange to me. Can you please explain?"

"Yes, of course. The increase mandated by the government is a *legal* barrier – to control spending, you know. Everyone feels they have good reasons to increase their budget. They are afraid that if they don't spend all the money allotted and ask for more, then their budget will be cut. That is why we are there – to prevent their padding their requests."

"I see. You keep them in line – but then the Chief Magistrate's people overrule you and let the excesses go. Is that it?"

Colonel Ramilleaux lowered his head. He did not answer.

"I understand." Mercal glanced at Fournier.

The unspoken message this time was *I've heard enough.*

"You are dismissed," Mercal said.

The advocate approached the magistrate. "I know that it is early, but I request we adjourn now. My reason is that I have several witnesses who require transportation since they have no means of getting here without our assistance." The magistrate nodded his approval. "Further, I request that the chief legal officer of the French Armey be present tomorrow, accompanied by sworn soldier police. After what I bring to light, there will be some arrests."

"Would you care to explain?" the magistrate questioned.

"With respect, indulge me this once. I cannot, for reasons that will become evident tomorrow."

"This time I will." Fournier answered. "But I will judge whether this convenience is pertinent or just courtroom strategy."

"Thank you," the advocate answered.

As they were leaving, Mercal whispered to Per "Send someone to get the gravediggers – both of them. Here is a list of the copies I will need from these jurisdictions – they will still be open by the time we get out of the building. Task your people with getting them – no excuses. If they have to break in after hours, tell them I will defend them after they are arrested."

"Now Bernard, you don't *really* want me to tell them that do you?"

"I need those documents. I want to send a few men to hell tomorrow – and I will not be denied. Get want I want Lola; no excuses."

The Attack

He planned to recall three witnesses tomorrow and perhaps a fourth. That depended on how quickly he could break down the one he would be questioning first. The most important aspect of his strategy was to accuse the first witness of wrongdoing and have him led away by police. The others would then be pleading for mercy and quickly reveal the entire scheme before the jury. The last would be accused even before he was asked to take the stand.

Wife Christine, again seeing that look Bernard had when he was on the hunt and knew he had his prey cornered, supported his night-long effort with frequent cups of coffee, food and the occasional word of encouragement. It would be a long night for both, but hopefully, a fruitful one.

Lola, on her assigned mission, was engaged in expediting the material her mentor wanted. She maintained contact with all of her cadre, demanding they check in every half hour to report their progress. Success was the order of the day. Every task she set for them was completed. All that remained was the ordering of the documents in the sequence Mercal required and marking the areas he would need. Unlike her mentor who had a companion, she had to provide her own stimulation and nourishment. Time flew by. As the morning sun brightened the premises, she found herself not at all tired, having managed to stay alert and focused for over fourteen hours. Amazed at her own stamina, and proud of it, she stuffed the papers into her brief, and laid down on the divan for a short nap. Two hours later, Bernard Mercal was shaking her foot attempting to awaken her. Once again, they were going to be late for court.

The train gently rocked back and forth most of the time but, on occasion, severely. Superstitious to the core, the gravedigger who had given testimony took it as an omen of impending doom. His friend seemed not to care at all. He was asleep. The first tugged at his friend's sleeve.

"Wake up, wake up," he whispered.

"What now," the other growled, "You've been nervous since we left. You're not going to your execution, just to say a few words at a trial. You've done it before. Calm down."

"But that man said I would go to jail if they found out I had lied."

The third occupant of the compartment was Mercal's investigator. He leaned forward and put his hand on the worrier's shoulder. "Nothing is going to happen to you. Just tell the truth. That is your most powerful weapon. Tell the court how they offered you money to say what you did. If you do that, then they will be in trouble, not you."

"But. . ."

"The advocate I work for would never let anything happen to you – on that, I will swear on my mother's grave."

"Is that enough for you? Now will you let me sleep?"

"On your mother's grave – well, that's enough for me."

Suddenly, the train ride home seemed much smoother.

~

As they climbed the stairs to the court, Adjutant De Voux was bombarding Advocate Beriot with his concerns.

"Did you see what happened when they left the courtroom? Mercal was whispering to his lady advocate as they left. After that she raced down the hall and left as if the devil was after her. What's that all about?"

"He may have forgotten some material he might have needed tomorrow. I don't think there will be any surprises," Beriot opined.

"How did Magrid's testimony go over? Was he convincing?"

"He held his ground. That is not easy when one is being questioned by an advocate as skilled as Mercal. Gouget, on the other hand, utterly failed to convince anyone, even me, that the decision to start and continue the assault was the right choice, or, for that matter, *ever* the right choice. He failed us – his testimony might even have cost us our case."

"Then it's over."

"Not yet. We still have the testimony of the gravedigger. We still have Magrid. If necessary, I'll recall him and have him repeat how serious it is to ignore the lawful command of an officer. That is no small thing, you know."

"Have you ever been in service?"

"No, I paid my debt by working for the army as an advocate."

"Then you don't know that orders are frequently ignored – not openly, but secretly – whenever that order is stupid or irrelevant to the situation. Most who serve in the field have the knowledge and experience to say the right things at the right time. It's those brand new academy graduates who issue the orders that shouldn't be followed. In time most learn, but some – well, they are hopeless."

Beriot stared at De Voux. "*Never* say that in court."

"Now I see – you're a fraud. You pose as an advocate, but you don't know your ass from a. . ."

"That's enough."

"I've heard about you. I can't tell you how many friends of mine cautioned me not to take you on as counsel for this case – but I ignored their advice. They were right after all, you are nothing but a. . ."

"I said that's enough, you pompous ass. You're a soldier? I was assigned to this case, not because you chose me. Now it comes to me that we both were chosen for this case – so that we could commit legal suicide together. My peers and superiors hate me – they hate me as much as I hate you and what you stand for, an overfed, self-aggrandizing imbecile in a uniform that almost anyone could wear more competently than you. It's people like you who are responsible for the deaths of many – too many – good men dying on the battlefield. You say I am incompetent; perhaps I am, but look at these hands and look well at them – there is no blood on them. What about yours?"

"You don't have to remind me, I know what I did. If it means anything to you, I regret what I did. Almost from the moment I sentenced those men I knew it was the wrong thing to do. But where could I hide, where could I go? Nowhere; I was in charge, it was my decision – and I erred, gravely. On the way back to Paris after it was all over, I wept, do you know that? I wept, not only for myself, but for all those whose lives I ruined because of my cowardice, being afraid to stand up and do the right thing. Those soldiers weren't guilty, it was the decisions thrust upon them by those who made them – *they* were the guilty ones. But who would stand up and say that? Not I – I had a career to build, a ladder to climb. I had to avoid embarrassing situations that might jeopardize my ascent. I couldn't have that. Certainly you understand that, don't you?"

"Thank you, De Voux, you cannot imagine the good you have done just now."

"How? I have just admitted that I am a coward, I am incompetent, and that I have committed the gravest of sins at Soissons."

"In my own way, I have walked every step of the path you have trod. And, now that I have finally admitted it to myself, I find there is no need to hide from everyone in order to protect myself." Beriot threw up his hands. "I am free, De Voux – for the first time in my life I am free."

"What about today? How do you think it will go?"

"We shall sit in court and let Mercal tear our argument apart. I will enjoy that. It deserves to be torn apart."

"What?"

———

Representing their side, only Beriot and De Voux entered the courtroom. Their opposition entered with nine individuals: Mercal, Per, the two gravediggers, two investigators, and three clerks wheeling two carts stuffed with documents.

The magistrate entered and all were seated. "I assume the defense has concluded? Shall the plaintiff begin?" His gaze drifted over to Advocate Mercal. He nodded.

"I wish to recall Captain Magrid." The officer approached and took his seat. Mercal smiled. "How old are you, captain?"

"I am 48."

"And how long have you served in the army?"

"It will be twenty-five years eleven months and three days tomorrow."

"That sounds very precise. I knew several men who were close to retirement. They kept track of days the very same way you are. Are you going to retire?"

"I am. I put my papers in. In 27 days I will be a free man."

"I suppose you've set a little aside to carry you through the years ahead?"

Magrid smiled. "*Oh yes*, I have."

"May I ask how much?"

"That, sir, is a private matter." He turned to the magistrate. "Do I have to answer?" The magistrate nodded. "About 18 thousand Francs – I think that's about right."

"No more – are you sure?"

"You can check my bankbook if you wish."

"Are you married, captain?"

"No, I have a writ of divorcement from my wife – cheating, you know."

"Did you, or did she?"

Magrid grinned. "I was the one."

"Do you have another woman?"

"Yes, I do. We are very much in love."

And what is her name please?" Magrid glanced at the magistrate. "Helene Badere."

"Does she also have a bank account?"

Magrid's face reddened; his breathing became troubled. "Y-yes."

"And how much is in her account?"

Magrid lowered his head and mumbled.

"You don't have to answer, captain, I already have the amount." Mercal waved his hand. A clerk rushed forward and placed a sheet of paper in his hand. "Let's see, eighty-three thousand Francs, is that correct, captain?"

Magrid nodded.

"You never told me the amount you approved funding for the prisoners at the chateau. How much was it?"

"I can't remember."

"Of course you can't." Mercal nodded. Again the clerk came forward and placed another sheet of paper in his hand. "You approved 1700 Francs. Was that for the year, or every month?"

At first, Magrid did not answer. "A month, it was for a month."

"It cost over 20,000 Francs a year to feed and clothe three prisoners? That seems exorbitant; were they staying at the Riviera?"

"Those were the amounts I was directed to send."

"Who directed you?"

"I don't recall."

"Based on what this court has heard, I recommend Captain Magrid be taken into custody until this matter can be pursued further at a later date. The amount of funds available to him could allow him to flee to a location outside the country."

The magistrate nodded to the clerk. He left and returned with two police. After Advocate Mercal dismissed the witness, they escorted him out of the courtroom.

"I call Lieutenant Jules Ronda."

"You were at Chateau Germain while Captain Gereau was incarcerated there?"

"Yes I was."

"How was the food?"

"Simeon and I were on starvation rations. We never had enough to eat. I was free to go out and get something after hours, but he never was. I had to sneak food back for him to eat."

"But Charles Brousseau was given seventeen-hundred Francs a month for your care. What happened to the money? Have you any idea?"

"He was spending some on his girlfriend Lily. What he did with the rest I don't know."

Brousseau arose and attempted to leave the courtroom. The magistrate raised his hand. The court officer blocked the door. He returned to his seat. Surveying all this, Mercal commented. "I will be getting to you very soon."

Turning back to his witness, he asked "Did anyone find out about this?"

"Yes. One night I was so sick of all of this I went out to the café and got drunk. A man helped me back to the Chateau. I told him everything. He informed Father Danilou. He came to the chateau and threatened Charles for not having given us proper rations. After that, the food was better."

"And when did that happen?"

"It was in the ninth year of Simeon's imprisonment. By that time he was so ill, nothing could have saved him. My God, he was a good man." Ronda lost control and broke into tears.

Mercal paused to allow the witness to regain his composure. "Do you recall the name of the man who helped you?"

"Yes; Marcel Du Parque. He will come and testify if you want. Father Danilou has passed away."

"Thank you, Lieutenant. You may step down." The advocate turned and stared at Charles Brousseau. "It's your turn." He came forward.

"You and Captain Magrid are complicit, that's plain to see. But you couldn't have received that large a stipend without some cooperation from upper echelon. Who were they?"

"I don't know what you are talking about. I had no accomplices. I simply did what I was told. There was no pilfering of funds. Perhaps Magrid did skim a little for himself, but every franc I received went for the care of Captain Gereau, Lieutenant Ronda, and me."

"You said you did what you were told – by whom?"

"I will never reveal that."

"Even if it means that you might go to prison?"

The witness did not answer.

"Very well, then, you are excused." Brousseau went back to his seat in the court room. He found himself sitting between two policemen.

"Lily please, can you come up?" The attractive, slightly-built, middle-aged woman took the stand.

"You know Charles Brousseau?"

"We were lovers while he was at Chateau Germain."

"You were lovers - for how long?"

"About ten years. He said he was going to marry me when it was all over. He did, but later he left me – after our little Moira died."

"Did you know he was married? Did he ever tell you that?"

"No, he never told me."

"I understand you used to run errands for him. What were they?"

"I used to get the groceries for the three of them; 12 Francs a week was all he would spend on them. He was very frugal with the food money – *very* frugal."

"Did you run any other errands?"

"Yes, twice a month I would go to the bank and put money into one account for Charles and the others. He said he was saving for our marriage."

"Do you recall the name of the persons who had the other accounts? Please, don't mention the names right now, just tell me whether you know them or not."

"I know the names."

Mercal turned to the sound of a loud thud, as if someone had fallen.

"He's fainted," someone called out.

"Who fainted?" Mercal asked.

"Adjutant De Voux," was the reply.

"That was one of them," Lily replied, "that was one of the names on the accounts."

Magistrate gaveled the court adjourned. "I've heard enough; court, tomorrow at ten." he said as he left the courtroom.

—

With Brousseau and Magrid detained, Mercal wondered what the fate of De Voux might be. He was sure that Magistrate Fournier was mulling over the same question. The entire situation was complicated enough. The corruption had been revealed. In addition to the disgrace, two of the offenders would be going to prison. Again, what of De Voux? Already responsible for the Soissons debacle, how much more serious had his situation become with the pilfering of funds from the military? He saw it plainly; not only was the adjutant a coward, he was allegedly greedy, and unequivocally stupid.

But the advocate understood that De Voux possessed neither the intellect nor the drive to have masterminded the embezzlement, nor the intellect to craft the intricate web used in the fund's disbursement. He was simply a pass-through pawn. It had to be someone higher, much higher, in the hierarchy, perhaps a prominent government official. From the information he had, and the revelations he had heard so far, he could not imagine who the ring leader might be.

It began to dawn upon him; how widespread was this misappropriation of funds? How many other disbursements of army funds were inflated and misdirected? The thought caught him short of breath. Suddenly he envisioned Magrid approving thousands, perhaps tens of thousands over time, of false approvals for payment. How many *other* bank accounts did he have, and under what other names? The advocate paused: was he making too much of this, could he be placing too broad an interpretation of a few soldiers cheating France out of a significant sum of money? *It is an isolated event,* he began to reason, *why make more of it than it is?* Satisfied with the events of the day, he went to bed.

At two, he arose and went downstairs to once again search though his notes. He was correct in his initial premise; there was indeed a rat under foot, a *big* rat, and he, Mercal, was going to find and expose him.

—

A courier arrived at the home of Magistrate Fournier. It was late; only a matter of the utmost urgency would have justified such a visit. He read the message and then informed the courier he would comply.

The meeting was to take place in an outdoor café on the west bank, not the most elegant location for a meeting, but it did ensure privacy. He wondered, *why there?* That thought plagued him as he made his way to the rendezvous. His intuition alerted him of danger, but he ignored it. After all, if one can't trust the Chief Magistrate, who then, is left?"

Chief Magistrate Clemand rose when his subordinate approached. He asked him whether or not he would care for wine.

Fournier's intuition nagged at him. This time he paid attention. There was something about the scene, the setting; it rang hollow. The questions kept surfacing: *why here, why tonight, why so late? What could the Chief Magistrate hope to accomplish?* The answer cascaded through his stream of consciousness like a torrent of rushing water. *I have been asked here because I am going to be assassinated. If his pleading to my better side and offering a high position doesn't work, then what is left? Only the territorial imperative – and that is deadly force.*

Fournier began the conversation. "I know why I am here. The press is having a field day with the trial. It's bringing into question the integrity of every high-ranking individual in the army, and they are strongly inferring that the higher echelon may be a cabal of thieves. Too bad, they brought it on themselves. I would be interested how many *are* compromised. I suppose we will never know."

"You have gone too far – you never should have allowed it to go this far. You are jeopardizing yourself, and, everyone in the profession. There are pressures being exerted – and they have nothing to do with jurisprudence."

"You mean we have picked up a rock and found snakes underneath? And they are becoming uncomfortable? What a shame."

"I have found two witnesses who will swear that Captain Gereau was the instigator of the mutiny and that he shot two soldiers who argued against what he proposed. That should turn the tide. You can have Beriot put them on the stand tomorrow."

"How much?"

"How much what?"

"Are they being paid for their testimony?"

"You don't understand. You think you are fishing in a pond. You are not. You are fishing in an ocean, and you are fishing in a monsoon. The fish are not flounder, they are. . ." Fournier interrupted.

". . . Sharks. Tell Beriot not to have them appear or I will have him, and them, arrested and jailed."

"You must do this. You have no choice. You *must* do this."

"And, if I don't? What are you going to do, kill me?" Fournier watched the magistrate closely. While his lips did not move, he thought his eyes telegraphed a 'yes.'

"Au revoir," Fournier said. He left.

The way back was dark and lonely. Few ventured out at this time of night. It was not the place to be, alone, and unarmed. As he turned the corner and entered a poorly-lit street, he heard someone approaching from behind. The person's pace quickened. He was trying to catch up.

Fournier turned to face him. The large man reached into his pocket and drew out a knife. He approached. Fournier froze; he could not think of one thing to do to defend himself; he was old. His assailant appeared young and extremely able. He reached out to grasp Fournier's arm.

A shot rang out. He slid to the pavement. Someone rushed out of the shadows, hooked his arm under Fournier's and whispered, "We must go – now."

His rescuer took the magistrate to a place unknown to him, a flat in the poorer section of Paris. After being ushered into the parlor and given several goblets of Courvoisier, the magistrate calmed down. Bernard Mercal entered. After discussing events with the investigator who shot the assassin, he thanked him and sent him home.

"Are you feeling better? You have been through quite an ordeal."

"And it has been quite a revelation. I never expected that from him."

"You would, if you had discovered what I have. The Chief Magistrate is a rich man, *very* rich. He has 32 bank accounts, only two in his name. They are the ones that contain the paltry sums. The rest are simply bulging with money, army money."

"Why didn't you tell me about this?"

"It is because I have a case before you. There would have been enough time after you ruled on this one."

"How did your man come to be there when I needed him?"

"After finding the evidence about the Chief Magistrate it became apparent he was involved in the money-laundering scheme. He didn't wish to be exposed. I believe he was the mastermind who orchestrated the entire operation."

"You had me followed."

"Day and night; it needed to be done, and without having you know."

"I owe you my life."

"Good jurists are hard to find. I thought keeping you on a little longer would be a good thing."

"I must go home. I have court tomorrow."

"I will have someone escort you. Do you have a pistol?"

"Yes."

"Keep it under your pillow – and have it on your person when you go to court. Now we have some idea just how desperate these people are."

Fournier nodded.

It was late when he returned. Wife Eloise was waiting for him.

"Is everything all right?" she asked.

"Yes – I'm fine – a little tired, perhaps, that's all."

"Come, let's go to bed. I'll rub your back – you like that."

As they mounted the stairs, he leaned over and kissed her.

She is a good wife, he mused.

Magistrate Fournier took his seat. Court was in session. He noticed Beriot behaving strangely, as if his trousers were teeming with ants. He had difficulty sitting still. He arose.

"The defense has come upon two additional witnesses. We request that they be heard."

Fournier turned to Mercal. "Counselor?"

"Oh, yes your honor, I believe it is imperative they be heard."

"Before you call them forth, I would like to ask you a few questions."

"Of course," Beriot replied.

"Did you have any contact with the Chief Magistrate regarding this case or any part?"

"N-no,"

"Did you find the witnesses or did the Chief Magistrate provide them for you?"

"I-I found them – my people found them."

"I spoke to the Chief Magistrate last night. Are you aware of that?"

"No, I am not."

"He told me that he would be providing two witnesses whose purpose would be to blemish Captain Simeon Gereau's honor by telling falsehoods about his behavior at Soissons. Are you aware of that?"

Beriot did not answer. The two witnesses skulked out of the courtroom. The advocate watched them leave.

"You should have gone with them," Fournier stated, "But you cannot. You are still counsel for this trial. I will deal with the two witness issue later. Are you prepared to continue, Counselor Mercal?"

"I recall Lily to the stand."

"She came forward. It was obvious she was not a person of means. Still, there was a certain elegance and strength about the way she carried herself.

"What is your full name?"

"I am known by only one name – Lily. I have never known another."

"Do you know Charles Brousseau?" Mercal pointed to the man.

"I do; we were lovers for ten years."

"Why are you not with him now?"

"He lied to me. I didn't know he was married. He promised he would marry me – as soon as we got rid of the prisoner. He did – but then he left me."

"'Got rid of the prisoner,' what do you mean by that?"

"Charles had to remain as his jailer until he died. After that he was relieved of his responsibility. He was a free man."

"What did you think of such an arrangement?"

"It was terrible – why would anyone choose to keep a man like Charles in such a position – he had better things to do than to be a nursemaid to a convict. That's why he cut the food rations. We wanted him to die – as soon as possible – but he didn't. HE JUST WOULDN'T DIE. Can you imagine? We were so angry."

The magistrate cautioned the jury to control themselves. They were whispering – one of them shouted a curse at Brousseau.

"If he didn't use the money for food, what *did* he use it for?"

"He bought me nice things – pretty bracelets and necklaces – we dined out many evenings – it was wonderful – and he promised it would be much better when we were free from this yoke around our necks."

"Did you ever have any money left over?"

"Oh yes, lots. Charles had bank accounts where we put the extra money. Three – no, four – yes, four – I'm sure it was four."

"Do you remember the names on them?"

"I just thought they were all for Charles but under false names."

"Do you have any idea how much was in them?"

"Not in the beginning, but when we had deposited so much each month for so many years, I took a peak at a few."

"How much was in them?"

"One had 40 thousand, another had 50."

"When the prisoner's health started to fail, what did Charles do?"

"He cut the rations even more – the prisoner would have died too, if that guard hadn't told the priest what we were doing. He changed everything – he made Charles increase the rations. Why, he even made him provide medicine. He should have kept his nose out of our affairs."

Mercal turned to Beriot "Questions?" The advocate listlessly waved off the request.

"Thank you Lily." The woman went back to her seat.

"I would like to recall Alfonse Duchard."

"Is he the gravedigger?" Magistrate Fournier asked.

"I object," Beriot shouted, "He's only a gravedigger – he already gave his testimony."

"Why are you recalling him?" Fournier asked Mercal.

"He wants to change his testimony."

"I OBJECT," Beriot screamed, "He's lying."

"We'll see who's lying," Fournier said, "proceed."

"Monsieur Duchard, tell the court; have you come here of your own free will?"

"Yes."

"Why have you come?"

"Because I lied the last time I was here – all for a pair of shoes and a few Francs. It's bothered me ever since I did it. I've been drunk every night. I have to stop. I want to make things right – there's no other way but to tell the truth."

"Please, go on."

"There was no military funeral for the captain. It was just Father Danilou, my friend over there, and me who laid him to rest. He didn't even have a coffin, the poor soul, it was burlap rags. That's what they laid him to rest in, rotten burlap. And I couldn't say a word about it because I'm *only* a gravedigger."

"And who was it who suggested you give this false testimony?"

"It was that bastard over there." Duchard pointed to Beriot; the advocate squirmed and looked away.

Mercal turned and looked at the magistrate who was having a great deal of difficulty containing himself. Vesuvius about to erupt on an unsuspecting Pompeii must have appeared in like fashion.

"DO YOU HAVE ANY MORE WITNESSES?" The magistrate bellowed.

"I do not." Mercal replied.

"COURT IS ADJOURNED. THERE WILL BE A TWO DAY RECESS. WE SHALL RESUME ON MONDAY," the magistrate announced as he stormed out of the courtroom. He did not attempt to hide his ire.

"Perfect," Mercal whispered to Per, "Perfect."

"Why?"

"Now we have time to find out the names of the others."

Mercal glanced at Per. She was beaming.

Early the next morning Advocate Beriot responded to someone knocking on his office door. The messenger handed him an envelope and left. He opened it. The declaration mandated he appear before a panel of his peers to review 'Your recent behavior as defense council for one Adjutant Henri De Voux.' Beriot had not expected such a swift response to the failed tactics he intended to use to discredit the deceased Captain Gereau. Then there was the false Duchard testimony openly rebuked by the witness who showed remorse and accused the advocate of being the person behind the deception. His actions had now been made public. It reached those who might decide to destroy his career.

He had underestimated the integrity of Magistrate Fournier; he expected to receive a slight reprimand for his behavior. Instead, his license to practice law was now in jeopardy. *What can I do to deflect this?* He contacted his secretary. "No more calls today, please. Tell everyone I have gone home for the day." The battle to retain his credentials as a jurist was on. He retrieved several books on jurisprudence; the expected and proper behavior of an advocate while at trial. He poured over each page hoping to find some sentence, some statement that would offer him relief. After many hours of intensive searching, he could find none. The strategies he had used were identified as 'unethical, criminal, flagrant, deceptive,' or 'beyond the limits of ethical conduct.'

The truth was apparent - he was finished.

———

The adjutant was in a worse state than his advocate. He envisioned his career, his reputation, in short his world, crumbling. The 'ignorant bastard' he had hired to defend him had failed, and miserably at that, to present any sort of viable defense for his actions. He knew it would be hard, but he never expected the utter collapse that had occurred. He took his revolver from its holster and laid it on the desk before him. He surveyed the weapon for some time, noting how clean it was, and how long it had been since it had been fired. Grasping it, he raised it to his right temple. His thumb pulled the hammer back. After several seconds he slowly released the hammer. It returned to its 'no fire' position.

"There's a better way," De Voux muttered to himself. Placing the weapon back in its holster, he went home.

The next morning he arose, dressed and made ready for his testimony at court. He knew Advocate Mercal was going to ask him those questions which would reveal his nefarious connection to Magrid and the others who were involved in the theft of army monies. There was no defense for his behavior; he had already acknowledged that. But would he, should he, reveal the names of those above him who were also engaged in the theft, or refuse and suffer the consequences? It was a question that would remain unresolved until the very moment he would be asked for their identities.

De Voux drew his revolver. He flicked open the magazine and determined it was loaded. He returned it to its cradle. He was ready.

———

It was Monday. The trial resumed. Advocate Mercal called Adjutant Henri De Voux to the witness stand. The formalities being addressed, the questioning began. De Voux appeared unperturbed – Mercal could not fathom why.

"You were the officer in charge of the cadre sent by command to quell the uprising in Soissons?"

"Yes I was."

"Were you successful?"

"Completely; we had to execute some, imprison some, and reprimand the rest."

"Did you execute the leaders of the mutiny?"

"Yes – that is – some of them. The rest we imprisoned."

"How many did you execute?"

"I can't remember."

"Your honor, here is a list of those executed," Mercal indicated, "Did you notify their families?"

"Yes."

"Did you inform them why they were being executed?"

"No; we simply said they lost their lives while in combat. We didn't see any need for the families to suffer any shame."

"That was kind of you," Mercal sarcastically commented, "And what of those you imprisoned, what did you tell their families?"

"That they were missing in action – that's all we told them. When they had served their sentence, they would be 'found' and be able to go home."

"Again, how kind of you." Mercal paused. "Were all given that option?"

De Voux stared at the advocate. "You know they were not *all like that.* Now we're going to talk about Gereau, Ronda, and Brousseau, is that what we are going to do?"

"It seems you've read my mind, adjutant."

"No, we didn't inform their families of their fate - no, we didn't make known their whereabouts - no, we didn't inform the Gereau family that he had died – yes, we did lie about having discovered Ronda and Brousseau after they 'miraculously regained their memories after suffering amnesia.' The whole affair with them was a charade, a lie, theater. I wish I never went to Soissons, I wish I never heard the name - and yes, it was my fault, mine alone that all those good men were imprisoned, or shot, or secretly jailed. I'm sorry - so sorry - may God forgive me. I'm a good soldier, I've served France for many years – but this, this, was my worst assignment – I TAKE FULL RESPONSIBILITY FOR MY ACTIONS."

"Well said," Mercal responded, "We here, *might* almost pity you – except for the money. WHO RECEIVED THE FUNDS YOU STOLE FROM THE ARMY? ADJUTANT, WE WANT THEIR NAMES. WE MUST KNOW THEIR NAMES. WE ALREADY KNOW CAPTAIN MAGRID WAS ONE OF THEM. WHO WERE THE OTHERS?"

De Voux squirmed in his seat. He glanced everywhere except into the eyes of the advocate. Every sign: his jerking and fidgeting, his heavy and erratic breathing, the wagging of his head, indicated he was in crisis. Finally he straightened – he had come to decision.

"I refuse to tell you who they are. I am faithful to my friends."

"You are faithful - to whom? To those who were robbing your country? To those who were taking the food away from the very men you command? To those who were filling their coffers while others were barely surviving? JUST WHAT KIND OF FAITHFULNESS IS THAT?"

"CALM DOWN, Counselor, calm down. Even if he refuses to name them, rest assured we will find out who they are." Magistrate Fournier, attempting to control Mercal's behavior, was having difficulty controlling his own.

"Are you saying you will not cooperate? You know what that means."

"I accept my punishment, whatever it is. For me, the sun is setting, my career is over. I regret only that I did not do right by Captain Gereau and Lieutenant Ronda. Brousseau is another matter – he will self-destruct where he is or wherever he is going – it is just a matter of time."

"I have no more for this witness."

De Voux left the witness stand.

"I call Advocate and fellow counselor Lola Per to the stand."

"Was counselor Beriot informed about this witness?"

"No, he has not. She has come upon several documents that need to be brought to the court's attention – the gravity of the information they contain requires this extraordinary strategy on the part of the plaintiff."

"Proceed, but remember the press is present. There will be grave repercussions if your evidence lacks credibility. I will address this unusual behavior later."

Mercal nodded. He motioned Counselor Per to come forward.

"You came into knowledge of these documents when?"

"When I went to Saint Germain en Laye to search for the woman named Lily."

"She has no last name?"

"To my knowledge she had none, or had not used it in so long that she could not remember it."

"How is she relevant to this particular evidence?"

"We know she was Charles Brousseau's lover. That is of no consequence to this proceeding, but what is, is that she was the courier for the funds deposited in various banks whose accounts were under several names."

"You mean those moneys stolen from the funds designated for maintenance of those incarcerated in Chateau Germain?"

"Yes, I mean the same."

"Are you holding new evidence?"

"I am."

"How did you come upon it?"

"Lily couldn't remember the names of the accountholders, but she did recall the names of the banks and the last four numbers of each of the accounts. I went and obtained copies of the accounts. While the accountholders could not be identified at first, they periodically withdrew moneys from the accounts Lily deposited, and transferred them to others under their real names. That was how we found out who they were. One of them is very well known, so famous in fact that several of the tellers referred to him by name."

"And who is that?"

Per did not answer. Instead, she handed her employer the document. He in turn, brought it up to the magistrate to read. After the incident with the assailant, the name was not a surprise. He handed the document back to the advocate.

"Chambers, please," The judge requested. Beriot arose to join both men.

Once there, Fournier turned to Mercal. "Are you sure of this? This is the gravest of accusations. If it is true, it could threaten our entire society for years to come. Such a stain on our system of jurisprudence will not easily be forgotten."

"Who is it? What is this about?" Beriot asked. Magistrate Fournier did not answer.

"My investigators took up posts outside the bank," Mercal said, "They saw him enter and perform exactly the transactions my associate described; transferring money from one account to the other. Just to be certain, they obtained copies of the transactions and deposed the tellers, the manager, and the bank guard. They did this several times. He is very punctual, precise. He comes in several times a week, exactly at ten minutes after 13, not five minutes earlier and not ten minutes later."

"Of all men I know, I would never have expected him to be the culprit. You know what this means, don't you? He is the ring leader. He is the one who rules on any complaints referring to budgetary matters, he validates the amounts – Mon Dieu, what has this all come to?"

"Who are we talking about?" Beriot asked. Mercal and the magistrate ignored the question.

"It seems Captain Gereau will have received more than the restoring of his honor; his passing has also resulted in a great service to this nation."

"You, of course, will not make this public – at this time. I will handle this myself. Then you may do as you wish –and I believe I know what that will be." Both advocates and magistrate reentered the courtroom.

"You may step down, Counselor Per," Mercal directed.

"The plaintiff rests."

"This case is adjourned until Monday. At that time, I will render my decision. The witnesses are directed not to leave Paris, under any condition. Those that have not already been put under guard are directed to be present at court at that time. Court is adjourned."

—

As the train sped back to Saint Germain en Laye, Alfonse Duchard had his nose pressed against the window and was looking at the passing landscape. Worried as he was on route, he had neglected to observe its beauty. Now the situation had changed – he was a free man – he had told the truth and everything that scoundrel Beriot threatened had not come to pass. His friend sitting beside him patted his friend gently on the back.

"You see, it's just as I told you, when you tell the truth, they can't do anything to you. It's only when you lie – that's when they have something to hold over your head."

"And I still have my new shoes, plus the money they gave me – and someone else stuffed an envelope with another ten francs in my pocket. Not bad for a gravedigger."

"You mean not bad for a gravedigger who tells the truth."

Now Saint Germain would be a happier place for two truth-telling friends.

—

Claire Gereau was at a precipice. She had opened the front door and found Bernard Mercal and Lola Per standing before her. She held her breath. With children Jean Pierre and Nicole clinging to her thighs, they all seemed suspended in time, waiting . . .waiting. . . . Their travail had been so extended that any answer, whatever it was, would be greeted as a blessing, closure – the final act in their bizarre existence.

"May we come in?" Mercal asked. The softness of his tone calmed Claire. By some unknown telepathy known only to mothers and their children, they also became less tense.

"On Monday, the magistrate will render his decision."

"You mean we still have to wait?"

"Yes, but I think it will be in our favor. Just how much in our favor, I cannot tell."

"What do you mean by that?"

"Let's wait and see."

"Is there any way I can make you more comfortable," Claire asked.

"Being who you are over all these years has already done that," Per answered.

Claire blushed. "Perhaps now the children and I can be free of this burden and resume our lives."

Per turned away and rummaged through her pocketbook.

"You will never know how, but your husband has done France a great service. I wish that I could tell you all the details, but I can't. Follow the papers, especially the headline stories. They will be there because of what happened to your husband."

"How can I thank you? I cannot afford your fees. We are managing, but there is not much to spare. Over time, perhaps I could. . ."

Mercal raised his hand. "Madame, it is all taken care of. A generous donor has seen to the cost."

Per glanced at him. "Yes, Madame, someone who knew and admired your husband has taken care of it. They have even given something for you – that was one of the reasons we came." Per reached into her purse and handed Claire a thick envelope.

"We must take our leave now. There is much to do before Monday," Mercal observed.

"Thank you, thank you both."

Sure they were clear of anything that might be overheard by the mother, Lola Per opined "There is no cost; you liar. You are going to pay for all of this out of your own pocket."

"And you, 'they even left something for you.' Where did that come from?"

"I was saving for a dress. I suppose now I will have to wait."

"I hope it was an expensive dress."

"It was, but I will never tell you *how* expensive. You would faint."

Mercal smiled. "Now that is what I call a generous person."

⁓

The phonograph's Triumphal March from the opera Aida was making delicate crystal figurines on the china closet vibrate, but Magistrate Fournier ignored the cacophony. *There must be a place in hades for all who have torn asunder the trust placed in them,* Fournier opined, *Radames betrayed his, and Aida was complicit. Look what happened to them.*

The world is a kaleidoscope of charades. Everywhere individuals mask their true intentions to achieve a purpose – onerous or exemplary. The worst of these actors are those who appear to be pillars of the community – but are actually ravenous wolves. Their greatest vulnerability, their Achilles heel is being able to maintain their public stature and not be exposed for who they really are. And this is the type of individual I must now face, Fournier mused. *In addition he is a close friend, one who has for years, for almost time immemorial it seems, fooled even me.*

Experience had taught the magistrate that those of this ilk went to great lengths to protect their disguise. But, when all the coverings were removed, they suddenly turned vicious, demonic – seething with anger and threatening harm to those who had revealed their true identity.

These were not the common criminals - there was honesty to *their* criminality. When someone asks you for your wallet, you know he is trying to rob you. When someone steals your horse, he is proclaiming to the world he is a horse-thief. These are easily charged and convicted.

Such is not the case with the actors; they are clever. They hide their true intent, they move in the shadows, they obscure everything that might impinge on their public image.

He turned off the phonograph. He was tired of strategizing. There was only one avenue to pursue: attack, attack, attack. But first, he had to render a decision, Monday. *Serve the innocent first,* he mused, *the scoundrels can wait.*

—

The courtroom was overflowing; Reporters, well-wishers, some who had served with Simeon, even several court clerks, no doubt sent by their superiors to see how Magistrate Fournier would rule – it would be setting a precedent for future cases of this type. Most prominent of these was the clerk associated with the Chief Magistrate – not unnoticed by Fournier. Mercal, Per, and Beriot were already there – half an hour early. Tension was palpable, even in those who had no involvement in the proceedings. Adjutant De Voux sat slumped in his chair, as if he were awaiting the call to the guillotine.

As certain as he was for a favorable verdict, Bernard Mercal requested that Claire and the children remain at home. This was not the place for a grieving wife and her young children. Reporters would have converged and bombarded them with a never-ending barrage of questions.

The Magistrate entered. A hush fell over the courtroom.

"It has been established that the witness who accused Captain Simeon Gereau as being complicit in the event that occurred in April 1917 was not in any position to state what he said. He was in hospital and whatever he heard was hearsay which he recited as his own personal account. He will be charged with perjuring himself.

Sentencing for this crime will occur at a later date. Since his testimony is false, it invalidates the charges against Captain Gereau."

"Since Captain Gereau has been cleared of all charges, I rule that all back pay and benefits for his service as an officer be paid to his widow, Claire Gereau, and family. I also rule that punitive damages be assessed and paid to the family, the amount to be determined at a later date. Advocate Beriot is to appear before the Council of Jurisprudence, date to be ascertained, for certain strategies he employed while defending Adjutant De Voux and others in this case. In the interim, he is denied the ability to practice law before *any* court in France. The aforementioned will appear before this court, at a later date, to defend against charges that he unlawfully engaged in the theft of national funds. Captain Magrid is also charged with the same crime. I wish to make it clear these are not allegations. This court has seen enough evidence to charge and prosecute these crimes. The court is aware of several other conspirators. The court will reveal their names in due time."

The courtroom was buzzing with excitement. The magistrate raised his hand. Once again the court was silent.

"My last ruling is that the Army plan and execute a burial with full military honors for the remains of Captain Simeon Gereau." The room erupted with cheers and exclamations. "It is the least we can do to honor an innocent man who was so unjustly treated by his superiors. This case is dismissed."

Lola Per was crying; Bernard Mercal was elated - it was over. Justice, occurring much too late, had been served. Though satisfied with the result, he still awaited the final blow – but that rested within the purview of Magistrate Fournier.

There was a clamor at the doors leading to the street. Reporters and photographers were shoving and pushing to get to the street and their newspapers. As Lola Per had predicted, the case of Captain Simeon Gereau would make headlines and, most likely, become a pivotal example of jurisprudence for years, perhaps centuries, to come. And, once more as she had predicted the names of advocates Bernard Mercal and Lola Per would be associated with the brilliant defense they presented.

As they left the courthouse De Voux and Beriot pushed their way through the crowd of spectators and reporters surrounding them. Embarrassing questions and curses went unanswered. The evidence had stripped them of any response.

Neither spoke as their chauffeur drove them back to Beriot's office. What provoked this silence was open to speculation. Was it anger, frustration, the overwhelming sense of defeat – or something far more sinister?

"You betrayed me – I thought you were an advocate, a *skilled* advocate. Instead, I find out that you are an arrogant cabbage *posing* as one. You have ruined me."

"No, I have not ruined you. That, my dear adjutant, you have accomplished all by yourself. I doubt whether anyone, even our brilliant opponent could have pulled you out of the fire. It's your stupidity, you see – yes, that's it – your stupidity that has caused all of this. If you had remained in the line, as a serving officer, without your ambition, then you might have avoided this. All of your superiors are aware of your incompetence. That was why you were assigned to an office, why you were sent to Soissons – to get rid of you. For the same reason, I was given this case – to shine a light on my incompetence."

Beriot approached. "It is plain to see that you and I, each in our own area of expertise, are not fit to hold the positions we do. They are over our head, beyond our capacity, far beyond our mental acuity to perform. We are lepers, De Voux, you and I, lepers. France and the army will be better off when we are gone."

"Don't say that."

"My father and mother intervened every time I got myself in trouble: in school, at play, in my first job, in my second, in law school – they kept telling me it wasn't my fault. But I knew better – I knew it was. But I didn't tell them I knew. I just kept riding the wave, the one they had made for me and not the one I had earned for myself."

"I have dug myself a hole - so deep that even they can't save me. And do you know what? I am happy. For the first time in my life I can be myself, incompetent yes, but for once, myself."

"Why didn't you tell me all this when I came to hire you? It would have resulted in my choosing someone else. We might have won."

"You fool. No lawyer under God's heaven could have made right what you did. Don't you see? It was not the act that was profoundly bestial, it was *you* that was profoundly bestial No beast of the jungle would have stooped to what you did. Animals kill to eat. Fish kill to eat. *You* kill to advance your career. And you kill *silently* – so no one will know. I despise you."

"I have had enough of your insults. This time the killing will not be silent." De Voux drew his pistol and shot Beriot. Then he turned it on himself and squeezed the trigger once more. Perhaps history would judge them more mercifully than they had each other.

⌒

Claire Gereau had raised her children properly, that was plain to see. Made more difficult without the presence of a father, still, she managed. Bernard Mercal and Lola Per had decided to take the family out for a celebratory dinner in one of the better restaurants. The children seemed perfectly at home with the ambiance and the tasks required – when to use the salad forks, when not to, the use of spoons, the proper use of the knife. Claire had taught them well. This gift reduced the tension in the adult sector to the point where everyone felt they could enjoy themselves and not worry about some unforeseen catastrophe.

"An army officer came by today. He was very nice. Apologizing at every other word, he told me that a portion of Simeon's back pay would be coming within a week and that the rest would be in my hands by the end of the month. Isn't that wonderful?"

"Then we can eat here all the time," Jean Pierre opined, "That would really be nice. Then you won't have to work so hard cooking."

"It seems your children understand a great deal," Lola observed.

"Yes, that's true. Sometimes they surprise even me."

"Will you be staying in Saint Germain?" Mercal asked.

"With our finances, I didn't dare consider anything else. Now other choices are possible. My parents have passed and I haven't been to my home in years. I don't know how many of my friends will still be there. It's a nice place to grow up, much nicer than here. I will give it some thought. Perhaps spending a vacation there might be a start."

"Have you thought of marrying again?" Per questioned.

"No, I haven't. Now that I know the circumstances of Simeon's incarceration and how near he was to us all those years, I will have to face that and find some peace. At this moment I am not, no matter how much money the government gives us. It was a terrible thing they did to my husband – and to us."

"Have you decided what you two will be eating?" Mercal asked the children.

"Whenever we go to some place special, Mama decides what is best for us," Nicole offered, "and she never makes a mistake."

"Oh, sometimes she does," Jean Pierre counters, "But we eat it anyway because we don't want to hurt her feelings."

"Aha, we have a truth-teller," Per observed, "Keep him that way. They are much in demand."

All secrets having been revealed, the rest of the evening was spent in much eating and little talk, all in all a pleasant time.

Justice

Eight cavalry pall bearers stood alongside the coffin bearing the remains of Captain Simeon Gereau. The ragged burlap shroud covering his body had been replaced by a more suitable sarcophagus. The flag of France was draped over the casket. Son Jean Pierre, always the one to look more closely at everything, noticed that there was not one crease in the flag. Claire and Nicole stood silently, awaiting the loading of the casket into the caisson for transport to a more appropriate resting place for the hero.

The two lines of bearers began moving ahead slowly, respectfully. In attendance were the two gravediggers. Alfonse Duchard saluted as the procession passed. Not to be caught wanting, his friend quickly did the same. Alfonse was now silently reveling in what he had done – told the truth. He made himself a promise that he would never lie again – no matter the cost.

In a short time the ordeal was over. The Gereau family rode in the car directly behind the caisson transporting the remains. Rolling down the window, the children were entertained by the numerous songs of the birds that had returned to herald the coming of spring. While not a military band, somehow it seemed appropriate. Claire was wishing she could see Simeon just once more, to kiss him on the cheek, to touch his face, to kiss him and say goodbye. Suddenly, a bird flew into the compartment. It alighted on Claire's lap. No one moved.

Claire crooked her finger. The bird jumped on. She raised it to the level of her eyes. "Adieu, Simeon, I will love you forever," She whispered, "Now, go."

The children were speechless.

What remained of the cavalry battalion who fought at Soissons were at the gravesite. They were there not only with their families, but with others: friends, well-wishers and citizens who felt an obligation to honor the hero who had been so unjustly maligned. A small stand had been constructed to provide comfort for the group that came to view the interment. By the time the funeral procession arrived, it was overfilled to the point of catastrophe, but it held. The front row was reserved for family and close friends: the Gereaus, Rondas, Mercals, Per, and several distant relatives.

Claire chose Jules Ronda to give the eulogy.

It was sunny. The clouds were a brilliant white, the sky a special hue of blue. That was what Jules Ronda perceived as he rose to give the eulogy. Somewhere, up there, his friend was looking down on him – Calista was there too, with her parents. He felt that whatever he would be saying, it was for both, if not many, worlds – this one, heaven, and who knew how many others.

He had not taken the time to prepare; he had no notes, he had not rehearsed his speech – he felt it would be inappropriate to do so. God had placed him here, at this time, at this place; and He would provide the words he had to say.

He arose.

Everyone stopped speaking. A hush fell over the crowd.

I am here. God has been merciful. He has allowed me to survive the Great War. If there was a reason for that, I am not aware of it. I will always be grateful for His mercy.

Here lies my dear friend and superior officer Captain Simeon Gereau, one of the finest men I have ever known.

But as honorable as he was, he became a pawn in a scheme to hide the incompetence of others. He suffered and died through no fault of his own. He endured, to the last moment of his life, the injustice that had been placed upon him. You see, he respected and loved France. He loved his country so much that he allowed those who misused its laws to remain unchallenged – even though they had corrupted it.

And now, this saga has come to its rightful conclusion. Simeon's honor has been restored. His family knows where he rests and France can once more be proud of the justice her courts mete out.

Make no mistake – this issue has not been resolved - there is a greater challenge. We must never allow what happened to my dear friend to ever happen again. We must never allow an elite group to administer the law as they wish – not as it is intended. In Simeon's name, I call each one of you, man and woman, to battle – to stand for what is right, for what is just, for the justice God intended for all of us. Stand with me and swear, swear now before God that you will fight for what is right – so help you God.

All arose – even the children.

A strong breeze wafted through the cemetery – the trees bowed to its force. They all swore, too.

～

Lola Per entered Bernard Mercal's office; she found him peering out of the window. His protracted silence indicated he was deep in thought.

"Well what is it; family trouble? Are you and Christine at odds again?"

"No, it's nothing like that."

"Well, then, what is it?" Lola stomped her foot for emphasis. It was unlike her, but the trial and the long hours it demanded were finally taking their toll.

"I am thinking about Fournier – what he must be experiencing. I wonder what he is feeling about having to go to Arnos Clemand's home and confront him – France's Chief Magistrate. Can you imagine what that must be?"

"I must confess I can't."

"Why did you come in today? I thought you would be resting. It has been a long road – and very arduous."

"I came in to inform you that I am ready to let you take me into your arms and tell me that you love me. It is not infatuation."

"Can you wait? I have to get over what I am feeling about Clemand – and Fournier. I would be very bad company right now."

"I will respect that. Is tomorrow too soon?"

"I need more time than that."

"I can be patient."

"I must call Magistrate Fournier now."

"Ta-ta," Per intoned as she sauntered through the doorway.

～

"Thank you for calling."

"Have you done it yet?"

I will be delivering the final stroke today."

"Are you going to his home?"

"I believe that would be the appropriate place. De Falle and Fens are accompanying me."

"Playing it safe, are you?"

"He did try to have me killed."

"It's good that you are prudent. Are you taking a revolver?"

"I don't feel I have to resort to that."

"I would. You really don't know him anymore. He's not the one you once knew."

"I will take your advice." He reached into his desk drawer, grasped the weapon and placed it in his coat. "I hope I don't have to use it," he lamented.

"But it's there if you need it, and that's a good thing."

As if he were carrying a huge bag of coal, a weary Magistrate Pierre Fournier left for his rendezvous.

In order of hierarchy, Chief Magistrate Arnos Clemand was principal. Directly subordinate was Magistrate Fournier first, Magistrate Bonaparte Fens second, and Magistrate Armand De Falle third. All were capable jurists and well respected in the halls of jurisprudence. Fournier had briefed them about the mission. They did not believe him until he showed them the indisputable evidence and the notes of the investigators.

After that, the two agreed to accompany him to the Chief Magistrate. Since they had sent word ahead, he was expecting them.

When he opened the door, he seemed unwell. His face displayed a grey pallor and there was a whitish halo circling his lips. "Come in gentlemen," he invited.

"You know why we are here," Fournier offered, "I need not be more explicit – or, do I?"

"I know full well why you are here. It seems the man I sent to dispose of you failed. I will have to talk to him about that."

"He is dead."

"How did it happen?"

"Mercal and Per found out about you – it was the bank accounts that revealed your involvement. Once they found that out, they realized how dangerous it was for me. Without my knowledge they assigned me a bodyguard. He was the one who saved me."

"Tell them I said bravo, good work. I always had a great deal of respect for Bernard. I can see him one day as Chief Magistrate. May I offer you something?"

Armand De Falle pulled a bottle of wine from his coat. "We brought our own, thank you."

"Then I'll get you some glasses."

Bonaparte Fens produced the glasses. "We brought those, too."

"My last name is not Borgia, you know."

"You are not the person we thought we knew. You are someone else; perhaps even a Borgia."

"Touche'; I suppose I can't find offense in that. It's true I have had - other interests aside from being Chief Magistrate. The war, you know, it offered great opportunity for some while others had to struggle to survive. I was one of the fortunate few to have prospered from it."

Fournier stared at the Chief Magistrate. He noticed.

"And I am not ashamed of it," he snarled.

"Now that you are about to be exposed, what are your intentions?" He questioned.

"My intentions are to enjoy a glass of wine with my colleagues. There is time for the rest."

"You seem very flippant. Why is that?"

"It is because I know that you all are men of good will, of integrity, and that you will not utter one word of derision about me after I am gone."

"You mean after you are tried, convicted, and hung?"

"Come with me." The three followed the Chief Magistrate into his arboretum. He approached one particular plant.

"This is an interesting species. It is beautiful, don't you agree? Yet, hidden in this lovely plant is a material so toxic that, if ground to a powder and swallowed, will cause death. And do you know how? I know because I have read of it. It reduces the ability of the lungs to process air. A grey pallor forms on the face, a halo of white surrounds the lips. After several hours, the victim becomes drowsy. This occurs because of the lack of oxygen. He lies down. He never awakens."

The Chief Magistrate turned and faced his accusers. "It is considered disrespectful to speak ill of the dead. I would be honored if you, Armand, would be one of my Pallbearers. You also, Bonaparte, would honor me by being the same." Turning to Jean Baptiste, he placed a hand on his shoulder. "And you, my principled advocate, fighter for truth and justice, I would be pleased if you performed the eulogy. After all, we have known each other for a long time."

"Yes, but you didn't tell me you were a snake."

"Be compassionate. What you see before you is a dying man. Have some pity."

Fournier spit in his face. "That's for Captain Gereau, one of the men you robbed. Yes, I will give your eulogy. It will be about the man I once knew, not the scoundrel who will be dying today."

The Chief Magistrate produced a handkerchief and wiped his face. "I thought you might do something like that. But I dismissed the idea. I didn't think you would. My, but you *are* a principled bastard aren't you."

"Let us take our leave, gentlemen. He must have his rest."

The three left Clemand's home. They had come in Bonaparte Fens auto.

"We are being followed," he said, "they fell in behind us as soon as we left the premises."

"Drive normally," Fournier instructed, "but don't let them get any closer, understand?"

Fens nodded.

The machine that followed made no attempt to close the gap between them. Thus, the ride back was more or less normal except for the anxiety the situation provided. Fournier's life had been threatened once. He was well aware of his adversary's capabilities. The one consolation was that he still had his pistol. If it came to that, he could still defend himself.

They arrived at his home. He invited his colleagues inside which they hastily attempted to accomplish. Just as they were about to enter, the auto arrived and stopped in front of Fens' machine. Two men were about to get out when a speeding truck appeared and crashed into their car. Both men were injured. Resisting the natural instinct to run over and offer assistance, the three stood in the doorway and did not move. Mercal's investigator, the one who had saved Fournier, jumped out of the truck and assessed the two assailant's condition. Satisfied, he climbed back into the truck and waved a goodbye. Before long an ambulance appeared. Both injured were carted off to the hospital.

"I must buy Advocate Mercal a good bottle of wine," Magistrate Fournier said, "He deserves it."

~

Clemand directed his valet to carry his bags downstairs to the front door. He had already telephoned and requested a car be sent to this home. He needed transport to the railroad station. It had all worked out better than expected. Public knowledge of his crimes would be delayed after Fournier and his colleagues were assassinated by his cohorts. The letter of credit in his inside pocket would give him unchallenged access to funds which guaranteed a leisurely and luxurious remainder of his life.

He would be meeting Greta his paramour at the port where they would be leaving France and going to America. A short ride on the train and he would be at her side. His wife would be surprised by all of this, but it didn't matter. He had left her the house and a few thousand Francs. He could have left her more, but it was his way of punishing her for being such a boring companion. Greta was much better at satisfying his needs.

His ride arrived. On the way out, he glanced at himself in the mirror; He still had the gray pallor and the white halo around his lips. He did not understand why. The dose of the poison he ingested was not very large, certainly not enough to kill him. It was meant to impress the trio that had just visited him. He calculated that after a few hours, its effect would wane and he would return to full health. His plan was working perfectly. The poison should have started to dissipate. Why hadn't it?

Upon seeing the Chief Magistrate the driver seemed unduly alarmed. "Sir, are you well?" was all he could manage.

The trip to the station took almost an hour. As the driver eased the car to the curb, he turned to inform his passenger they had arrived. The Chief Magistrate lay unconscious slumped against the door.

The driver sought assistance.

~

"Is it done?" Eloise, his wife asked.

"Yes, Fens and De Falle accompanied me. I think he is going to commit suicide – if he hasn't already. I expect to hear something of that nature in the morning."

"And you – all three – are safe?"

The magistrate did not tell his wife about the attempt on their lives, nor had he chosen to mention the first, the one after meeting with Clemand that evening at the bistro.

Eloise slept well, but her husband did not. He was being bombarded with a series of bizarre dreams. The last and most intense was the one he could not forget. It plagued his consciousness.

At breakfast, ever-sensitive Eloise noticed his discomfort. "What is it?" She asked, "You seem dismayed. Would you care to discuss what is bothering you?"

"I had a dream last night, a terrible dream - I was chasing Clemand. We both had fast cars and were racing at high speed. We came to a bridge. Torrential rains had washed much of it away. He did not stop. Instead, he went faster and catapulted over the opening. I did the same. The road ascended, we went up into the mountains. There were many curves and at times he almost went over the side. Then – in a flash – he purposely steered his car toward the precipice. He went over. I stopped and looked over the edge to see where he had crashed. Then, far below, I saw him going down another road. He waved. He was laughing – at me - I realized that I had been duped. I cannot forget his laughter. It still bothers me."

"It does because he tricked you. He made a fool of you." Eloise opined. "You think, somewhere deep inside, that he may be the smarter and that thought upsets you."

"Perhaps that is the case. Yes, that may be the case. Did he dupe us?"

"What do you mean?"

Fournier did not answer. He was already through the door and on his way to court. His dream still affected his thinking. *Did he dupe us,* he mused, *and those men, why did they follow us? Was he really going to take his own life?* Those same questions kept surfacing. He could not shed them.

As soon as he entered chambers a clerk ran to meet him.

"Have you heard? The Chief Magistrate is in hospital – they say he is going to die."

"Take my briefcase to my office," he instructed. He took a taxi to the hospital. He needed to see for himself. *Why in the hospital,* was the question, *why not at home?*

As Fournier approached, several of Clemand's clerks and associate magistrates were milling about outside his room. The gloom was palpable. One of them greeted him by explaining "They say he doesn't have long. Are you with Lieutenant Brousseau?"

"Why do you ask that?"

"He was here earlier. He had some documents he said the chief Magistrate had to sign. It was very important. He said he would be back later, or send someone to see how he was doing."

"Do you know what they were?"

"He didn't say, but I saw one of the envelopes – it had a bank's name on it."

"Thank you." Fournier braced himself. It is not pleasant to see one's associate dying – and in a most terrible way. Once again the two faced each other, but this meeting was different. Now he was in command – not the Chief Magistrate.

"You have come – that is good. I duped you and De Falle and Fens. I took only a small dose of the substance I mentioned – just enough to give me the symptoms of the poison. I intended to flee – I already had my rail ticket and steamship cabin. My paramour was going to meet me at the ship." Clemand lowered his head. His chin touched his chest. "I must have miscalculated the amount. It seems it is I who has been duped."

"I still don't understand. Why did you engage in this behavior – you have prestige, you have a reasonable social presence, you have enough money to live well, you have a beautiful wife – why, why?"

"There are those who are satisfied with all that – but I needed more, much more. Why should I be satisfied with meting out verdicts to men who have wealth hundreds of times more than I? Can I not be one of them, too? Why should I go home every night and spend my evenings reading briefs and going to bed with a wooden wife?" Clemand raised himself and stared at Fournier. "I wanted more – I deserved more."

"And now you have nothing."

"A good burial and a quiet place where I can spend eternity damning my own stupidity; that is what I will have. That, I have earned." His sneer was unmistakable.

"The money will be confiscated, you know, all of it. I imagine there must be a lot."

"It will surprise even you when you see how much I have laid aside. I have been a *very* bad boy." Clemand paused. "You may not have a chance to confiscate it, after all."

"What about Brousseau? Do you know him?"

"His family was instrumental in my being appointed as Chief Magistrate. He and I have had a relationship – very positive - for a long time."

"Was it from his time at Soissons?"

The Chief Magistrate attempted to answer, but his voice was fading. His breathing became labored. "You will make a fine Chief Magistrate, Fournier, better than I. France is fortunate." Clemand closed his eyes. The death rattle followed. He was gone.

Outside the room, the group awaited the magistrate's exit. They wished to enter and pay their respects and comfort their mentor. Fournier informed them that their encouragement was no longer necessary.

～

Reporters crowded the hall and courtroom. They were all waiting for the magistrate to open court. As he approached, he noticed their unpleasant glances. "I apologize for the delay. I have just been to the hospital. The Chief Magistrate has passed away." There were exclamations of comfort and condolence.

It was Magistrate Fournier's practice to dispense with minor motions and pleadings before opening the court to the more serious cases. Today the issue of Adjutant De Voux's behavior regarding the stolen funds was to be the magistrate's main concern. Because of lateness due to his hospital visit, it was thirteen before he cleared the calendar. He allowed himself a short recess before resuming court, which would be the De Voux issue. He reviewed the principal aspects of De Voux's circumstances, his behavior, intent, and military service; whether those aspects of his life might mitigate the sentence.

His determination as to the adjutant's punishment needed, above all, to be just – and that was the crux of his discomfort. How does one weigh military service, and faithfulness to the nation against unmitigated disregard for law, the military code, and the veil of secrecy he imposed when it came to judicial proceedings? It was a thorny question. And what would the parameters of a just sentence be? Should the magistrate make an example of him? Should he show lenience because of age, and service to the nation?

Fournier glanced at the clock on the wall. It showed the hour as fifteen.

He reentered the courtroom.

No one was present. "Where are they?" He asked the clerk, "is there some reason they are not here?"

Just then, Advocate Beriot's clerk, breathless, burst through the doors and ran up to the magistrate. "Advocate Beriot is dead. Adjutant De Voux shot him." Taking a deep breath, he continued, "Then he shot himself."

"Thank you," the magistrate said, "Rest; you have done well."

The magistrate returned to chambers.

—

The building might have been considered elegant in the past. Now it was a relic that lay between the industrial sector and an array of lower middle class homes. Everyone in the vicinity knew what it was – a brothel. Gaudily adorned within and painted flamboyantly without, it called forth the same impression one might have if he were observing the Follies at some famous and naughty bistro. Not wishing to be associated with the activities therein, those of a religious persuasion avoided using the side of the street it was on. Without explaining why, parents always chose a more circuitous route for shopping and escorting their children to school. Single men always made it a point never to be in that vicinity especially late at night – it would surely result in the destruction of their reputation.

Only those who sought its services dared approach the palace of pleasures. Neighbors knew who they were and often speculated about their home lives, and the innocent, naïve spouses that stayed home by the fire awaiting the return of their masters.

Clarisse had done well – in fact, she had over-performed. That was why her client had gifted her a 100 Franc note. As she tucked it into her bodice, she embraced and kissed him. It was a thank-you-and –hope-to-see-you-soon gesture. Satisfied and very pleased with himself, Charles Brousseau was ready to face the world. Of course, there would be his manufactured excuse to Jasmine - he had important business somewhere, a location and scenario he would concoct on the way home.

His visit to the expiring Chief Magistrate had been fruitful. He obtained the numbers and locations of all the bank accounts held in trust for him by his partner who would have no further need of them. The sum total of the six was well over 150,000 Francs, the proceeds from a number of successful embezzlement schemes over the past decade.

Clarisse helped him with his cravat, making sure it was just so, an annoying fetish of her client. Finally, he was ready to go. A kiss on her cheek, a pat on her bottom, and an invigorated Charles Brousseau was on his way. As he opened the door to the street, he found Bernard Mercal waiting for him.

"I didn't know you were a client here. Don't worry, I won't tell anyone. Your secret is safe with me." Looking past the advocate, he noticed two policemen. "What is this?"

"It has to do with six bank accounts. Do you know anything about them?"

The suspect frowned. "Someone once told me that advocates never ask a question they don't already know the answer to."

"Shall we go?"

Clarisse had been watching all this from the window. She ran to the door and opened it. "Charles, do you need help? Shall I call the police?"

"Madame, we *are* the police." One of the policemen offered.

"Don't tell her anything," Charles pleaded, "She doesn't have to know."

"What's wrong? Why are you taking him?" Clarisse was concerned.

"He's being arrested. He's a thief," one of the policeman said.

"Oh, OH," Clairisse replied. She closed the door.

"Now everyone in town will know."

"The fault is yours, not mine," Mercal replied.

The accused was placed in a police vehicle.

⁓

Morning found Charles Brousseau in a cell. Marcus Renier, the advocate his parents hired for him asked, "How will you plead?"

"Plead to what?" Brousseau asked.

"I will have my clerk read the charges," He recited all the crimes the defendant was alleged to have committed. The list was long – so long in fact, that the accused began to swing his head from side to side in cadence with the same crime being repeated over and over for the different bank accounts.

Finally, he finished. "That is all."

"How will you plead?"

"I will plead not guilty, certainly. I am a man of means, of noble blood. These charges are fictitious – I am innocent."

"Trial will be set for Monday, two weeks hence. I recommend that you request mercy from the court.

"But I am innocent."

"I doubt that."

"Once more, how will you plead?"

"Not guilty."

"I will see you on that Monday."

—

The day came. Advocate Renier was in Brousseau's cell trying to have him change his mind and fall on the mercy of the court. His client resisted.

"This is absurd – I shouldn't be in here. It's a gross miscarriage of justice. I won't stand for it. Have you called my parents? They'll know what to do. They know people."

"I'm afraid this is beyond their reach, Monsieur," The advocate answered, "*Far* beyond their reach."

"Are you saying you can't get this dismissed? What kind of an advocate are you, anyway?"

"A very good one, Monsieur, and one who sees that there is very little that can be done to defend you. There are records, signatures, communications; all written in your hand and signed by you. The evidence against you is overwhelming. You are going to prison. The only course of action left for you is to throw yourself down and plead for mercy. Kneeling might help."

"I'm not going to do that – and don't call me Monsieur – I am *Lieutenant* Brousseau."

"That's not going to help you either. Remember, you and your cohorts stole from *military* funds."

"SILENCE! You're not helping one bit. Who hired you, anyway?"

"Your parents retained me. It was their hope that they could salvage the good name of the family. They are already resigned to the fact that you will be going to prison. You have disgraced them."

"They do, do they?"

"Frankly speaking, Monsieur Brousseau, you have."

"I told you to call me lieutenant."

"I don't think you have the right any more to be called that. You have disgraced your rank."

"How dare you say that? I have noble blood. You're fired."

"You have disgraced that, too. And, you can't fire me. Your parents hired me. I speak for them."

"You speak for them – so rudely? How can you?"

"My rhetoric is mild in comparison to what *they* said about you. I don't think you would wish to hear what they think of you – and your activities – including your visits to the brothels."

"They know about that, *too*?"

"They have borne your indiscretions for decades. They hoped you would change – become an honorable person. But you didn't, you got worse. I have known your parents for years. Do you know how much anguish you have caused them? I am sure you don't – your mind is fixed on that trollop Clarisse. And now, after wasting away your monthly stipends, you have turned to thievery – THIEVERY! AND NOW YOU WANT ME TO BEND THE LAW SO THAT YOU CAN CONTINUE IN YOUR DESPICABLE WAY; NEVER."

The advocate's rant deflated his client's ego. He looked very much like a captain who had been informed that his ship was sinking. His eyes exhibited that dull, unfocused gaze of those who felt the end was close.

"Can't you do something?" He whined.

"I have already told you what to do – throw yourself on the mercy of the court. Beg, if you know how."

He stiffened. "I'll never do that. I am a Brousseau."

"Since that is all I have to offer you, Monsieur, and you will not take my advice, I will see you in court in an hour – and, I suggest, that you not be late."

"I told you to call me Lieutenant."

—

"I hope you will accept. While we are sorry with Chief Magistrate Clemand's passing and pray for his grieving family, I must tell you that many of us wished that you had been appointed instead of him. But that is ancient history. Now we have the person we want in the position – that is, if you accept. We will require an answer as soon as possible – are three weeks enough for you to consider our proposal?"

"I don't need any time – I accept. I have had to sit by for too long and watch decisions made that were not lawful – in my opinion. I think the time has come to reinstate justice to French jurisprudence."

"I didn't realize you felt so strongly about these matters."

"You do now. Does that change your wish to have me as Chief Magistrate?"

"Certainly not; I will happily inform the Board that you have accepted. I'm sure they will be pleased. Thank you."

"And you, for the good news. My valet will escort you out."

"As Magistrate, soon to be Chief Magistrate, Fournier watched the chairman of the judicial council make his way out, he mused, *At last I will be able to stop the court being corrupted by those who have had Clemand's ear. Many times he has ruled in favor of those in his cabal – I've seen it time and again. I know it will not be easy for me, for they will not calmly yield to my decisions – they will resist. But I must do this – I have dreamt of it for so long – it has been my goal in life. And just when I believed I would never attain that which I desired, a merciful God has opened the way for me in the strangest of ways*

Now the magistrate turned his attention to the last item to be resolved in the Captain Simeon Gereau case – the meting out of justice to Charles Brousseau. He thought again about the honest thief - the one who robs a person with a certain honesty of purpose – he is a thief and he robs – he does not cloud his intent – he is what he is. Then there is another, one who portrays himself as respectable, and *then* surreptitiously commits the act of thievery. He is guilty of two crimes – dishonest deception and the other. In the case of the present accused, he also broke his oath to serve France honorably. And as an officer, whom others relied on for leadership, honesty of purpose, and pureness of loyalty. In addition, he had falsely named his superior as a perpetrator of a crime for which he was not guilty.

On every level, the accused had failed – in his responsibility as an officer, as a citizen, as a son of a family, as a husband, and finally, as a speaker of truth. And now, Magistrate Fournier had to pass judgement on this person, but only on those charges that were criminal. It would be unfair to punish him for moral or ethical transgressions that carried no weight of law.

That is why the magistrate barricaded himself in his study for the evening; to do battle with his conflicting emotional and philosophical feelings running amok in his thoughts. In this case especially, the passing of judgement needed to precise, succinct, like the stroke of a surgeon's scalpel, so that anyone reading the sentence at some future time would have to conclude that though harsh, it was just.

While deliberating, he needed to set aside all of the contravening and associated occurrences that had passed before him in the previous weeks and months – there was the case itself and all its intricacies regarding military and civil law, the treachery of Beriot, the acts of conspiracy by De Voux, the use of the gravedigger in presenting false testimony, and, finally, the attempts to nullify any adverse ruling he might have made by persuading him not to preside over the case.

It would be incorrect to have any of these events contribute to the sentence imposed on Charles Brousseau. His crimes needed to be judged on their severity and nothing else. That was justice – the other, revenge.

Later that night the magistrate's valet entered the study silently and left food and drink. From previous experience, he knew it was going to be a long night for his employer.

———

It was time for the Tremaines to return to San Raphael. They had remained at the Ronda's home during the trial. Their presence proved to be a blessing for Madame, who would have otherwise been sentenced to a life of solitary existence while husband Jules spent hours and days supporting Bernard Mercal and Lola Per in their research and other needs. Many times he would return weary and uncommunicative, able only to make the climb to the bedroom, even skipping dinner. While Annette supported him as much as possible, the circumstances of their existence was taking its toll on her. Regardless, she persevered.

But now it was over. Jules seemed a resurrected man. A great burden had been lifted from his shoulders. Annette also prospered from this new-found existence. The companionship of friends only enhanced their release from the trial and its numbing commitments. One might even propose that the two couples were on honeymoon.

But, as someone, at some time, must have opined, 'all good things must come to an end.'

All packed and about to depart, it fell to the Tremaines to say goodbye. A great deal of sorrow permeated the parting. The four had experienced an event that few others would ever have. They had endured the many slights and inconveniences that came with Jules being so busy. They had stolen every moment possible to nourish their friendships. They had cheered when appropriate. They had encouraged when necessary, when they felt the tide had turned against the completion of Jules' quest – to regain honor for his dear friend Simeon.

"It is hard to say goodbye," Marie said, "I don't want to leave."

"I will never forget this. And it has been all because of you, Jules, and your quest for justice."

"We have all had our part to play in this. I am grateful that you were here to comfort Annette. I have not been a very good companion for her during this time; thank you."

"Goodbye; you and Annette must come visit us. It will be our joy to see you once again."

"Bon voyage. Until we meet again," Ronda replied.

———

Order; having it brings joy, peace, and a sense of fulfillment. Chaos, its arch enemy, brings unrest, anxiety, and a sense of fatalism. Mankind, at its own peril, oscillates between these two extremes. But someone once opined that the mills of God grind slowly, but exceedingly fine. And so it was that from the chaos that was Soissons, there emerged a trio of minor miracles – all because of the former existence of one Captain Simeon Gereau.

First, Providence, some might even say a loving God, had worked in mysterious ways to see that the widow Claire Gereau and her family were adequately provided for, in a much better way than had her husband survived and returned to take his rightful place as head of the family. Second, his reputation had been restored – more – he was now considered a hero, for not only trying to save his men but for having been imprisoned unjustly. And, third, the web of corruption that surrounded the disbursement of funds to the military had been revealed and torn asunder, with its perpetrators punished or facing punishment.

Charles Brousseau, the last of these, awaited his fate. Arrogant and a self-lover to the last, he still felt that his parents would intercede and save him. Day after day he sat in his prison cubicle awaiting their arrival. As time passed the thought nagged at him that they would not be coming. *It's not like them to behave in this manner. They have to come. Would they leave their son, their only son, to rot in some prison until he was an old, decrepit man?* He kept reinforcing that belief daily, hourly; fighting the creeping realization that he had finally drained dry their reservoirs of compassion and mercy. They were done with him.

The day came when he was to appear before the magistrate and be sentenced. The guard unlocked his cell door and motioned; approach. He was given the opportunity to bathe, primp, and dress. Now he was ready. As he and his keepers neared the courthouse, all that came to mind was the folly of the event. Now comfortably clothed and shaven, he was about to be sentenced to a place where that kind of comfort would be non-existent. The thought flashed across his consciousness that perhaps his parents had interceded at the last moment. That would not be the case – in his heart he knew that. In cold blood he had assassinated their love for him. He had no regrets. He knew who he was and if that was the way it had to be, then so be it. He *was* the ultimate iteration of narcissism.

Finally, there he was, standing before Magistrate Fournier. Time seemed to stand still. He studied the magistrate's expression; he found no evidence of displeasure, of hate, or vindictiveness. It was blank, appearing almost disinterested.

"Charles Brousseau, the court has found you guilty on all counts: thievery, twenty counts: perjury, four counts; behavior unbecoming an officer in the French Army, twenty-two counts."

The accused wondered at the placid tone of the magistrate. He expected anger.

"This court sentences you to forty years of hard labor, the location of your incarceration to be determined by those in charge of such matters. I wish to note for the record that the law states that the nature of your crimes provides only a maximum of thirty years. However in extreme cases the law allows the additional ten. In your case, I have made use of the option."

Forty years, Brousseau mused, *forty years.* He lowered his head until his chin rested on his chest.

"I have provided personnel to escort you to your home and elsewhere so that you can conclude any outstanding commitments you might have and to say adieu to your parents. After that you are to return to prison and prepare for the journey to your new home."

The accused glanced at the magistrate. This time he saw not anger, but rage.

"Dismissed"

Opportunity – that was the way he saw these last few hours of freedom. *Perhaps, perhaps, there might be a chance -* he began to devise a plan.

At the home of his parents he found cold indifference. As he embraced them, there was no transference of love or emotion. They could have been saying farewell to a corpse – and, indeed, they were. He was no longer their son.

He packed a few items in a small valise – less than he wanted, because he was told some would be discarded upon his processing to a prison cell.

He requested to be driven to the brothel. His escorts were uncomfortable with that. He parried by saying he had left some personal items there that he needed. After some discussion between themselves, they decided to allow it. After all, forty years is a long time.

The escorts waited outside while their charge entered. Clarisse was there sitting on the divan. She smiled as he entered.

"I need your car," he whispered, "Where is it?"

"It's where I always park it; in the back."

"Give me the keys."

An uncertain Clarisse handed them over.

Brousseau roared out of the driveway past the two dumbfounded officers. He was smiling.

They gave chase.

Where to, where to? He mused, *Switzerland or Belgium?* He glanced at the gas gauge. *Its Switzerland, They'll never catch me with the junk they're driving.*

Driving at an excessive speed has its own consequences. Soon, a police car joined in the chase. The accused reacted by driving still faster. A second police car joined the caravan. Approaching more difficult terrain, the roadway became more curving. Ascending higher and higher in the waning light, Brousseau, not a particularly adept driver, became hard-pressed to maintain his speed and stay on the road. The police, more skilled, began to gain on him. Their prey increased his speed even more. The chase dragged on, becoming more complicated with each approaching curve. Finally it led them away from countrified areas. They were now approaching terrain that was new to all of them. Reason mandated caution, but this was abandoned early in the chase.

Night enveloped them. At the speed all the autos were travelling, the winding mountainous roads became even more treacherous.

Arrogance has its own rewards. Under certain circumstances it achieves its goal and intimidates its target. But even this behavior has its limits. In this case the limiting factors involved were those of physics: centripetal and centrifugal forces. At the speeds involved, the tires of Brousseau's car could barely maintain their grip on the pavement as he flew around the ever tightening curvature of the road. A few telltale skids warned him of the peril. He ignored them.

Suddenly the race was over. The three following autos all came to a stop at the place where the accused had failed to negotiate a sharp curve and driven over the edge. All watched in silence as the car continued its journey down the side of the mountain, finally exploding into a ball of fire.

Charles Brousseau had cheated justice.

———

The occurrence and frequency of catastrophic events cannot be determined; they follow their own course and consume those who might not even be aware of their proximity. Their effect is unpredictable; they bring catastrophe to both the victim as well as the innocent bystander. The parents of Charles Brousseau fall into the latter category.

For those of good deportment and honorable intent, guilt is an unusually heavy burden. It is unfamiliar and treacherously draining on those who are not aware of its demands. And so it was with Monsieur and Madame, parents of their ill-fated child, Charles. Their shame was genuine. What more can one say when your child is sent to the best schools, given the finest tutoring, reared in the best of circumstances, and still chooses to behave in a despicable manner? No analysis can adequately answer the question. Children can be taught, but they, and only they, bear the responsibility of *learning*. This was their realization, coming too late. It gripped the parents fiercely and cast a cloud of gloom over them.

Being truly good people, husband and wife searched for some way they could counteract the devastation son Charles had caused.

The parents thought it best to avoid social gatherings. They could not face their peers, for they felt they knew the topic of the conversations that were swirling about privately, in many circles. Friends could be ruthless, opponents even more so. Derisive gossip, while toxic, was tolerable, but when there was an element of truth to it, and when that truth concerned their child, it was unbearable.

They retreated to their safe haven, their estate. No one visited and they did not see any advantage in inviting anyone. The essence of their struggle was not shame or pity for their son, for they realized all that was in the past and could not be changed. Charles was a scoundrel and, painful as it was to bear, that was that. What the parents were struggling with was how to make their son's wrong to be made somehow right.

Those most affected by Charles' behavior were the Gereaus: the widow Claire, and her children Nicole and Jean Pierre. What might be done to ease their pain? How could their lives be made easier? The topic consumed the couple.

The day promised to be a good one; the sun was shining, the temperature was mild, and a soft breeze was making its way up from southern climes. It was a perfect day for them to visit the grave of Simeon Gereau. While they had never met him, Charles had spoken well of his commanding officer, actually admiring the man. On the way to the cemetery, husband and wife struggled with the choice they had made. They were going to visit the remains of the person their son, their own son, had betrayed. The emotional ascent was proving to be very difficult. Still, they persevered.

It was approaching evening when they arrived. The sun, now low in the western sky, was on its way to the ever-nearing horizon. Still, the temperature remained pleasant even though the southern breeze, pronounced during most of the day, had abated. A conveniently placed bench near the grave provided an unexpected treat. Across the path stood another bench; it was occupied by a woman and two children. Their heads were bowed; they must have been praying. As they made ready to leave, all three approached the headstone, uttered a few words, caressed it, and left. The Brousseaus deduced it must have been his family.

Already well into the evening when they left the cemetery, the ride home was taken in silence, not because there was an absence of topics to be discussed. On the contrary, each spouse was busy formulating a plan to address the needs of the Gereau family. Their intent was the same; only the elements differed.

Dinner was usually taken at nineteen, but on this night, due to the trip, it began at twenty. It lasted until three. When the pair finally arose and made their way toward the bedroom, they had succeeded in drafting a viable answer to fulfill their need. To put it into motion required several maneuvers in two worlds, first in the financial, the second, legal.

———

There was someone at the door. Jean Pierre ran to open it. A man in a chauffer's uniform handed him a note and told him it was for his mother.

"Mama, Mama, a soldier gave me this note and told me it was for you."

Claire quickly went to the window and saw the man drive away. She smiled, adding "He was no soldier, he was just a driver of someone's machine. He is called a chauffeur."

"They shouldn't dress them like that. They look too much like soldiers," the boy opined, "Then they will look too much like Papa."

Claire unfolded the note.

Madame Claire Gereau

>   *Please accept this invitation for you and your family to dine with us tomorrow evening. To make your journey here as effortless as possible, we will send Henri and the car to bring you here. You may contact us by phone at the number listed below.*
>
>   *We sincerely hope you will accept. We have much to discuss. We are sure that it will prove beneficial to you and your family.*

Henri and Claudette Brousseau

What do they want? Their son betrayed my husband. He was his jailor for over a decade. He has stolen money. Why do they want to have a meal with us? Her first impulse was to excuse herself and not go. But she changed her mind. Perhaps something good might come of it. Her husband's death had impressed upon her the reality that truth has no bounds, it exposes what it must; it does not flinch at consequences. Perhaps this might be one of those times when a good results from an evil.

She went to the phone, requested the correct number, and accepted the invitation.

The auto arrived at the appointed time. Dressed in their best clothing and having been instructed at least twelve thousand times to be on their best behavior, Nicole and her brother climbed into the vehicle. Claire, helped in by the chauffeur, followed.

The ride was longer than expected. Leaving Saint Germain and then Paris proper, the view from the windows turned from urban to suburban to rural. Rolling hills, grazing horses and sheep, and impressive mansions served to keep both children occupied. Whenever Jean Pierre offered some illuminating comment, Claire would respond in a subdued tone. Her son received her message; comment, but quietly.

Both husband and wife were at the front door to greet the family. They were cordial. Their demeanor served to calm Claire's apprehensions as to why they were summoned to this place.

An uncommon silence was ruptured when the boy noticed a painting of Joan of Arc and asked who she was. Monsieur Brousseau quickly explained, mentioning all of her triumphs and at last her martyrdom. He concluded by calling her a sainted and noble woman.

Jean Pierre's response was "I didn't know girls could fight – I just didn't think they could."

Nicole's response was "Seeeee!"

The children's exchange proved to be just the right medicine. Claire and the Brousseaus relaxed. From that point on, the conversation was less labored.

Conversation during the meal was bland; Claire discussed the children and their schooling while her hosts discussed the weather, the quality of the grapes that were grown on the estate, and the market that had developed after the war threatened the price of local wines. After demitasse for the adults, for the children dessert, the group retired to the drawing room. Host Henri asked whether it would be permissible if their valet could take the children on a tour of the winery and stables while the adults remained behind. Claire agreed, sensing there might be another reason for removing the children.

"We regret deeply what our son has done," Henri began, "And Claudette and I realize that there is nothing we can do that can atone for the despicable treatment your husband received at the hands of our son."

"It was not your fault. He is a grown man. He alone is responsible for his behavior."

"We would like to do something – something for you and your family," Claudette added, "Would you allow it?"

Claire nodded.

"We will set the wheels in motion, then. Our advocate will contact you at the appropriate time. Will that be satisfactory?"

"This is very kind of you, but you should not feel. . ."

Henri Brousseau raised his hand. Claire fell silent. "Understand Madame that our debt can never fully compensate for your family's loss. We are doing as much as we can to erase the stain our son has caused to fall on your loved one; that is all we are doing. Please, allow us to do what we can in this regard."

"Then it shall be as you wish."

The children returned. Jean Pierre was bubbling with enthusiasm – he had just seen a *huge* workhorse called a Percheron, and "The man let me sit on top of it," he exclaimed. Nicole mentioned that "A lady showed me how they make wool thread from sheep hair."

Claire smiled. She was pleased that she accepted the invitation. Not only did it benefit her children, it also satisfied the needs of Henri and Claudette Brousseau.

Claudette raised her finger to show Henri the spot of ink. She had received it from signing the document at their advocate's office. He took out his handkerchief and wiped it away, in the same motion leaning over and kissing her on the forehead. What they had planned was done. The Gereau family would receive a tidy stipend for as long as the Brousseaus were living. After that, Claire, Jean Pierre, and Nicole would inherit the vast holdings of their benefactors. It was as much as could be done, but they knew not nearly enough.

It was late. Restless, Chief Magistrate Fournier found that he had difficulty sleeping. A short review of all his vital signs achieved nothing: he did not have a headache, his stomach and digestive tract seemed to be in order, he did not have to frequent the bathroom more than usual. What was it, then, that was not allowing him to feel in control? Leaving the bedroom, he made his way to his study. His valet, a faithful servant, had risen and followed his master downstairs. Fournier explained that no, he did not need anything, and ordered his man to go back to sleep.

> *Perhaps it is time for me to retire*, he mused, *I have restored Simeon Gereau's honor, his family has been recompensed and, after having exposed them I have seen to it that several thieves are receiving their just reward. These last months have been hard. Perhaps it is time. Still, I cannot forget that poor soul and what they did to him. It disturbs me.*

He noticed the copy of Simeon Gereau's diary resting on his desk. Picking it up, he turned to its last entry.

> *Calista will be coming for me tonight. She will be taking me to heaven with her. For those who might ever read this, they may come to the conclusion that I have gone mad. It is not so. I only dream of Calista when I sleep. She comes of her own accord; I do not summon her in my dreams. Would an insane person long to see his wife and children? Would an insane person long to be freed from this dungeon and resume his life, the one before he was imprisoned here? Would a madman long to see justice, to be vindicated, to be brought before a tribunal in public view so that he could defend himself? No, he would not.*
>
> *I am not mad, but I might have become so, were it not for the valiant effort of my good friend, Jules. He has visited me every day, sometimes all day – even into the night, when he saw my spirit falling. One time he stayed with me all night – until dawn; he on one side of the door and I on the other. We spoke of intimate things, those anecdotes that only a priest might hear - under the protection of the confessional. I learned he was not perfect,*

and I confessed to him that I was not, either. We laughed
at our stupidity - then we cried about our present state of
our affairs – that he would not be free from all of this until
I was dead. And here he was, doing everything in his power
to prolong my life.

Why am I here? Why did my comrades have to be
slaughtered in that field? What warped minds created the
circumstances where those young men had to give up their
lives; for what? All of us should be home, playing with our
children, loving our wives, feeling the wet mist caressing
our faces, turning our faces skyward and letting the
raindrops wash over us. We should be in the sun, feeling
its warmth; we should be standing out in the moonlight,
marveling in the pale light it showers upon us. We should
be looking heavenward at the stars. Which insane cabal
has robbed us of all this; the beauties we will now never
experience. I am not mad – they are. They hide, they
scheme while we fight for them - and die. Perhaps it is we
who are the ones that are insane – for allowing this to be
done to us.

I made Jules promise that if he survived, he would visit
Claire and the children and explain what had happened.
I thought more about that; I changed my request. He
should not tell Claire everything. He promised he would
do as I asked, but that perhaps this might be over and I
could tell her myself. I glanced at him. He knew what I was
thinking – that will never happen.

It pains me to cough – I spit up blood, and have for
some time. I still feel it was my fault that Calista died on
that April day as well as the other children and villagers.
Still, she comes every night and pleads with me - she says
I am not responsible and that God understands and has
forgiven me.

I do not want to sleep any more – the thought of her
death haunts me.

I wish I could see Claire one last time and tell her I
love her. I think she knows that, but I would like to tell
her anyway. I saw my little daughter – I even played with
her. My son I saw only as a baby – he will not remember
me. Will anyone remember me after all this comes to pass?
That thought refuses to leave me. Sitting here in these rags,

in this dungeon, unable to see the sun, unable to see the sky – it terrifies me.

All I have to cling to in all these years is Saint Jules - yes, he is a saint – in disguise.

I am tired. She will be coming soon. I hope there is no pain in this journey: I have had enough. What if God does not forgive me? It is too late for that now. I will throw myself on His mercy.

I must sleep now. Adieu Claire; Adieu Nicole, take care of your brother. And you, my dear friend Jules – you are a saint. May God bless you for all you have done.

Adieu.

S.G.

The magistrate reverently returned the diary to its former resting place. Going to his record collection, he chose Gabriel Faure's *Requiem*. He turned on the phonograph and placed the needle in its proper position. He returned to his chair. He leaned back. As the last segment, *In Paradisum*, began, He wept.

Epilogue

Thus the Tempest trilogy comes to an end, the result of our sojourn, in beautiful France at the turn of the century. Eugenia my wife and I decided to visit Fort Douaumont at Verdun. We were doing research for my first book *The Tempest: Calista's Song*. The day was overcast and it had rained the night before. As I walked through the memorial and along the graves in it, I felt a deep sense of sadness and pathos. I found myself grieving for the souls interred there. I had difficulty breathing; I was mourning as if the remains of these souls flanking me were my own kin. Reflecting later, I concluded they were. The visit to the fort resurrected a notion I had been dwelling upon for years. These combatants who gave their lives defending France did so in the belief they were doing something good, saving France; that this war would be the one to end all others. After this there would be no more strife, only peace. Were they alive today, I would painfully inform them that their noble efforts were in vain, that we all had not progressed one iota beyond murdering and maiming one another when it suited our purpose.

Standing in a graveyard alongside the Chemin de Dames on a windy, breathtaking Spring day, I looked down the valley at Soissons, the scene of one of the most terrible massacres of French military personnel in recent history. I was taken by the inconsistency of it all; being at peace and wonder in a place where almost a century ago there had been agony, the screams of the wounded and dying, the roar of cannonade and the deadly rat-tat-tat of machine guns.

There were two sections in the graveyard, white crosses for the French who had fallen, and black for the German. I looked closer. I saw what appeared to be an anomaly; a white stone not in the shape of a cross, but a simple slab. The interred was a Muslim – a crescent was carved in the marker. I marveled; at a time when the Muslim was not well-accepted in France here was one who gave his life in the ultimate allegiance to his new home. That gift was recognized by others; he being interred with his comrades-in-arms. As I walked among the white crosses I noted the ages of the dead: 19, 22, 20, one, 18. These were novices to the profession of war. Walking among the black, the ages were different; 24, 27, and 32. These were seasoned fighters; career military. France's youth had taken on professional German soldiers. How well were the French trained, I wondered? There was no doubt in my mind their opponents were. I came away from our trip deeply moved – I could not escape the sense of utter French futility and incompetence I felt in what I had seen. I was motivated. The trilogy 'Calista's song,' 'Wings of Courage,' and 'The Diary of Simeon Gereau' was my response to seeing the graves of those youth at Soissons.

Those who seek to engage in the destruction of their kin, humankind; how shall we identify them? They devise ways to annihilate – why are they doing this? Are they hateful, are they angry, are they insane, or, simply evil? Perhaps one day we will understand the reason for their behavior. For the present it must serve to say that while humankind makes remarkable progress in the fields of technology, medicine and the study of human behavior, it still has not gained an understanding of the darker side of its psyche whose symptoms are greed, avarice, arrogance, hate, deception, delusion, narcissism, and a host of other calamitous leanings.

We continue to pay a heavy price for their existence.

Printed in the United States
By Bookmasters